THE
INQUISITOR'S
TONGUE

Aquellos polbos.

THE
Inquisitor's
Tongue

A NOVEL

ALAN SINGER

TUSCALOOSA

Book Design: Illinois State University's English Department's Publications
Unit; Director: Tara Reeser; Assistant Director: Steve Halle; Production
Assistant: Brooke Burns
Cover Design: Lou Robinson
Typeface: Baskerville

Portions of this book previously appeared in the following publications:
"A Severed Leg," *Golden Handcuffs Review* 2, no. 11 (Spring-Summer 2009).
"Vinous Tide," *Western Humanities Review* 61 (January 2007).
"The Chastity of the Wine Taster," *Golden Handcuffs Review* 1, no. 6 (Winter 2006).

Frontispiece: "Those specks of dust: Perico the cripple, who was caught giving love potions to lovers," plate 23 of *Los Caprichos*, pub. 1799 (etching), Goya y Lucientes, Francisco Jose de (1746-1828). Private Collection, The Bridgeman Art Library International

∞
The paper on which this book is printed meets the minimum requirements
of American National Standard for Information Sciences—Permanence
of Paper for Printed Library Materials, ANSI Z39.48-1984.

Library of Congress Cataloging-in-Publication Data
Singer, Alan, 1948–
   The inquisitor's tongue : a novel / Alan Singer.
      p. cm.
   ISBN: 978-1-57366-167-6 (quality paper : alk. paper) 978-1-57366-831-6
(electronic)
   1. Inquisition —Spain —Fiction. 2. Marranos —Spain —Fiction. 3.
Confession —Fiction. 4. Deception —Fiction. 5. Identity (Psychology)
—Fiction. 6. Spain —History —16th century —Fiction.
   PS3569.I526 I57 2012
   813/.54
                                        2011043109

FOR NORA

I am not myself.

You might say, "I am not myself today." But for me, day after day, the days possess their own character more than I do. They are more themselves than I am. I am the colorless air they breathe. The days pass through me—the ghostly presence—as if to urge me to run after them. Their swifter and swifter passage is an admonition to me: to make haste. It is a rout.

Portents abound in the ringing chamber of my vacuity. Yes, "run," "run," "run" is the sound resonating most wordlessly in that ring.

And now there is a leg. An omen? A warning? It has been laid at my door, bent at the knee. The runner will miss it. Still coutoured in its turquoise silk finery and booted to mid-thigh, finished at the top with a cuff of burgundy calfskin—alas the wine taster's color. Livid at its unsocketed stub end, the leg portends what I have already seen in such frenzied imagination that it might have rushed at me from out of my own nightmare.

Who in this *ciudad*, after all, has not been a witness to the quarterings in the Plaza de la Salvación? Who doesn't know the legs fly first, even before the proverbially winged arms, the shoulders feathering the air with the whitest flutter just before the crimson spray? It is a sight like no other. It twists the braided thread that hooks the eye to the pit of the stomach.

My not being who I am does not distinguish me from all others with respect to this revulsion. But neither does it make more of my presence in the world than the leg itself which is a mere meated bone.

My body (mine?), by its revulsive spasm, filliates a passionate solidarity with the crowd in the Plaza de la Salvación. The throng rings the spectacle of public execution with the most violent peristaltic contractions. The noise of so many wagging tongues has a resonant stench. Garlic, anise, salty anchovy. We—I say this without having decided to join them—are pressed into one skin, perspiring and tensile with excitement, all the better to feel the imminent dismemberment of the victim squirming in the eye of the arena. The victim is already flexing the ropes that tether him to sixteen drumming hooves. Amidst the heat of the surrounding throng there is the sodden, squelched blare of the sacbutt. A crimson kerchief is released from the pinching fingertips of the bald headed bailiff. All of our breaths commingle in the rhythms of the excitable blood, as hot and vehement as the fierce breath of lovers' maws soldered into the double rictus of climax.

The ermine robed tribune of the Auto da fé stands above, upon a balustrade scaffolding. He is stillness itself.

And the first tearing of the joints is so like the orgasmic body, submerging under a translucent flood tide of frothing wavelets, the eddying muscles of pleasure released from their deeps. The crowd steps back from the clearing at the center of the Plaza de la Salvación. The odd foot lifted like a question mark is snatched from the frigid tidal line that separates us from the spectacle of victimization, but ripples through us now, routing any thought that we could wade deeper into this act of witness. The ropes snap taut with the restiveness of the horses' hooves. The blood hisses and spits from the grinding sockets. The nostrils of the horses as large as stone basins bubble and seethe with the heat of the exertion. The muscular chords stretched taut from the tossing manes to the victim's wrists and ankles bleat faintly as the sheathe of white skin begins to fray and unfurl from the raw corpuscle of muscle and ligament underneath, more like shucked leggings and gauntlets than legs and arms.

The revelation that we are all of us held together only by fine crimson threads—they are sprouting like grass where an instant ago the joints were as smooth and firm as the maker's moulding thumb—leaves a gritty dryness in the throat, as if a scorching wind were whirling. Before our eyes the trembling limbs are drawn to viscous filaments, long and scintillating as a grim mash in the maw of some devouring beast.

But I feel nothing by myself. Nothing *as* myself. Nothing myself. I must look around me at the other faces, engorged with indrawn breath, whites of their eyes whipping the air with disbelief, cheeks rouged with the shame of their own bodily frailty. I look at them to know I must be like them: a doll so easily broken.

A doll! It is the perfect conceit at last—one knows who one is by conceit in the best of circumstances. My wooden head. My glass eyes. The limbs hung slackly inside my silk bloused sleeves and woolen leggings may not even be crudely modeled by the dullest of knife blades to resemble the curvature of life, flexed beneath an impermeable skin. But I am just that. A doll's self.

See the doll propped in his chair at the wine maker's tasting table. See what I see, if I were *I*.

With the wineglass raised before the doll's lifelike visage, darkened by the blood tones of this lifeless *rioja* that will shortly wet my tongue with its tears, I see the convexical face of my brother, my mirror, turning in the glinting belly of the goblet. Our mirror eyes were always so sparkling and perhaps as brittle and sharp as the shattering glass. But the goblet is full. It is not broken. The goblet is as full in the cheeks as the bursting of the glass-blower's fermenting breath. The stem of the goblet is roundly modeled and pearly smooth rolling on my fingertips that I may better appreciate the ruby hue of this portraiture in light. My features swirl with the bubbling liquid. Myself and not myself. But no other. And peering into the velvet clarity of those hallmark features— hawkish nose, primped lips, dimpled chin—that twined us together in life, I know how my brother's death has killed me.

Isaac de la Concepción, my twin brother. Dead of the bite of a horsefly, just one day ago. Infected it was, as I am now by such capricious fate.

I drink to you.

Tell me, Samaritan, to whom would the glass be raised if the gesture were yours? To whom would you show such savory compassion? Does the face in the Plaza de la Salvación, the victim's grimace, seem a better choice for your charity? Does the blood pump in your heart for the dismembered victim, more crimson than anything brimming to the lip of the raised glass?

Deceiver. You felt no shiver of communion with that shivering frame. What feeling do you feel capable of yourself? And why should you imagine that the words of Osvaldo Alonzo de Zamora could give you confidence to give an invidious answer to that question? Would you strive to be better than he? Are you more innocent? More unblemished by selfhood?

Will you tell me that your deeds of compassion are more generous, to a fault? Is the pride of such selflessness not a fault?

I am not speaking to Osvaldo Alonzo de Zamora. I am speaking to you. Not him.

He is only the character to you.

It supporates. The skin splits. A gash of lush fragrance. A tannic bite in the air. The air drinks before the simmering nectar has moistened any human lip. A greenish pulp. Impossible not to think of its guts. A grit of seed. A grain of sugar's pulse on the tip of the tongue. A fermenting spawn. There is always a harvest. It is the grape that yields. The expressed juice of the novitiate berry awaits its transfiguration. The must is first. And then the yeasty cloak thrown off to reveal the ruby-bodied seducer.

And then we yield to it. I am the taster after all. My taste. Yes, this if nothing else is mine. My nature. My tongue tells of it without any dissembling lilt in the voice. My taste, after all, is mute. But it is indisputable. Since the age of thirteen I have known it: age of manhood for *my* people, though the pronoun possesses nothing in my case. *Los conversos* only *people* the earth. They are not people of the earth, let alone the self-righteous legatees of any God's favor.

And yet, at thirteen years of age I was blessed by the grape to know it as myself, twinned more perfectly than the unexpectedly fair features that sutured me to my brother's identity.

✦ ✦ ✦ ✦ ✦

Imagine the scene. Three grapes dimming their ripeness in oily reflections upon the lacquer sheen of my father's tasting table. Then there was the goblet still trembling at its crimson rim. My father's lips parted dryly with a whisper of encouragement.

My hand was not the object though the short reach of my thirteen-year-old arm threatened to make it so, fumbling after, rather than grasping, the goblet's firm stem. But I held on. Yes, I succeeded in bringing the trembling goblet to my lips. The first taste yielded a lisping recognition. But it was spoken proudly in the buzzing sensations that were as alive as a swarm of bees bearding my tongue.

"Canaiolo and Tempranillo."

With one severe finger I parted the first grape and the third from their lonely semblance.

"Six months in the clay Tinajas. Nothing of oak." I did not lift my eyes to render this judgment.

The words effervesced from me. No need to think about it. It was a fermentation as inexorable as the plunging sword. Perhaps I was my father's son after all. The thought was levered by the pressure of his praiseful hand upon my shoulder.

In the same instant the castrato tones of my brother's empty mouth rose upon song in a distant room. Was that accompaniment I wondered? Or the familiar rivalry?

Was there familial relation among us after all? A family despite the monstrous masquerade of our Christian brotherhood. The converso tastes like nothing, smells only like the empty stall where the shattered cradle is rubble underfoot. He is converted into an appearance of likeness and for that reason disliked by all. But tolerated. Tolerated by law: the bull of Toledo. Such tolerance is kindred to oblivion. Such kinship is the sloughed skin of forgetfulness. Something brown and shriveled. I have always imagined the foreskin nipped at birth. Forbidden birthmark. But that is only my imagination, not my body. My manhood wears the hood of my disguise at the age of twenty nine years with all the quiet zealotry of a monastic devotee.

The boy becomes a man at thirteen. I became a taster. Over time, the renowned possessor of a prestigious nose, an invaluable tongue. Without doubt a possession to be sought by others. If not a self then a sense. I have always been told that the gifted tongue, the rarified sense, is a fine thing to which nothing can be compared. Perhaps that is why it is nothing to me, no counter for myself. Itself only. It. Alone. Untethered to anything but its own nature. *Unnatural.*

Let me explain then how it abides.

✦ ✦ ✦ ✦ ✦

The Cardinal's cellar was said to be as vast as the catacomb of Santa Inés.

Though I was still physically small by the measure of my years, and seemed the least mature of my fellow apprentices in the retinue of Cardinal Mendoza's tasters, the maturity of my gifts were evident to my masters. So much so that the envy of the other apprentices—yellow teeth biting through the thin lipped smiles, the fermenting breath of a greeting spittled upon my upturned face, the fart-smothering bows by which they gave fetid place to me at the tasting table—was all they showed me of their society. Hooded as I was in the

burgundy mantle that was the livery of the Cardinal's service, I might indeed have been a member of some monastic order sworn to silence: the tongue lolling as uselessly in my mouth as the pendulous organ forsworn in damp folds of the monk's unbelted cassock. Lonely as I was in my monastic apartness, how well I knew this palace was no place of ascetic pursuits.

So when I was summoned from my apprentice's cell I was surprised to be called to change out of my brotherly vestments. A galoot of a page brayed the command with a brutal mouth, lips swollen in gross proportion to gigantic teeth. They were as large and blocky as dice—thrown as crookedly, as if by chance alone along the stone sill of his jaw. His arms held forth the piled plush of a richly textured, brightly colored attire. Even a ruby cap tassled with a golden braid.

And when I presented myself so magnificently outfitted in the anteroom of the Cardinal's dining hall I realized I could not make a competent bow without disarranging myself. All of the garments, and especially the top-heavy cap—too large for my slender frame—cascaded from my limbs with the slightest tilting forward or backward.

"And yet they fit your brother." But by this utterance the Cardinal slighted me further, calling everyone's attention to the startling contrast between Isaac's body and my own when he was convinced to stand beside me in impromptu mockery of my shameful haberdashery. The skin was the same on our bones, but in his person it was filled out with such well exercised sinew and muscle that we would hardly be recognized as twins: even stood side-by-side for the mystified guest to

whom the question might be posed as a riddling of the identity of our indistinguishable faces. And so we were.

Was I not made even more sensitive by the knowledge that it is the taster's duty to mark distinctions with the most precise powers of observation?

These were now against me in the narrowing eyes crowded about myself. My brother had been taken aside, his shoulders cradled in the Cardinal's embrace. Compared with myself, the ladies and gentlemen who made up the company were impeccably appareled. They wore the fit and cleanliness of fresh paint upon their silk and organdy dappled skins.

I sensed the prickling attentiveness of our audience. Their faces sifted me from my surroundings. Something salubrious moved in their murmuring throats. And then I realized. I was being tasted. And was I expected to return the favor?

I could see—by the regimental order of bowls and glasses set out in brilliant display upon the long claw-footed table, feet too far apart to serve the lunging instinct of any beast it could have been modeled on, and sheathed in a tapestry woven of gold, silver and vermillion threads (yes, of course it was a hunting scene!)—that I was.

Yes. I had been called. Myself? My taste. It. Was it not groomed to be at the Cardinal's beck and call?

"Perform a miracle."

These were the words that watered Cardinal Francisco Mendoza's mouth from then on, whenever he wished the wine to flow. Because on that evening, unbeknownst even to myself (have I not persuaded you that this was already a vessel long since drained of its meaningful elixir) miracles were possible.

The crowd parted to reveal the specific nature of the challenge awaiting my nascently legendary powers of taste. It trembled at the long table's precipitous edge. A goblet of crystalline water. Behind it several carafes of the same colorless liquid stood in line. Beside it stood another goblet barely wetted with what could not have been more than a thimbleful of *rioja*, if one could judge by its ruby glimmer. A dozen similarly tinted goblets were ranked in single file behind it. That miniscule dose of the grape in each might have been the red quavering eye of a holed rabbit staring up at me from the depths of the impeccably blown glass.

I immediately guessed the gambit in which I was already ensnared. I was the rabbit myself facing the probing nose of the dog whose toothsome snout was as wet as the bobble of wine inveigling my capture. But the rules of the game remained to be set forth before I was permitted to presume upon what I knew very well would be my fate. Or perhaps the rules were only belabored so that the fairly buzzing audience would come to attention and let the silence ring that much more portentously than the Cardinal's finger skimming the rim of an empty goblet that he now raised above his head. He needed an appeal to sight since the dulcimer tone spun upon his moving finger had merely become entangled in the hubbub.

This is how it would be. His voice was ponderous with authority. The words were squeezed from the tightness of his smile like sugary juice from the ruptured skin of the grape itself.

He instructed us all. "Osvaldo Alonzo de Zamora must imbibe the ethereal bubble of wine and immediately douse

its savor with a mouthful of water. Swallow. Then pronounce the names of the grapes so evanescently infused in the disembodied dram. Each act must be performed with the strictest economy: no swishing of the liquid in the glass, nothing of its aroma to be indulged in the nose, not a drop to be let loiter upon the palate. It must be washed away almost before the tasting buds of the tongue can flex their grip. Only the ghost of its vaporous fermentation can guide his judgment."

And what was being wagered against my talents? There would certainly be something in the balance for a feat weighted with such improbable expectation. I knew the wantonness of the Cardinal's tastes as painfully as I strove to realize my own.

"This is what I wager," Mendoza's lips sealed the answer to my question as oozingly as the molten pitch seals the barrel staves of the oaken cask. "My man Osvaldo's taste against Monsignor Boca's man's daughter: no doubt as savory a taste as any man's tongue could desire."

I understood immediately. Nothing of the Monsignor himself to be hazarded, but what was valued by his own servant above everything that poor valet could even imagine his master might already possess. And I, myself was nothing more than a counter, a chit, a blank line, upon which monetary value had already been affixed, as easily as the insignia of an official indictment by the Auto da fé.

I espied her. Now we were we.

She was the demur daughter, whose purple habit elicited an exclamatory hush when she was pushed into view to display the innocent blood of her novitiate self. I was my own foolishly attired selflessness, thereby deprived of even a

dignity to be violated. *We* were empty vessels waiting to be filled with the delectation of our betters. And yet we were not much more to them than the transparency of the spotless goblets that were arrayed on an adjacent shelf and that would soon be brimming in celebration of someone's certain defeat.

If it should be mine, I knew what salvation I would thereby accomplish.

But I am explaining how it was my taste, not myself, that stood to be tested. My tongue bristled—as involuntarily as a hair sprouting from the root of my tongue—with readiness for the challenge. By the rules of the wager the most difficult hurdle would be capturing the holy ghost of a flavor before its smokelike ascension from the quenching draught of clear liquid. The transparency of the water would be rendered more bodiful by the powerful gulp that was mandated "to wash away the blood of the grape's demise." Cardinal Mendoza's heretical conceit—the tight smile still wringing its salubrious juices from the moment—was nonetheless an admonitory finger wagging in my direction. That much I understood. But my taste remained an inscrutable force of this circumstance. I anticipated the eventual outcome with no less wonder than the gathering spectators.

I grasped the stem of the first goblet because I was so ordered to commence. But the hiving buds of my tongue were animated by a volition of their own. They gathered in a military phalanx giving an iron point to the spear of my licking incubus.

My self, shoved aside by the selfish protuberance of my tasting prowess, would be the first rent in the veil of the little sister's purity, whose eyes seemed to me sewn shut, though she was now the most prominently positioned witness to the spectacle. Out of the stinging corner of one eye I saw her slippers peeping out from under her heaving purple hem. They were as rounded at the toes as two beading droplets of blood. Or they were wrung from the plush fabric of her novice's raiment like the juice of the pitted grape. Are we not meant to believe that blood and wine are the same thing?

She believed, no doubt. But belief has no taste I am just as certain. For the guilty knowledge of her quavering presence only two steps to my right—we might have been bride and groom at the altar—was thoroughly erased from my consciousness by the lip of the goblet, slippery with the excitement of the moment, delivering up to my nose the ever-so-ethereal annunciation of the rubescent bubble, trembling in its readiness to crown my tongue.

By the rules of the wager my other hand was already in possession of the water goblet, quite deliberately full enough to require the swiftest of graces if I was not to spill and by that mishap let the firmly beaded droplet of concentration, just bobbling among the discriminating follicles of my tasting organ, dribble away into the indistinguishable reaches of my throat and esophagus.

But the truth was, I could no more spill than think. I could do nothing that was not the will of that vaunted taste, possessed as I was of its impetuous fervor.

The gulp of tepid water, designed to confuse wetness with wetness, only slaked an uncanny thirst for what it washed away. A grain of sugar, a blade-like sliver of tannic sharpness, the merest mealiness of fruit, as alive as the tendril of vine upon which it bobs, were all still savory enough. Clenched in the acrid flex of that muscle which is rooted in the capacity for regurgitation these sensations of taste now produced the mysterious grape in the word that was bursting with its nameability.

"Tempranillo." I permitted the blush of my tongue to be exhibited as the nuptial bed sheet is proof of consummation.

Something sharp as a pointed stick seemed to poke Monsignor Boca's eyes from within.

And then: "Sangiovese, at least ten percent. Zanuga less than ten."

There was an audible tremor of silks amidst the lavishly garbed guests.

"Water into wine my friends, and so I told you. The boy is a miracle." Cardinal Mendoza gave a bow, a flourish of his richly sleeved arm that seemed to scoop some invisible bounty from thin air.

I wished to believe that I had not spoken, though I could not have held my breath a second longer. And yet the words were out. Out of my mouth. And my mouth ached with the knowledge of their articulation. The slightly tipsy water goblet remained perilously in my grip, there had been so little time to find a resting place for it.

The little nun collapsed to the floor in a faint that was indistinguishable from the inebriate's stupor. Now, where the wavelet of her purple hem crested upon the shadow-caressed alabaster of her lower thigh, all could see the doubly embarrassed legs, hatch-marked to the knees with lacerations she had no doubt incised herself in the hermetic ferment of a dank and musty cell.

But in the course of the most fluid arpeggio of silently ticking minutes that followed, the miracle of my ever more discriminating taste multiplied itself like the goblets that had been ranked in single file upon the table: wine and then water, water and wine until all of the known grapes of our most luscious Castilian landscapes had been rendered of their juices in my pounding pronunciation of varietal name after name, as if my talent were itself the mashing peasant's foot turning blue in the bottom of the all-consuming vat. When all of the goblets were drained and the table was cleared well enough to serve as a pedestal for my exalted, though still ridiculously garbed person, I was lowered from the tumultuous shoulders of the Cardinal's burly grooms so that I could be viewed by all. I realized that a smile had sprouted upon my stone face like a perverse mustard seed of faith in something that was not even mine to cherish.

I knew the little nun had already been revived and was now seated dejectedly in a throne-like chair at my feet. She had been the virgin in her majesty. Overshadowed, but no victim of an oversight. The magnificently intarsia cherry wood and ash throne gave her impending shame a perversely triumphant aura. And the encircling eyes that now almost probingly touched her sorrow, also lowered themselves, as if in some perverse obeisance to her condition.

Her condition, as I knew full well, was conditional upon the power of my taste though it had nothing to do with the sourness that filled my mouth as roundly as the indelible flavors of the wines. But in this case the roundness was no part of such perfection as I had been credited with only moments ago.

Does one doubt that what I knew of myself at that moment was reproachful and at the same time reproached?

✦ ✦ ✦ ✦ ✦

At that moment I should have *been* two people, as I had often felt myself to be, in the knowledge of my brother's existence, when he too lived so lavishly in the Cardinal's embrace. When he lived.

After all, my brother Isaac masqueraded publicly in the vestments of the church thus bearing my features into the world under false pretenses. He was always looking through the mask of the priest with the tunnel eyes of the Jew. But, on that account I, if I can say *I*, could remain featureless. Invisible. Safe in the darkest depth of the tunnel with no thought of passage through it. Still, I was the priest's brother, if necessary a convincing semblance of the priest himself. By a torsion of this thinking that seemed perversely disembodied—it was so strained—I realized that I was the perfect mate to the little nun. Priest and nun. But the little nun was already struggling against the vile moments that were hastening toward her in some inverse measure of the slower and slower ebb of applause upon which I felt myself buoyed. A false priest on so many counts.

Her posture, for they had turned the chair so she might look upon me, already wore the disfigurement of her face. She was no doubt troubling the fate of the very organ of her sex that she was otherwise never meant to know as something belonging to her. It no doubt reared its head out of the tightest folds of her gown. She beheld the bearded seam fraying the flesh between her legs—and which she would otherwise never have recognized as her mirror image—now grimacing in her direction.

Just this well did I understand what it is to know yourself for the first time as something already taken away from you. Though I certainly must have looked like her tormentor through her eyes, I was myself tormented with the knowledge that what she saw was not. It was not me.

*W*ould you test me *if you could? Would you risk infuriating me more than you already do by the questioning furrow you have made of your brow? It makes me think of the merry fool's mustachioed guffaw, or of the nervous woman's most tight-lipped secret gripped in the clutching folds of her ample gown. Read me? Do you imagine you have the words?*

Perhaps you find it less distressing to judge the wine taster? Hasn't he given you the cue, even a grip upon the club with which he is so strongly tempted to beat himself? The little nun! How you sympathize too? How would you know with what? Did the detail of the little feet, the "peeping slippers," trod upon your heart? Then put your hand upon it and feel it beat as uselessly as the candle drips. Does your feeling flame? Then let me snuff it with this question. I'm full of them aren't I? What do you know of her but what he has vandalized? Is she really as incapable of villainy as his guilty conscience is capable of pious lamentation?

Tell me what you know.

I'll tell you, because I know you better. You are the confidant and consoler of all who suffer. Samaritan-smitten you are. You are renown to the most beggarly priests of this ciudad—shriveling in their filthy cassocks like food spoilt from such poor wrappings—as the selfless restorer of spoiling lives.

I have seen you stooping to wash the bleeding knees of supplicants to the punishing basalt steps of our Old Cathedral. I have seen you, your nostrils unswathed against the contagious fetor, pushing upon the unlocked door of the leper's compartment, little more than an animal pen in the muddy yard of the monastery. And don't imagine I have not seen you bearing meals to the latest widows of the plague. You are ever alert to the sobbing that tolls from bedroom windows. You are like the black fly upon the back of my hand, rubbing its sticky paws in anticipation of feeding an insatiable appetite. For what?

But in all this time that you have been renowned for the passion of your Christian sympathies I have never seen you at the wine taster's gate. You did not know of his suffering? You did not know.

An annunciation. At once I recognized the tableau vivant upon which I opened my chamber door. The knock upon my door a moment earlier had not seemed so portentous.

Since my installation as the official taster of the realm my door gave way into a marble balustraded courtyard, an interior garden spot in the green reaches of the palace grounds, extended toward the terraced vineyards.

My apartment was the Cardinal's gift and was itself the wondrous aperture of an artful view. Beyond the low balusters that marked off the colonnaded corridor, I daily focused my eye upon a perfect aisle of emerald ycws bisecting the courtyard and pruned into the conical milestones of a shockingly foreshortened distance at the end of which stood a miniature figure of Medusa, quite literally turned to stone by nothing less than the sculptor's hand. The short path between the emerald pylons led the curious viewer too quickly to discover the secret scale of the illusion. Upon approach, the menacing object of one's attention grew almost small enough to fit one's hand. It was a vegetable conceit fashioned by a mathematical genius who haunted the library in the monastery of San Juan de Oviedo and whose appetite for naturalistic application of the most abstruse geometrical theorems was nourished by Cardinal Mendoza's patronage.

And so I was accustomed to the prospect of infinity whenever I decamped from my rooms in the Cardinal's palace.

Today it was the antithesis. Today I opened the door upon quite another scene.

Who is not acquainted with the conceit of the annunciating angel? How often it is painted as if the virgin, her face a pool of perplexity, had not heard right the first time, or the second? How many times has the painter visited the image upon us? Time and again we imagine she shakes her head in the direction of the sound as if she were voiding her ears of an insect's buzzing instead of straining more ardently after the elusive sense of the voice that is trumpeting its news before her. Time and again the archangel flies through a gilt-drenched window, leaves the door swinging soundlessly behind him, bursts upon her meditative enclave. It is an ivory colonnade. It is a chamber closed but for its ceiling's opening to the sky. It is a rocky wilderness promontory. The archangel's wings are as lustrous with their downy feathers as his armour is made resoundingly bright by the painter's mania for putting reflecting surfaces before our eyes. Does he not trumpet his own powers to let there be light?

Above all there is the space between them, between the angel and the milky girl. The space. Empty. It must be crossed but not trespassed against. It must be known without any means at her disposal. Without any visual means to be sure. She must realize that the emptiness is what will fill her up.

In these scenes the painter frequently calls our notice to familiar objects that occupy the space in our world and which thereby make us so forgetful of the clear emptiness through which we see such opaque things: there is a startled cat, a cut flower, a querulous mouse, a chair, a carpet, a distant riverscape, a shoe, a sash, a wooden table, a basket of fruit, and upon the spotted skin of the apple that crowns the pyramid of peaches and apricots and plums, a black fly painted in such a scandalous manner, that perhaps it seems to perch upon the surface of the canvas itself revealing the illusoriness of our gaze through space and our proximity to the decomposing nature which is the fly's repast. What piety our pictures procure for us!

Such artfulness is, of course, nothing more than the painter's most wanton pride.

But that morning, when I myself was startled by the scene that seemed so far from the familiar long expanse I ordinarily threw my door open upon, I was brought up short by my immediate recognition of the players, not to mention the time-honored play.

Before me stood Carlito Zanzuella, advancing across the proscenium of my doorway, fully armoured in the costume of the warrior angel, sword well-scabbarded and swooning upon one knee with his arms thrust out—albeit more in sup- plication than annunciation—in the direction of his virgin. And more surprising still was the undisguisable moustache and goatee of Fajito Moscadura, my other apprentice, who was over-generously gowned in the virgin's meridianal hue, billowing blue skirts, a white bodice shining against the re- bellious black hair of his chest, and the blond postiche aslant of his wrinkled forehead with braids dangling wildly astride the head that would not cease its violent back and forth motion. Such a vociferous negation exposed the profusion of real hair bristling from what seemed auditory nostrils, though they were in truth his ears. Crossed as they were over his chest, his arms held a riotously mobile bosom in place.

Could it have been more farcical? Indeed, it remained for me to witness the demurring virgin's fatal step backward, catching the telltale boot heel upon the inner hem of her gown. It upended him, revealing naked legs, like black thorns among the satiny folds. Naked legs and the hint of what joined them in the hidden depths of the gown.

But annunciation it proved to be. I could see the words effervescing upon Carlito's lips, a simmering spurt of enlightenment surging behind the cork of morning silence with which my ears were stoppered.

No, there were birds chirping like the sound of the cork torquing in the neck of the bottle.

Perhaps the strained birdsong gave Carlito's words the profane propulsion that my two minions, so intoxicated with resentment, would have concocted between them: the poison with which to dispatch their master and so master his domain.

In the paintings the Angel often speaks in a glittering relief of Greek or Roman script. A scintillating aura raised like a scar on the surface of the canvas, suffused with its own halo of gilt. "DEUS!" The viewer of the picture might have to imagine its difficult passage out of the angel's throat. The "D" would be easy. But the "S" is a snag for the vocal cords.

Carlito's mouth seemed as tormented by the undisguised gleefulness with which he spewed the venomous words into the empty air, out of which his clumsy virgin had only just dropped to the pavement in a paroxysm of vindictive laughter: "Your brother.... Your brother is dead!"

*W*ould *you have been stung as sharply by the words announcing your brother's demise? But* your brother *is not blood, is he, Samaritan? You have seen such paintings in any case. Who has not? But for you it must be something too painfully enviable. What, after all, is the spectacle of the virgin's cocked ear to your own calling, Samaritan? When you heard it did you know, better than she appears to have comprehended, what flighty thing flutters its paper-thin wings in the labyrinthine darkness of the human ear? Or did you only shake your head like a wet dog?*

Well, of course. Why should it be a blasphemy to say you heard it too?

And yet you wear the habit of no holy order yourself, Samaritan. You seem to be a man of the world. You certainly wear no shame to exhibit such a taste for sartorial splendors. Your gold braided sustantivo. Your lavender velvet breeches. Your striped stockings of green and gold! I can only imagine the other choices.

We should think of those stripes as the bars of a prison, if I were preaching. We are both preachers of the shriving word. And so we would foster *our* brotherhood.

And the whiteness of your silken blouse. To carry your heart in a silken purse! Do you not worry that it bleeds so? Or do you intend to wear the stain all the more sportingly?

I don't mean to offend or accuse. Only to inquire. I am meant to inquire after all. I am a servant of our poor church, for all the public hostility I must bear upon my shoulder, if I cast an eye backward upon any path I travel through the streets of this city. Oh yes, I am known. My cross, you might say. You can say it. You can even smile when you say it. Smirk if you will. Nor would I shift the burden to anyone else.

Then do you tremble to know that you interest me?

✦ ✦ ✦ ✦ ✦

Well, there you were. I saw you. How could I avoid noticing? You averted your eyes like a man hastily palming two coins from a tabletop. You recognized me in a street you'd never have thought me to frequent. Turning the corner, no doubt you were looking behind you. It is the telltale blunder of the man with a guilty conscience. Not to think of what might be right in front of him, staring him full in the face, because he is always, always looking at himself, always imagining what others would see if he didn't block their view with his own crowding obsessiveness. And the most painful irony was your manifest lack of suspicion about what I was doing there, which would have been the upper hand had you flexed that muscle. Is it that the guilty conscience can imagine no greater guilt?

At least you found a shadow, a hovering darkness cast by a street vendor's breeze-molested awning. The constricting skins of the sausages so strangulated on the smoky grill sizzled and popped loudly enough to have caught any passerby's attention to your hiding place.

Not to mention the smell. Surely you had imagined surrendering to the allure of other perfumes in this gaudy street. You in your green and gold stockings! But now you yourself were impregnated with the rancid juices of tumescing meats, roasting on their skewers. Perhaps you felt the point of the skewer in my persistent eye.

But of course you didn't see me anymore, blinded by the garish light that fringed your shadowy oasis. Indeed I was still there. Not twenty steps from your stock stillness, not hiding, but no doubt hidden behind the statue of San Sebastiano impaled at his withered stump where the narrow street dilates into a modest plaza. The alabaster statue was no less immoveable than your safest self, tethered to the darkness. Or so you thought. Or so you thought. You waited long enough that I felt a stiffness in the limbs of my own body.

But then we walked together, I your bright shadow now. Because you still clung stealthily to the dark side of the street. My shadowing steps, overexposed in the flood of sunlight that carried me in its glittering current along the cobbled passageway of the Calle de Fernando, would have been an obsidian blur—upright and unskulking to be sure—in your dilated pupils. It's true, sometimes black is white and white is black. I counted on the failure of your eyes to serve me well.

That is how I followed you to number 6, though you, still cloaked in your furtiveness, your eyes still as averted as if they jostled in your pocket, must have felt you were already safely behind the door when I watched you deliver your rhythmic knock. False confidence, Samaritan. It is the devil's lucre you trade in when you presume not to be seen.

I am supremely confident to be seen and known, as I was in the sprawling shadows of that late afternoon. How else would I have followed you up those stairs? The latch man didn't ask any more of me than he had expected of you.

Blessed ascent. There was nothing on the ground floor of that establishment but a dark, septic, humidity. Foul air trapped beneath a realm of bliss. No, it is not an unfamiliar conceit to either of us, though in our faith the passage to that higher plane was never meant to bear the body's dead weight. But no man who ascended the stairs you trod then would have placed his body upon the Weigher's scale for fear of destroying the balance.

What about me?

Now your face is convincingly alarmed with the very expression you wished me to believe was your grief at the announcement of Osvaldo Alonzo de Zamora's brother's death. Perhaps now I begin to believe in your capacity to empathize, Samaritan. Even the corners of your eyes are puckering convulsively—greedy fish mouths at the surface of the pond—to produce the tears in which you want me to believe your emotions naturally swim. Now I can see you are capable of at least the signs of compassion. I might even compliment your ability to sigh, as if you would give your last breath to the dying man. I might even confess that you are in love with God's creation, that you would even give your compassionate look to another, asking nothing in return.

But by the silvery shine in your eye I know you are only the mirror of sympathetic grief, indulging the crumpled features, the wrinkled brow, the hollowed cheeks, the long chin, for only another chance to look at yourself, whatever disfigurement such pathos might arouse.

You are your own twin perhaps, in that reflection.

I was my twin brother's image of myself. My face is longish, brownish, with a nose that cuts the air snappishly. High cheekbones to offset the appearance of such rapier protuberance. The nose has almost no bridge. The eyes, thus deeply set, are brown, velveteen. It is a brown women have praised for its "luxuriousness." The hair is as jet as the pupils. The brown and the black scintillate in darkling harmony. The lips are full and wide and unexpectedly so when they succumb to smiling. But an air of seriousness prevails most of the time. It is a gift of the dark hue that the one who bears it mystifies.

When I call our family life a mystery I don't claim to possess its secret. We were deceivers of course. Conversos. We were the converted. We professed ourselves to be other than we were. No longer the Jew, though the name must never be mentioned, not to say breathed in all its tell-tale odor. We appeared otherwise. In dress, in act, in speech. We were sanctioned by law to be deceivers. The question in such cases is whom do they deceive more, the world through which they make safe passage by their deception, or their consequently ever more dangerous selves? Vigilance is the pressure behind the knife-blade of that question. They live with it always at their throat.

And now there is a leg. The blade that severed it was sharper and heavier to be sure than the one hovering at my throat. But the leg is also a question. Severed at the hip and crooked at the knee it resembles nothing so much as a question mark inscribed upon my doorstep.

It is not the leg of my brother, though it arrived within a day of my news that he was dead. Such wicked punctuation. But what was the question? Was it being asked of me? Or was I being prompted to ask myself? And who would then answer?

What I feared most was its being merely what it was, a token of flesh and bone. No part of the body that might have thought upon how it looked was in evidence. And judging by the elegant turquoise drapery of the single embroidered pantaloon, the radiant show of gilt stocking shimmering between the hem of the pant and the height of the boot, the purplish luster of the boot-leather cuffed above the knee, the exaltedness of its heel, I imagined what intense scrutiny the looking glass that had held this body last in its slippery embrace would have inspired for the one who beheld himself there. Thinking: that's what I look like.

It was clearly up to me to think about what it meant. A severed leg must be a question, even if it were straight as an exclamation! Was it a warning that I should run while my leg could carry that thought? Was I already falling under the shadow of a blade held aloft by my brother's enemy? My enemy? A highly placed advisor to the Cardinal of Sevilla has enemies in proportion to what intimacy with power he enjoys. My brother never masked his enjoyment. To be a converso renders susceptibility to such envy an ever more convulsive twitch of the via nervosa. It is the way of the converso to understand this. And I know what every converso knows, like the release of some luminous gastric juice flaming in the gut without warning: that one is already found out by those whose hatred one has so hideously aped in order to elude it. And so I begin to think that I am finally recognizable to myself as a dead man. Am I not already recognizable as my twin brother? What worse portent must I, clandestine Talmudicist that I am, decipher?

Yes, I am a dabbler in mysterious books, books more forbidden than the name of the god forsworn in their pages by brilliant encodings, as much as I am the scion of a mysterious family harboring the double-meaning of twin brothers like its own codex. The key to the code is even more elusive. For I am neither the apparition of the Jew nor a believer in the very black magic whose secret I protect with a disciplined mastery. In the dank cellar of my apartments I labor to disclose the secret meanings of mystical texts, only to mock the code of their mystery by publishing it to the world in anonymously distributed broadsides. I keep myself secret from myself by this convolution of my faith. Would my brother have sought to understand me if he had lived to discover this, my most perverse private practice? Or would he have sought to correct the angle of the mirror to safeguard our fragile reality?

As I say, the leg is a question mark.

But there is nothing more to be said of it. Something must be done. I had decided.

I determined to approach the leg. Hearing my chary step ring as feebly as the tapping of the blind beggar's stick, I wished for the cloak of an impenetrable darkness as protection against the deed that was before me. Who would want to see it? Who would want to go closer? But I couldn't escape it. The limb was not even within my queasy reach before the tapping of the blind man's stick had set up a grisly resonance in my arms. The unflexed muscles, the bicep and the forearm, even the ligaments that made a small harmonium of my whistling rib cage were gruesomely prescient with the ghostly weight of that portion of the body meant to support its whole heaviness. If I took another step I would feel it most in my own leg, a nibbling at the kneecap, a lightness to the foot that was the furthest thing from a dance-step. I was already toppling from the precipice of my stomach.

It was by that involuntary motion that I stooped, now close enough to take the leg into my already shivering embrace.

And how can I describe the touch? I stooped even lower. I reached for the jointed section. You might have thought I was about to casually swing it over my shoulder with the nonchalance of the hard working butcher. But lifting it I felt a gentle jaw bite softly upon my hand where the knee joint closed involuntarily upon my palm. It was still limber with the life that was so garishly missing. Its breath, that warm upon my grip, told me how recent was its dismemberment.

So the leg held me as much as I held it.

I would have to think about this. It was certainly dead. But how was it so alive? I might have been face-to-face with its phantom personage stammering an introduction of my trembling self. But it was no more meaningful than if I were addressing myself to a dog with the pat of my hand.

So I resolved to carry it. I would not keep it in my rooms.

I carried it into the street like a sleepwalker. I can barely picture it myself. I am struggling like the dreamer recalling the most frightful dream. But I do remember feeling the cool shade of the arcaded courtyard in which I dwelt pushed back from my forehead like a hood by the brusque heat of the sun advancing to the meridian. In broad daylight I was a man fully dressed for the business of the world. Walking. Cradling a severed leg in my arms. Its hinged extension, awag as a puppy struggling to be free from my grip. And yet no one looked upon me. They averted pale faces. No crowd gathered, not even a gaggle of roistering street urchins rushed to taunt me with rude gestures or hard stones.

And as I progressed down the narrow street I began to hear my own footsteps as if they were following me. Those whom I passed had let their abruptly averted gazes be drawn into the slack shadows hanging curtain-like upon the facades of houses and bodegas where under that cover of shade they then stood stock still. Horses tethered to their posts are more animate. A street of statues. I might have been a noble general upon horseback myself, strutting past the heroes of the nation immortalized in stone on either side, already feeling the bevel of the sculptor's chisel at the base of my neck. Weren't all eyes upon me, if the cheering chorus of their voices remained choked within the narrow throat of their dark refuge? No. I shuffled through my dream state as one thrown from the horse and only now regaining consciousness.

For most of the street by this hour was awash in blaring sunlight.

Yes, I should have sought a shred of shadow to cover myself. I should have hastily unburdened myself of my gory armful already warming with the fetor of its carnal reality.

I should have awakened more briskly from the dream state in which I had walked too far already into the glaring reaches of the real world. For the narrow street was just a dusty cobblestone passageway. A gritty stream of filth followed its desultory trickling course between my feet, straddling as they were the deep groove against which the cobbles of the street were so carefully banked. It was always thus. And the light was just the day growing longer, and hotter to be sure. In a few moments there would be not a tatter of shadow left to anyone as the noontide ravished their shameful bodies of the shade and we confronted ourselves once again, this time inescapably creatures of the same world.

At that moment the street became the needle of a steady compass, and my purpose pricked me at the needle's point. It was the conscious prickling that awakens one in all the limbs of one's body from a sleep as still as that of the dead. My head turned abruptly away from the glaring whiteness of the sleeper's pillow with the same reflex that one averts one's gaze from direct sunlight.

So, impaled as I was on the compass needle, was I my own destination?

I knew where I was of course. The street that was now fairly blazing with the noon sun was but a tributary to the becalmed sea of reflected heat that yawned before me in the Plaza de la Salvación.

And because I knew where I was, I knew who I was. I was a pilgrim. Yes, with the leg still dangling from my aching arms, a pilgrim. A pilgrim sojourning to restore a holy relic to the place that made it sacred. I could already see the stones of the Plaza de la Salvación shining back at me from the end of the street, molten and quavering with the portent of a brazen afternoon. But as I approached I also realized that the plaza was even more empty and hence even more ominously silent than the street that unraveled behind me. Indeed, the plaza had been swept of its human shadows by the dispersive rays of golden straw scratching brusquely across the coarse stones spread out in concentric rings to make up its circular expanse.

Every summer afternoon was the same.

Usually only the vendors on the periphery of the Plaza de la Salvación remained in repose beneath their striped canopies awaiting the flood tide of shadow into which the crowds would begin to assemble again in the latter reaches of the day, like dry animals come to drink at a muddy bank.

As I stood on the marbled curb of the Plaza de Salvación I could see there were no vendors. There was no one. No thing. The heat rising from the beaten copper stones blurred my vision, but I could see everything.

Yes, I could see nothing. I felt a reptilian scaliness harden upon my unblinking eyelids. I had always felt that my blood runs cold. My mouth was parched. Not even perspiration seemed possible in such suppurating heat. But I wanted more sun. I wanted to submerge in glare, so completely that the burden I hefted would at last float free of my arms, would bring a proper end to my procession.

For it was just so. A kind of religious procession: a piety, unintended to be so, yet now inescapably holy, holy, holy. Baptismal. As if the light, not the water, harbored the more desirable purification. Only the converso is spiritually limber enough to conjure such an inversion of the elements.

But the converso stands on his head in every situation, does he not? Is it not a special talent?

I simply let the leg fall from my aching arms. Less a thud. More a knock on the door.

That door opened behind me. The hand on my shoulder. The breath hotter than what radiated from the stones beneath my feet. I sensed the gurgle of an indecipherable pleading. That's why I thought I saw everything when I saw nothing. Everything was behind me where one does not naturally see. Everything *converso*. Converse, convert. The words turned in my mind like a burning muscle, until my body was face-to-face with the hand that had seized me. I was at last looking behind myself where, during the entire procession from my rooms to the Plaza de Salvación, I had imagined the prosecutorial footsteps echoing from the soles of my own boots, were those of another, as if my shadow were my pursuer. To look behind is to be behind yourself, a cowering figure, eternally at the mercy of the light.

Now fearful of looking up, fearing the blade of light that would be wielded by the Inquisitor's guard as harrowingly as the blade that might have severed the leg, fearing the irrefutable eyes of the incriminating witness, fearing an accusatorial wrath more purgatorially flaming than the omnipotent sun, I confronted instead a shadow figure even darker than myself.

Hunched under a woolen shawl, black as a sleepless summer night, and from which I imagined barbs of gray hair would protrude, an iron crown of thorns, the mouth—no longer the hand—became the supplicant. Toothless it surely was, with the lips bunched and crenellated as if a thread had been pulled. A purse-string meant to keep its modest treasure safe, though the words would out and fairly whistled through the livid orifice.

"Señor, Señor."

Were we really alone? I quickly scanned the perimeter of the Plaza de la Salvación and saw no one else whom she so strenuously struggled to address. This meant there would be no one to witness my deed but this dwarfish crone whose bones I imagined were already turning to a white powder, though perhaps she possessed more strength than I fancied, as I felt her hand creep upon my arm, the counterweight of her speech, as heavy a brick as might smash a man's jaw. At least *he* would have to remain silent!

"Who are your leg? Who are your leg?" With each repetition a harder tug upon my sleeve. And again: "Who are your leg?" I felt like a bellpull though I could not ring out an answer to her question.

Nor did I wish to stand any longer at the knee of the dismembered limb in the middle of the Plaza de Salvación like a bug under a magnifying lens. Waiting to be seen in such circumstance was surely waiting to be incinerated by whatever mysterious scrutiny lurked behind any of the darkened windows facing into the sun. Now the awkwardness of the small woman's plaintive presence became a strain upon my own legs. I needed to move, to shake the stiffness out of my stance. I needed to be gone.

"My legs are sore mother." I heard myself become a querulous child as I was unexpectedly seized by the iron grip she then closed upon my stooped shoulder.

She persisted in her quizzical inquisition.

"Who are your leg?" And as she extruded the incomprehensible words in a pinched whisper that made me think of the unconscious droppings of a sheep or a goat in mid-stride, the other hand, flapping free from some deep black fold of her skirts, arose and clenched my thigh in its talon.

The woman was upon me like a scarab upon a velvet drape. But the nimbleness of the muscle that gave her such aggressive purchase on my person excited just enough dishevelment amongst her clothes that I caught sight of a shapely leg, naked and flexed with vigorous youth down to the scalded flush of the naked foot. A marble arch made all the more seductive by the certain knowledge of how it burned. She was walking on coals. Perhaps she was only seeking relief in the physical commotion that now seemed like nothing so much as an attempt to mount me, her knees scuttling about my hips, her own hips riding to the tops of my thighs and sliding down upon what I realized was the silken chemise of her own nakedness squirming within the coarse weave of the black skirt, viscous wings of the butterfly abrading the chrysalis from within.

With a gesture that seemed to loose her hands into the sky she threw off the cloak exposing the whiteness of her body, frothing with vigor. The aureole of her small breasts beaded a violent line of sight as focused as the knife-tip of her bearded sex in its jabbing thrusts upon my supine form. Then she clapped her hands over my eyes. Or was that only her struggling to keep her grip on my upper body, she was riding me so perilously? The clapping made a crazy musical accompaniment to the blinding sense of her questioning refrain: "Who are your leg? Who are your leg? Who are your leg?"

So out of the fluttering, slapping alternation of light and dark dazzling my eyes, a pattern at last emerged. It was more exquisitely startling than the first unfurling of a butterfly's wing. For in my embattled blindness I had tripped over the very leg I had borne into such self-mystifying significance here at the very center of the Plaza de Salvación. It was a significance more frightening now than the specter the leg had presented upon my doorstep at the very start of this ever more purgatorial day.

I had tripped over the leg and fallen. And, now, lying athwart of the bone of it, so that it made my stomach seem to roll, and with the nubile incubus still so unrelentingly upon me—she had shed the black disguise of her robes so entirely that she was fully naked astride my collapsed form—I finally came to the sense of her question like the poor inebriate, sick to the point of an obligatory regurgitation.

Call it oblation if you like.

Yes, I began to understand the direction of the catechism which my hobbling inquisitor compelled me to follow. I had two legs, of no use to me now. "Who am I now?" I was forced to ask myself. I was forced to confess that I was more than one and less than two. Thus I was ready to admit the fact that I could not be what I was. How did she know it was a confession that I could be forced to make?

I was the priest's twin. Two legs. One man where formerly there had been two. Who was she to be the demon of such knowledge? Or was she set upon me to drive the demons out, an inquisition unto herself?

Now that I knew the meaning of her question however, I had to wonder: what had she to do with this other leg, which was certainly the remainder of quite a different body than my brother's but was, just as nakedly as herself, an essential prop of her outlandish theatrics?

The deliberativeness of her plot to this point ruled out madness. But the madness of the moment was as insurmountable a reality as the recognition that her mounting my physique had won. Feeling the heat from the stones of the Plaza tattooing my cheek where it was pressed flat at the lowest point of my proneness, I was of course reminded that the provenance of that leg might indeed be bled into the mortared ground beneath me. The quarterings in the Plaza de la Salvación were the most notorious in the ciudad for the crowds that could be accommodated.

And who would have transported this relic from the holy site of its dismemberment? My agile incubus! Hadn't I known it, the whole time of my pilgrimage, that I was bringing the leg back to the place where it had parted from the company of its brother limbs?

She had to have placed it where I found it. It was she who had set the stage for this whole ridiculous and ridiculously incriminating spectacle in broad daylight, where both of us would be easily espied as guilty parties, trespassers and transgressors of the official rites of the Inquisition and by that guilt, offering ourselves to the Auto da fé upon our own eminently breakable knees.

When I turned vehemently upon my back, freeing my hands in order to seize her by the shoulders, I knew that I was strong enough to still everything except the firebrand eyes. Shivering with the reflex to protect my own eyes from the shower of sparks she rained upon me with her accusatory stare, I realized that she wanted no such protection for herself. She wished to be as exposed as she was, and she wished me to share her fate.

Another twinning of fates I could not endure.

So I used my strength. I flipped her onto her own back. This time I held her shoulders against the stones of the Plaza de la Salvación as if I heaved their weight in the hammer of my torso.

But she would not be still. I lost my grip. In losing my grip I was gripped again by the fear that had been only a squeamishly sensual thought when I first entered the arena of sunlight. Now, astride the naked girl and naked to the discovering eye of the world, that thought became a lascivious surge of blood in my brain.

So much violence conducted to the body from the brain convinced me this was no dream. None of it.

Here I was with my fists squeezing the life from the slender throat as easily as I might mash a handful of cactus meat to slake my thirst. Here I was for all to see perpetrating a crime more public than even the leg would have confessed. How many times today had I already imagined the accusatory eyes amassing around me? How many times today had I already imagined what had *not* come to pass according to the edict of my most prosecutorial imagination? How many times had I escaped the fate that I deserved?

Now I had to wonder: was there anyone who, at this moment, could not see my furious enactment of the very criminality that the ordinary man, shut within the prison bars of his recurring nightmare, shudders to think he will be accused of, because it is only a matter of time?

But they did not come. They did not summon the authorities. They would not see.

Then I would force them out from behind their closed doors with the final pressure of my knuckle against the young girl's trachea.

And still, no shadows moved in the windows looking down upon the Plaza de la Salvación. No cry went up. No footsteps erupted on the perimeter of the illumination in which my deed shone so glaringly.

So I might confess that I was dazzled by the blindness to my deed. I half believe that I was its perpetrator just to prove to myself the existence of those witnessing eyes to which I had at the very last clearly become invisible.

Am I exonerated at last?

*S*o even the taster admits his guilt.

Do you forgive the deed if it is confessed like a poultice for the gaping wound? Do you have love in your heart Samaritan, even for the criminal who robs the victim of the righteousness of her victimization? I see you annunciate your forgiveness with such a discreetly wrung tear-drop of lamentation. Nor did you expect this dilemma to appear on the doorstep of your conscience as provocatively as a leg.

But then you never expected me.

Really. Your face is such an open window. The wine taster would certainly have wished that you had been standing at one of those windows looking out over the Plaza de la Salvación. You have the accusatory finger that all maudlin sympathizers keep at the ready, scabbarded in the prayer-fully arranged hands of holy repose. Ah, you could have doubled your pity. You could have pitied the poor girl so possessed by her derangement. And then you could have pitied her executioner, led away in his coveted chains. Perhaps he was her savior after all. Both guilty in any case. Who is not?

If you rest that fingertip in the moist corner of your mournful eye, aren't you fearful that it might rust?

✦ ✦ ✦ ✦ ✦

Well I must tell you that I saw the crone shaking her finger at you at the top of that shadow-shrouded staircase at number 6 in the Calle de Fernando. I assume you know at this point what you failed to notice then: that I stood only two or three treads below you. But climbing like you, heavenward.

You owed her money from another time. She would not let you pass the perfumed threshold unless you paid in advance. She coughed raspingly between the imprecations she hailed upon your bowed head.

Doubly ashamed?

Doubly ashamed, you let her take the Escudos from your purse herself. Her long brown fingers foraging beneath the beady focus of one eye, she kept you pinned at the threshold with the other.

And with her leg. Bent at the knee, its ample nudity lunging from the skirts that were like the curtains hiding the bustle of actors in the theater, her leg obstructed your passage. One would use one's leg in such a way to block the access of a dog to the kitchen.

Then I was right behind you, so that we would be admitted together, brothers of a sort. You would not have looked for my face would you— perhaps I was cowled in any case. Which made it all the simpler for me to pass you up, to find my alcove, would you believe it? Such poorly lit quarters, as you know avail safe harborings for every secret need, even the most craven, some would say.

It was a structure not even describable as a warren of filthy rooms. Once one passed through the guarded portal, vaguely an anteroom to some marble-clad architecture long forgotten, but originally imagined for purposes of some grand sociability, one had to slither along a seething hallway that ran parallel to two tiers of what could best be described as racked wooden lean-tos on silts. They hovered in a vertical space that seemed to be haunted by the aspirations of a vaulted ceiling. Several of its crumbling coffers were visible as speechless puckerings in the darkness. Perhaps twenty pigeonholes in all. Above ground catacombs. Serried cells of a wasp's nest. Each cell was shrouded with a curtain through which the silhouette of a simple pallet was made luridly apparent by a single candle. Always an imminent conflagration.

Beneath the supportive framing that arose from floor level into a criss-crossing of massive roof beams that must have been looted from some collapsed palace, lay murky recesses in which one could imagine there lurked beasts, grizzled with the rankest fur, for whom the burrow was their natural habitat.

Three moveable ladders were the only access to the niches above. A churlish guard attended at the foot of each ladder, slouched upon a lower rung, awaiting the call to shoulder the tottering length of it up and down the line.

In that space, every voice was audible, the harsh words of contempt, the urgent pleas, the accelerating repetitions of a ragged name, and especially the slick yelpings denuded of all articulate speech. Such a fervid din. So how did the ladder tenders do the bidding of whomever called them from above and below?

More to the point, how did I, witnessing from within the furls of darkness below you, hear every feathery word of your complicated solicitation teetering as you were, in more ways than one, on the topmost rung of the ladder?

Certainly you have my oath that I will not tell. This is no part of Osvaldo's story for us to interpret.

But this is what I heard:

"My dear."

"My honor."

"Can we speak of your virtue one more time? It is not too late, I assure you."

"Take my hand if you are unsteady." Did you drop a coin for the ladder man? Or just step off the ladder and let yourself be embraced?

"Not yet. Not yet. Not yet."

"Oh, I am sinful beyond any speech that can salve, let alone save. The words would blister upon our lips if we attempted it. Let me burn. The skewer is already through me. The fire is already lit. It is a just meal for He who judges."

"A meal?"

"But I'm sure you told me that He had an appetite as do we all. A tasty morsel am I not? You said so. You did. I've seen myself glistening on your lips as brightly as in any mirror."

"Not yet. No. Please. Show me that you think about your innocence. No, none of us is innocent. Show me that I've said exactly those words to you. Show me. Tell me. Be so innocent that you will be within my reach."

"But my time."

"We'll save time if you speak to me as I must hear it. It is my time now. Bought and paid for: mine for the time. Take my hand. Let my foot touch the threshold. But do say what I must hear."

"Oh, I am sinful beyond any speech that can salve, let alone save."

"Yes, yes."

"But perhaps. Do I dare say it now? But perhaps, only you. Perhaps only your forgiveness. Are you my only hope?"

"I am my dear. I am."

What I heard then was the chuffing and the slap of one chest heaved upon another. Perhaps a sob. The rest was swallowed into the gullet of a squalid din that unexpectedly reared up in that vaulted space, sound indistinguishable from the tumescing heat, the fetor of exercising bodies blaring: the menacing, suppressed roar of a beast turning in the oppressive confinement of its cage.

I try to make it sound hellish. I wonder if I succeed with you. What would Osvaldo feel? Aren't we meant to compare ourselves with our stories? With our favorite characters? You say you sympathize, Samaritan. Sympathy. Sympathy. Or do I merely sibilate, sowing the temptation to say what is not so?

Slithering me.

Perhaps I've always been invisible.

At the age of five my brother and I discovered the vanishing contours of our semblant selves. We played our first tricks on our parents whose notice we trusted most.

I came to his name. He to mine. Only on each others' lips did those syllables know their proper roost in the world. Ours were the only eyes that could see. The world was blinded altogether in its delight at seeing us both at once.

"But mother," I would say, "he is not here. It is only I."

"Who?"

"Whom did you call?"

I knew *whom* so much better than she. Knowing that much, my brother and I realized we could be anywhere we liked. Time and space had no boundaries. Of course we dressed alike. That was indispensable. But that is already a mother's preference, the better to distinguish her children from the rabble. Even in that way we would be indistinguishable from those who would not want to perceive a difference. The converso is so obliged. Togetherness was our realm of visibility. Apart, we were like mischievous ghosts, touching the shoulders of strangers in the dark, whispering out of the breeze, conjuring the homely familiarities with which our parents fleshed the barest difference between us, only to produce the response of the other.

"Oh, stop your incessant whistling," my mother would teasingly say, full of her pride in the choirboy's peerless voice.

"It wasn't me." I would answer through sibilant teeth, tuneless and tone deaf as I was known to be compared with my brother. Yes, there are always differences. But who can know them for whom they are?

At last I came to see this fact for myself and that day was the real precipice of my disappearance.

✦　✦　✦　✦　✦

The heat of the July sun pouring directly through the open window gave a yeasty animus to the chill of my father's laboratory. It stood atop the cavernous limestone cellars in which the Cardinal's grapes fermented endlessly. The stone floor which was but a shared membrane between the two domains, just as continuously radiated a damp coolness, clutching a tight cough at its core. I sat upon the tall wooden stool which was my father's perch when he worked, feeling the eddies of warm air meeting cold air and sharply attuned to the strenuous undulations of my brother's voice stirring the air in another of our rooms in the Cardinal's country residence, *Las Cuervas,* where another window was open to the light of a glorious day. Breath and tongue. We were brother senses of a body that resembled the most diaphanous spirit by our casual indifference to the distances between us.

On the massive oaken table before me a dozen tulip-shaped phials were racked upon a wooden frame. Each was upended and impaled upon a fat peg. A handful of unlit candles was laid out like a set of brushes beside a painter's palette. The boards of the table wore a sheen of still fragrant beeswax over the purple birthmarks that blotched its surface in testimonial to the labors of the vine. No one had worked here for days. My father had been called away to the most distant vineyards where a virulent mold spore was siphoning the juices of the Cardinal's most prestigious grape.

I was as alone as my brother would have appeared to be, should someone have come upon him at his vocal exercise. As ambiguous a presence in the world.

I was merely breathing. Idly inhaling. I was dallying with the pollination of the beeswax that was still abuzz in the wings of my nose. Then it seemed that the very prick of the stinger might have released the nectar of the wine stains sealed beneath its sheen, as though that frenzied stinger had pierced the skin of the grape itself. A bubble burst. Something gushed like a pent up sea englobed in a vegetable skin. I felt the throb of it in my tongue, smooth, spasmodic, and deliciously pleasant. It was a sensation without precedent that nonetheless seemed native. And was there a secret passageway between the nose and the tongue?

And now the room itself was suffused with the taste of that fragrance, though I had not stirred the air, heavy as it was with the condensation of sunlight. No. I had not stirred the atmosphere even with the ecstatic shiver which seemed to authenticate my sense that something was happening to me, perhaps without me. Like the weather, though the unclouded sunlight poured itself through the window without abatement.

But there is no such thing as internal weather. And rooms do not begin to sweat with their own glandular exertions. The world is outside the body. Or so I thought. So I thought.

The certainty of what my olfactory buds were tasting or my tongue sniffing, brought out the dog in me, homing to the scent. On the far wall, through a stone arch there were steps to the cellar. Their descent would be a footless venture into the dark. The obscurity welled up to the brim of the limestone floor upon which I had left my chair overturned like an abandoned shoe. I could make out a heavy mahogany banister that invited my unsteady hand to try the depths.

Down I would have to go. I went without the illumination that the torches mounted upon the wall would have permitted, with the dispensation of an adult hand. I had no fear of the dark, or the drinkable depth that I knew that stairway plumbed.

It was already inside me, as kindred as blood to the bone, you might want to say. And yes, it was my father's vocation. I was a familiar of these places, these smells, this wetness that is not water. But it was my nose, my tongue that yearned to swim in that fragrant darkness. It was not me. Nose and tongue. They were the real creatures of that undulant current whose flickering fins and flashing tails at that moment seemed to wriggle beyond the reach of reason's frantic net.

I continued my descent. When I felt my foot stop upon the most silent of stones I held myself ready. Because now, as if I stood where I could not breathe among creatures whose enviable life-breath bubbled invisibly around me, I knew I would have to adapt. At this moment, as I walked on the bottom of a vinous sea, what creatures kindred to my nose and tongue would swim before my eye, to convince me of my absolute strangeness to myself?

Though I was blinded by the darkness, I knew they were there, seething. Yeasts greedily ingesting and even more energetically casting off the sugars of the grape pith. Tannins bitterly sloughed from the shriveling skins and sheared bits of stick and stem. The gasses of fermentation erupting upon the surface of the acidic ponds like egg clusters from some empurpled amphibious species struggling into the realm of breathable air. By now I was all nose and tongue, as though the remainder of my human carriage were dissolved into the buoyancy in which both nose and tongue eluded any self-control.

From this moment on, I was present, but not to myself.

Still I touched wood. Or so it seemed, without a hand to prove it. Without a toe to stub against its bulk. Wooden staves. Within their circumference they held the volatile must. This I knew from sure-sighted memory. But what I experienced in the moment did not appear in the brilliant sunshine of that knowing mind.

I was a quick child. Fleet of thought. Everyone said so even before I became a tiresome amusement to adults forcing their smiles into uneasy accompaniment with my sing-song recitation of the fermentation process in Latin.

Now my only thoughts were immersed. Not in darkness alone. Nor in the dark juices of the crushed fruit. Unthought. I felt my body to be as bloated with what's inside it as the grape underfoot. Nor was that a thought, even unto bursting. It was nothing I could grasp with the word *mine*. Neither inside nor out. I was gone. Not. Not even *from*. *Was* is all I can say with honesty.

It was. The velvet dark, furred as it was with vinous bouquet, wet as it was with what I realized were the involuntary palpitations of a slavering tongue, was suddenly and overwhelmingly a tremor.

And that was not me either. I perceived that there was another person. Within the vat. Swimming. I knew by the clutch in the throat, the audible gluttony for a mouthful of air breaking the surface of the vatted pond, splashing, spattering my face with the kick of what I told myself must be human feet.

So anointed with that liquid, which had up to this moment been little more than the urgent tugging of nose and tongue, sensation became a world of its own entirely. It was no longer my sense of smell, no longer my sense of taste, but comprised of its own particles and germs of being, a runaway alchemy beyond the power of the wizard's frenzied wand. Now nose and tongue were themselves dissolved into the medium they choked upon. The word *intoxication* is used to steady the stance of the dizzy imbiber. I have to say that word is a broken crutch for the tumbling mind. Just so the body was no support for the headiness suffusing the space where I might have thought I stood a moment before, if I had not already felt myself lost to the featureless depth of this underworld.

Then came the bubbling of a voice from the otherwise becalmed surface of the vat that bulked invisibly before me. The body immersed within it was audibly trying to be as still as possible. Then movement, the shedding of the depth she swam in. Hands scuttling to a grip upon the iron rim of the vat. The body hovering above it, finding its legs, standing. Now her toes curling around the iron rim of the vat readying to make the leap. Yes, it was unmistakably a girl's voice that rang out and would have been barely a mist above the becalmed surface, if I'd had eyes to see such inquisitiveness.

She filled the word "who" with the same air that she would have held in her chest to submerge.

"Who is there?"

It was a bubble that burst upon my eardrum and left me breathless at the sound of her re-immersion.

Had she known I was there? Or had she been as confident of her solitude as I had been of my absent being?

The breath she took before the reprise splash, the kick of the feet over the head, the doubling of the body curling upon itself into a submersive somersault pitted the depth of her lungs against the bottom of the vat. For a moment there was the mewling silence of the ear plugged with wax. There was a barely sensible swaying of something in the air, the way a tidal shift can dizzy the beachcomber standing upon dry land only two steps away. Then another becalmed moment. Aura of the indrawn breath held to its limit. The sound of a knock on a door so far away the ear seems to be retreating within the vortex of its own coiled anatomy. Then she surfaced with the force of a fountain.

This time her breach was unbridled, propelled with a spurting yelp. No doubt when she spit, it was the effervescing ferment of the grape upon her tongue that struck the bell of her voice.

It struck me harder. For it brought my body back to me like a bloated corpse flushed to the surface from its captivity in a sunken hull. I had been dragged out to sea on a merciless tide. Now I was cast back upon the shore.

And what of the sea change?

I could see.

The gradual, involuntary dilation of the pupils performed its magic. The shades of black began to appear, edged with deep purple. If one peers long enough into the dark nothing, the wetness of the straining eye becomes indistinguishable from the quavering surface of the world it heaves itself upon, reflecting what is there in thin water. The turgid muscle beneath merely flexes to inveigle the most feeble rays of light to strike its stubborn tain.

Illumination is relative of course.

Though she was there like a muscle under a rippling skin, I made out the bird shape of her. Again she was perched on the iron trimmed rim of the vat. Her knees were tucked under her chin. Her shoulders were hunched forward. Her arms were straight to steady the balance of the whole body rocking against undulant darkness surrounding her. I thought she might unfold a wing. Her long wet tresses pulled at her scalp, tightened about the crown of her head until their tautness glinted an obsidian sheen.

"I knew you were there," her shadow smiled. Teeth are luminous too. Was that what made her smile? The better to see me see?

"Come." Because she used her hand to gesture I knew what she knew.

I shed my clothes invisibly enough that the sudden chill upon my flesh made me feel as if I were the shadow cast by the little pyre that rose up around my ankles. I shuddered more with embarrassment at the thought that her eyes were no less capable than mine of titillating the darkness.

Then another splash. She had kicked off from the rim of the vat again. Submerged. Surfaced. Spurted a fountain of warm liquid upon my gooseflesh. Yelped. Paddled to the rim again, now within reach of my quaking anatomy. Her brazenness was utterly past me: the thing we are blind to because it is too quick for blinking sight.

"I've already peed in the wine. So you will have to consider what you can contribute." She didn't giggle to say it.

And with those words she reached over the rim of the vat, through an opacity as impenetrable to me as my own thought of it happening, to grasp me in the place where I could not be expected to make a decision of my own. She had my presence before I could rush to catch up with it. And then there really was nothing to think about.

I followed myself meekly up the four rungs of the ladder swagged against the walls of the vat. She had reached down. Up, I wavered, hovering over the vinous pond. I could not make out where the air stopped and the vaguely membranous skin of the must no doubt shivered to admit me to its depth. But for the moment I was perched above her upon the cold hard rim of hammered iron where her own feet had been only moments before. Now I would do what she did. Her grip upon me was only strengthened by the rigid stalk of my bodily excitement.

I would be plucked and fall. Easy fruit. Perhaps a kinship with the vaporous grape with which she was already drenched and dripping.

So I lowered myself into a crouch like hers, steadying myself with cold talons hooked over the metal rim. For the second time since I had immersed into the artificial darkness of this sun-drenched afternoon I felt absent from myself. But this was not the pleasure of disappearing into my brother's skin, the games we played with our resemblance. I could always find my way back from the other side of that mirror.

This was altogether the pleasure of my own skin, as pulpy as the peeled grape, as full to bursting and, at this very instant, rolling as helplessly in the palm of the master's hand before it must be tried mercilessly against the palette.

The wetness of her mouth where it replaced the grip of her hand was indistinguishable from her splash. Then I was only aware of the porcelain smoothness of her lips grinding out the seed of the pulpy mass that was myself, still perched, naked and alone upon the rim of the vat, feeling like a swelling frog-body, becoming aware of the clamminess that was my own skin tightening all over to bring out the bulge of the eyes the dorsal ridge, darker lozenges of color lumping upon the curved back.

Nor did I want to suffer the green embarrassment of being turned back into a fairy-tale boy, however princely. I wanted simply to burst like a bubble. Which I did.

I say "I". Who else would it have been then, whose fleshly remains throbbed so with the bruise of ecstasy? And from that moment I knew something about myself that was not my brother too. It was "I."

Yes "I." But not what you think. Not what I have disavowed from the first words of my narrative. This "I" was different. Its very moment of inception, after all, guaranteed that it contained nothing. A sloughed skin.

The fountain spray of grainy grape juice upon my face reminded me how much I was a creature of the skin.

She had emptied her mouth twice and was still brimming with something to express. She spit twice. She laughed twice. And then with barely a flick of her wrist she pulled me in. An empty wineskin at best, I did not float. I could not swim.

I should have simply let myself drift peacefully to the bottom of the vat, filling up with liquid as I sank until I weighed like the proverbial stone. But with the first sensation of weightless depth I began to flail wildly in the dark, unintentionally hampering her attempts to come to my rescue. I might have rescued myself by calmly and deliberately putting both feet to the planks of the floor. However slick the floor of the vat might have become with the sedimentation of the other shucked skins, I would have found my head above water, bobbing like a coconut. I was tall enough. Gulping the seething wine-juice with the spumy air that was within easy reach if only I had raised myself upon the tips of my toes and stretched the frantic supplication of my stiffening lips into a veritable chicken neck of convulsive pecking at the air, I would have enjoyed the intoxication of knowing I was in no danger. Instead I struggled for an entanglement with her limbs that surely put us both at risk, though I was indeed intoxicated with the knowledge that there was something I ardently wished to save from drowning. There was something of mine, even if she had wrung it from me like the chicken's poor neck.

"Your seed. The seed of the grape. They are brothers now," she laughingly declared as she helped me to my embarrassed footing.

The mash of seeds and skins and stems that oozed between my toes were a kind of earth however much the watery surface of the vat was lapping over my chin. Earth, water. And she was a kind of fire. With our arms around one another we were steady enough against the fuming wavelets to sip their brew in harmonious rhythm with mouthfuls of cleansing air. It was a kind of world where the four elements combined to make an elixir of life that was beyond compare.

And that is what pleased me most. For where there is no comparison there can be no difference. For my brother it would be different, and I forever singular. Perhaps, I was myself at last. The girl's irrepressible laughter sealed this knowledge with the molten wax of an impetuous kiss. I waited for the insignia of my self to harden in its aftermath.

+ + + + +

But I was deceived. She was not alone as I had thought to have found her. And so she was no more herself than I.

"They drowned my father in these vats," were her breathless words upon breaking the bond with my lips. I heard the splash of her dive, the breath of her feet kicking the air. I felt her feathery transit between my legs and when she surfaced behind me I turned to hear the reason.

"He was denounced. To say what you are is one thing. He who will not confess what he is not is an intolerable nuisance to the Inquisition. The *Califacdores* wish for all of us to dwell in the land of what is not. Speak for yourself and become someone else or be what you can be called. It is the same thing of course. Jew. The word with two voices. I am and I am not. Well my father never said anything. That was his nature. So he was dragged from the vineyards like a stubborn mule by a rope around his neck."

And in the shadow that her speech cast upon the already impenetrable darkness lapping between us, my eyes were somehow stirring in their blindness. What is it like for the bird unfurling within the unpecked shell? Will there always be light if there is something to be illuminated? My thoughts were an aura around the invisibility of her voice. It made me think I could see. It made me think I could see the aureole of her breasts flashing purple reflections upon the impassioned liquid in which we stood across from one another. It made me think that her breasts had eyes. I did not want to see what they would say. But she testified out of the ever more breathless witness of her buoyant flesh.

"They mocked my father's silence by aping the confessional word they sought to draw out of him with intonations and inflections that mimicked the dog, the rooster, and the pig. The circle of jeering voices became as filthy as the rope around his sweating neck and stained his skin with its shadow. They kept him dancing on the end of the rope with sticks that prodded him from every side. They taunted his black power to turn himself inside out and show the animal he was hiding under his skin. One of them proclaimed that baptism was the answer.

"They were his perspiring friends from years of toiling amid the grapes and it took them no time at all to be wicked enough to think that you could marry communion to baptism. And didn't one of them have the heretical hair to chortle, 'Our mother Maria would be tickled?'

"'Into the vats with him and the heathen shall be washed blind of his sin.'

"'Body, blood, and *spirits*,' as they would say of the flammable vapors that rise in invisible clouds from the unskimmed surface of the musting vats.

"There was no such transubstantiation, let alone resurrection for my father. They held him by his bare feet. Even before they immersed him his head was bowed under the enormous yoke of a plough horse they had hoisted upon him. It smelled of hay and maybe even some sweat kindred to the ring of perspiration that was the noose of his daily labors. Like all of them, he wore a scarlet and gold bandana to soak it up.

"The heavy yoke made an anchor of his head. He came to rest at the bottom of the vat, all movement slackened in the legs, in less time than most of them had taken to position themselves for a good view.

"No one seemed to see me drowning myself in the deep shadow of the staircase that descends from your father's tasting room. I was like any child confused by the childlike antics of men whose exhaustion or drink or both made them giddy with game.

"With droplets of liquid beading up like a spontaneous squint of tears on their cheeks they each stepped back from their action as though enveloped in a sudden fog of incomprehension. They tottered. Their arms gestured without purpose in the ominously stilled air. Their breathing was as labored as if each of them bore the weight of a *cuba grande* of grapes upon sagging shoulders. The sounds of their heavy boots were muffled and seemed to have lost the rhythm of the dance that had whirled them into the stunning sobriety of a stone wall. Then a voice like the sound of breaking teeth rattled with the syllables of my father's name.

"They appeared to be abruptly awakened from the dream of their rabble rousing, rubbing their eyes and yawning with disbelief at the deed they had performed. 'Fernandino! Fernandino! Fernandino, awake!' Staring in disbelief at one another's deed, they wept in one another's guilty arms. And then they worked out the official language of their denunciation.

✦ ✦ ✦ ✦ ✦

"The denunciation was reportedly delivered by an unidentified man to the representative of the Suprema where he sat in his black cassock soaking up the shade of the well head, islanded in the sea of sunlight that flooded the *Plaza de los Hermanos*. The young priest was waiting for his horses to be brought to him. He would mount the saddled steed and depart. The vision of the town's cathedral shimmering in the heat would soon evaporate completely from his mind.

"But of course my father was not the Jew. Perhaps not enough of a Catholic, though who would know that? I am certain he did not enchant a chicken to sing the Angelus at the commencement of the Hebrew Sabbath. And in any case, the denunciation was of little interest to the itinerant priest who only wished to move on to the next hill town where the beds were perhaps not so infested with lice. He only breathed the name to the hosteler who delivered his horses. He answered the accuser with nothing more than a question about why he should be bothered with accusations at this late hour. The word, the name Fernandino hung listlessly in the air between the two men. It mingled with the dust of the horses' hooves that arose at the priest's departure.

✦ ✦ ✦ ✦ ✦

"So I swim. I am my father's daughter though the nuns call me orphan. The Cardinal commends their mercifulness to me. They know little enough. The denunciation did not follow me. The murderers had wiped their lips of it before they took their leave of this cave. Now that my father was dead it mattered to no one. The nuns have designs on me though.

"So I swim. When I am not doing the bidding of the nuns in the laundry, or in the kitchen. I swim in these vats and when I break the surface for air I fill my father's lungs with it. I will never see him again.

"But I will see you Osvaldo Alonzo de Zamora. I will see you and darken my eyes with lowered lids and such luxuriant lashes. You will see me in the sunlight and think I am the most beautiful girl you could have imagined in the darkness. You will know me by my voice. You will desire me more than you have already confessed in the utterance of your stuttering seed, soon to be sown in barriques for the ages.

"Will you ever taste yourself, I wonder.

"Not I. I will continue to swim. I will soak up the juices of the crushed grape until my skin is indistinguishable from the wrinkled skin of the grape when it is finally sloughed into the must. I will exude its bouquet. I will swim until the nuns cannot scrub the fruity blush from my skin and must confront me as the demon I would have to be to be so colorful. For, surely, I will become their demoness. The empurpled skin is impregnated with shame.

"Every young girl is already under suspicion when she begins the bleeding. One always suspects the pretty ones like me. The pretty faces look the most fearsome with horns. The horns are protuberances of the nubile body that no girl can hide from public sight unless she keeps her own face averted from the world.

"The horns come out and it is no longer for the nuns to decide our fate, any more than our blossoming bodies were decisions taken by us to be wicked.

"No. I will finally be delivered up, not in a word, but in the colorful flesh to the itinerant priest who will be forced to send for a barred wagonette with wheels as large as cheeses. I will be transported. Not like Santa Theresa, who is no sister of mine for all her titillations, but like the barriques of finished wine belabored over the barren hilltops to Sevilla by senseless mules. Naked upon the dais in the Plaza de la Salvación, my denunciation will come from my own mouth as incontrovertibly as the tip of my tongue. The Auto da fé will see to it that the fires of my demon lust have wood to burn."

So she was no less a doppelgänger than I, no more herself. She was her father's daughter. But she fathered his fate upon herself without knowledge of whom she might have been otherwise. Though I had already possessed her, she was beyond my reach.

Soon the privilege of invisibility would be hers as well. My sister.

*Y*ou say you know what he meant by the word "sister," do you, Samaritan? That he would have sat stalwartly beside her at her trial, a sworn witness to her innocence, incurring by that loyalty every conceivable suspicion like the contagion of a pox, if one were swaddled in the bedclothes of the recently departed. Yes. You believe that familial feeling is more than the pigmented serum that throbs through us and makes us blush. Mankind is your brotherhood, so you say.

Admirable. Very admirable, Samaritan. And you do not blush to say it!

But you have your sister, don't you? Do you take pride in the whiteness of her habit? In the absolutism of her vows?

Yes, the sin of pride is habitual too. You make a witty point. But I take no pride in knowing so much about a man who is so intimately a family member of mankind as yourself. Love of mankind is a humility I may humbly share in my knowledge of your family.

I have spoken with your sister, after all.

You didn't know I am her confessor? So when I say I know her, I am speaking of the real world, though the glare of her habit tells us she has renounced it.

She did not denounce you if that is your worry. Why, what would she say?

No, she only told me of your youth together. You were children to the brooding stepfather, as if by immaculate conception. Your mother plighted your fates to him. You bear no imprint of a resemblance to him unless the color that has rushed into your face is the shadow of his open hand upon your cheek.

Your natural father was dead.

You were a young man of nine years. Am I remembering correctly?
Well, I only spoke with her yesterday!

The tears brimming in her otherwise cloudless blue eyes certainly
honored the helplessness of that nine-year-old child who suffered the loss
of his father before he could be a proper guardian to his sister. So perhaps
those tears were salted with a bit of selfishness as well, to make them so
savory. What else does one say to one's confessor, after all?

He was a wine merchant, your father. The grape had made him
a rich man, even flamboyant with his wealth, as if he were a reckless
imbiber as much as an aggressive retailer of such intoxicating wares.
Perhaps he even boasted of the number of casks he could accommodate
in his cellar where he trusted that the sun would never point its revelatory
finger. Who knew in truth how many casks, how many bottles, what a
high tide of riches buoyed this man of fur and emerald embellishments.
He would have been wise to understate the facts.

You have his nose I'm told. A nose is nothing to speak of unless it
calls attention to itself. He called attention to himself—your father the
wine merchant—to his rings and medallions, to the double loggia of his
city house that permitted a guest to look out to the street or into the impec-
cably cultivated garden with its alabaster fountain, to the gold-striped
livery of his house servants, to the beauty of his wife, the beatitude of
his children. His nose was a veritable scimitar.

Who could envy such a nose? But such a nose could arouse the al-
ready envious soul to see what kind of root would be exposed should one
pull on it. We look at the line of the nose, at the set of the eyes, at a smoky
cast to the skin as though we were looking at the internal organs of the
body which, if so exposed, would be the spectacle of a horrifying death.

That, after all, is what we intend. We look for the outward sign
that will release the yearning within us all to make a denunciation so

terrible that the lash, or the carving knife or the rack will be applied without mercy. The spectacle will lead us to the knowledge that other people possess interiors as dark and as turbulent as our own, the writhing made finally peaceful in the lifeless cords of sinew and shapeless mire of muscle and soft tissue, that, given time, pools upon the stones of the Plaza. The shine of blood reflects our fearfulness with a proper gaiety under a blazing midday sun, a miraculous wellhead. To see ourselves smiling in the blood, that is our true salvation. And to think, it can all be accomplished with the utterance of a single word.

Who denounced your father? It is a question still. Of course your sister could not tell. And the widow, when she was well enough did not speak of the past. Her new husband was a Councilor of State who has now given his stepdaughter to the church. What else could be expected of him?

I am told the denouncer was a child.

When a child is interrogated it occurs in a private room. The walls are so thick. The massive stones might be impacted with ice they throw off such a chill into the room. It rattles the spine. The windows are shrouded with heavy drapery. One hears footsteps echoing in the halls. But the door is shut and barred. A man in a black velvet wimple which the child has only ever seen adorning the face of a woman, speaks in soft tones as if the woman had a beard. The words of the questioner rub coarsely against the child's smooth cheek. For the face of the child is kept close to the face of his questioner. The chair in which he must confront his questioner seems as closed as a confessional, fitted as it is with massive wooden arms and heavy mahogany panels. The child, passing his hand nervously back and forth over one of the panels feels the carved relief of the cross in his palm as a prickling sensation. His fingertips pick at star shapes and a half-moon. He is restless.

He thinks of the heavens hung with stars and a moon. His feet hang loosely in empty air above the floor. But he feels leaden. For he has been told that he is duty bound to speak. *He has only to look again at the iron crossbar on the door, battened with roughly hammered nail heads, to know what this means.*

He does not wish to speak. But he cannot say so again. Or the hairy wrist will be bared from the questioner's sleeve again to find leverage enough upon the child's arm to make it snap. Thus the child will begin to think how he is made of joints and sinews that can be easily broken.

The questioner leans forward so that his voice barely brushes the air with its coarse purpose:

"Have you seen him hurrying to his cellar as if he could stop the sun from falling on the roof of the cathedral by quickening his own footsteps?"

Or some such question as this. There are so many questions that could be posed.

"Does he dart a glance over his shoulder before he re-enters the shop which he himself had closed only an hour before? Does he descend the stairs where you are already hiding in the darkest recess soaking up the shadow spilt over the railing of the stairway? Do you see that he stands ceremonially before an unadorned stone wall where a wobbly table used for business is prepared with a single candle, a bottle, a goblet. Does he pour? Does he raise the glass above his head? Does he intone words in a language that is like a mouthful of food that has already been well chewed by someone whose plate is not your own?

"But how could you secrete yourself behind the stairway to the cellar awaiting his nervous footfall, if you had already espied him from behind when he re-entered his shop?"

The questions are meant to be confusing. Can you imagine a child lost in the fog of such questioning? You might reach for help and grab hold of the most dangerous arm.

Was it you, Samaritan? Were you the denouncer of your own father by an accident of the slippery tongue?

Is my intuition that good? No, for the second time I abjure pride. Do you really think so little of me, Samaritan?

Of course I have the story from your sister. Growing up in the gloomy shadow of an older brother who wept without provocation, she absorbed the story like the effects of perpetual dampness, a water stain on a peeling wall, though we live in the land of the unblinking sun.

The questions were confusing. The questioner was merciless to put them to a child. The child could not have guessed that there were other voices, faces never seen, to prime the pump of suspicion. The child could not have known how a glass of wine should incriminate a wine merchant. But others knew.

Judaizer.

The boy could not find the word in his memory. On the lips of the questioner it sounded like a lozenge to be sucked for its sugars. How sweet it would be to hold it under his own tongue and think of nothing else but the slivered thinness of it dissolving until it was gone, until the questioner was gone, until the stones of the chamber melted away, until the way home was already under his feet, until he could let the words in his mouth go free. He had told them nothing.

But the word did not dissolve in the questioner's mouth. It sat on his tongue. Like a small toad that might spring at the boy if he kept his silence. So the child said "I do not understand sir, what you mean?"

The hairy wrist lunged from its shadowed sleeve again and the boy felt his forearm burn in the questioner's grip. The word sprang off the questioner's tongue. The stickiness of its tiny webbed toes made the boy want to spit. His mouth was befouled with it. But now the word was his.

"Judaizer, yes, my father makes the juice of the grape dance on his tongue. He says so. It is his trade. Many others follow him. They follow his lead. He is a leader of the dance."

We know the boy did not know what he had said. Does it matter? The father was a wealthy man. He was a man who mirrored his wealth in every public appearance he made. Richly cloaked. Dazzlingly bejeweled. Preening in his speech and gesture. A too proud man. His richness, proportionate to his nose, was hook enough to hang him on. Others called his sin by another name perhaps. But the boy unwittingly spoke the truth. For a sin is a sin whatever name it flatters itself with. There was a kind of blind justice in what the boy would forever think of as his crime. For the father was condemned. But not to the garrucha. *Not to the rack. Not to the water torture. Not to confiscation of his worldly goods. Not even to banishment. Certainly not to the stake.*

For performing a rite of the Jewish Sabbath this man—whose Christian blood was indisputable, but perhaps because it was allowed to continue to flow through his veins was inadmissible evidence—was condemned to wear the sanbenito.

It was ordered that he exchange his sartorial finery for a sack-like yellow garment arrayed with black diagonal crosses. In his case the crosses were to be embroidered over the breasts, the genitals and the buttocks. The sentence was for life.

So the man hanged himself. He hanged himself rather than humble himself to what, after all, is the color of the sun. Don't you see, Samaritan? His pride would not be so illuminated. The suicide proves the sinfulness of the life taken: however wrongful the name of the crime, however ill-fitting the raiment of the accusation. After all, he wears that for eternity.

Go to your little sister, Samaritan. Do not accuse her of denouncing you. Because she does speak sincerely on your behalf. She wants to save you from the conscience that she says you wear like a black hood beneath which only the eyes have ever been visible to her. She says they are the eyes of an animal who lives in a burrow. She wishes me to coax you from your dark habitat. You do not know this. You think that the heart that beats within your breast beats for all mankind. Yes, the family of mankind. You think you live among blood relations, because you have never been anything but the charitable man, the helping hand to those in need, the heart that bleeds. They are droplets of sweat, Samaritan. You do not realize that you dwell fearfully in the filth of the earth where you do not have to turn around to know that you are safe. Let us see if we can coax you out into the sunlight, the very sunlight that your father shunned out of such blinding vanity. Let us see if we can persuade the son to doff the black hood and let the sunlight shine upon your aching head.

Your sister weeps for you. But she has words only for me.

She tells me that you conceived a punishing folly: that the vindictive father had been resurrected in the wife's second husband. This you believed because the stepfather's rage at you was so monumental and because the endowment of muscle upon him was so much like a wrathful hammer. There was no resemblance whatsoever to your father's soft eyes and wide mouth, not to mention the nose which was already growing hawkish between your receding eyes. Retribution is not meant to look like itself after all. That would be mere revenge.

The stepfather stalked you from the first days of his occupation of your father's house. He only bellowed your name, harrowing the halls of the grand city palacio. His footfall was an avalanche which overtook your fleetest step. The redness in his eyes was a fire that could only be quenched with a blow to your head or his boot upon your stomach.

Nothing distracted him from his preoccupation with your physical vulnerability. He imagined that he raised his hand over an anvil to feel the full force of his presence over your person, his fist hovering, dropping, sounding its fearsome metallic fervor. Your patience upon the hate-forged point of the anvil only goaded this violence. Perhaps this salved the guilty conscience you exposed ever more ardently to the fever of his blows.

But in time there was a ripening of his interest in the stepdaughter's blushing fruitfulness. It was inversely proportionate to the indifference to pain you exhibited in all the most welted regions of your body. You had learned to swallow your tears. You stiffened your muscles in paroxysms of self-discipline that mocked the stiffness of his birch rod. You made your person into a sculpture of indifference to his hand so that at last his eye turned elsewhere for a shape he might deform.

The stepdaughter was already his.

By now, the mother had gone deaf and blind in the aftermath of a mysterious illness which forced her retirement to a room dominated by a carved marble fireplace. From its flanks the heads and forehooves of wild stallions reared up in a flaming rage. A blaze was stoked in the firebox even in the months of molten sun. She might have been burning at the stake. Did the stepfather even hear her cries? No the stepdaughter was the flame of his passion.

The stepdaughter had been remanded to the care of governesses. She had matured in an almost cloistered silence in a deep and curtained recess of the house: beyond an interior courtyard with its high gardenia hedge and its central fountain. The sound of its waters was her constant companion throughout adolescence and somehow filliated with the sobbing of the lachrymose brother ever present behind the wall of an adjacent room.

At the age of thirteen her stepfather began to regard her with a more proprietary eye. He supervised the sewing and the fitting of her clothes. The choices of fabrics were determined by the value of the richly colored threads that tightened their weave. He found the patterns for their design in paintings: the portraits of aristocratic families descended from well-burnished thrones. He ordered that enormous freestanding mirrors framed with gilt be installed in her rooms so that there would be no place from which she could not regard her own form.

Yes, the stepfather wished the stepdaughter to see what he did, so that she might recognize the look in his eye when it finally took its predatory roost. Did he imagine that by cultivating a streak of scarlet vanity in her heart he might win her sympathy for his own most livid desires? No doubt he wished to contaminate the bewildering sensations of her changing body with the sight of it, as if the light of the mirror could give off a spark of lustfulness for her own beauty. Stepping absentmindedly out of her night shift into a pooling ray of the most fiery daylight, the sulfurous sheen of her naked skin might ignite her womanhood. Then he would not have to bring the torch himself, though the way to her was through a dark forest of his mind. He imagined her flushed with his sinful thoughts.

Though she didn't know it, she was a captive of the house. Under the pretense that her chastity was being guarded against the prying fingers of the world, the stepfather rendered the house impenetrable. The rumor that ran in the street passed his threshold on footsteps hushed with pious respect for a stepfather so devoted to the spirituality of his stepdaughter's beauty, which was all the more renown for the stepdaughter's never taking the most tentative step into the public eye. And so was the stepfather deemed to be all the more virtuous himself.

Unseen, he watched. The window of his private studio looked inward upon the gardenia scented courtyard where his daughter's rooms opened upon the only unshuttered air she was permitted to breathe. The sounds of Ciudad Real bustled remotely in that air. But she did not strain to hear them. The sight of his stepdaughter flitting about the fountain, leaving an undulant wake in the gravel path upon which her footsteps danced, inhaling sunlight, exhaling song, tried his patience. Apparently she was made for sequestering and might live happily oblivious of whatever life buzzed against the glass pane that divided her from the outside world. He who had sealed her behind glass now heard the battering of his own wings where he hovered helplessly over his prey.

He would certainly have to put his fist through the glass.

And what of the brother? Did the brother warn her?

Of course she did not need to be warned. The sight of her brother's body, still shivering in the metronome shadow of the stepfather's cane, or the strappado, even when the skies had cleared and the sun flamed, the sight of him carrying his limp across the graveled walkways of the garden, the sight of him holding his head in his hands upon the roughly hewn steps that led up and down, steep as a cliff, to his stepfather's studiolo, filled her eyes just like the scalding water that collects under the welted skin.

Yes, her sight was blistered with the knowledge of her brother's pain.

No she did not need to be warned. Though the brightest sun shown right through the billows of her white shift as she cavorted around the alabaster fountainhead of the secret courtyard, to reveal the swell and curvature upon which her stepfather's eye was a storm-tossed vessel, she was not naked prey. A closer inspection would have seen her armored in her developing body, her shoulders stiffly squared, the soft outline of her breasts metal tipped, even the pubescent shadow between her legs outlined like the lunging jaw of a fierce dog, toothed with a sharp angularity.

She was already the warrior in the brother's cause.

And she kept the knife well hidden, even as she let the stepfather see the seeming nakedness of her body through the soaking veils of her childish frolic in the spray of the fountain.

She knew he would come in the dark, as she slept. He would creep as insensibly as an ant upon the back of one's leg. He would be confident that the brother, who slept on the other side of the wall, would be sealed behind the enormous cold stones of his recurring nightmare, beyond the reach of any sounds of this world. A sleep potion would be administered by the family priest in sly mockery of the communion rite.

In any case whatever cries might arise from the sister's sibling chamber, the brother would probably mistake for the murmuring of his own grief, so muffled would they be by the dungeon recesses of the memory from which this weakling no longer struggled to escape. The stepfather would come without his sword, without his heavy footfall, without the jangling of medallions that hung around his neck in honor of his official powers. He would come in susurrous ermine slippers, perhaps convinced of the svelte gentleness of the deed he contemplated by the feline padding of his soles upon the stones of the corridor, the stones themselves fairly rippling toward the stepdaughter's chamber.

But the knife slept as lightly in the cradle of the sister's hand. Neither would the stepfather anticipate the presence of the ancient but wiry nurse waiting beneath the bed frame where she quailed in the nest of rags she had been instructed to gather for ample absorption of the blood.

The young lady had spoken almost sharply to stiffen the nurse's resolve. Her words were like wind over water in the ripple of incredulity that spread across the servant's eyes, as this woman of a thousand wrinkles, who had borne the infant in her arms so many years before, understood her duty. Perhaps she felt the pupils coagulate in her eyes. The small mistress's own stare was already ice. The brave sister wished there to be no misunderstanding. Yes. There would be blood enough to overspill the rim of a barber's bowl, if the barber's hand were so unsteady, as the unwavering girl promised her own hand would not be.

But there would be no real murder. Not even a death. Only the shadow of a death.

There was of course no sun to cast a shadow extending the stepfather's reach when the moment arrived. The darkness was unmolested by the merest shard of reflected moonlight breaking the windowpane. The shrewd child had thrown a velvet cloak over each of the tall mirrors that stood about her room like minions of her father's bidding, now turned against his cause and waiting furtively for the collision of darkness with darkness.

Somehow the stepfather's unstumbling foot eluded these sentinels. He might have been a floating spirit descending from the raftered ceiling instead of trodding upon floorboards to find his way.

The nurse in her crib forced a fistful of filthy rags into her mouth when she was sure of the master's hand upon the shuddering bedpost. The young mistress lying invisibly beneath him clenched her teeth. The shadow of a shadow hovered above her, buoyed by its own breath. And then the ghost materialized. The indrawn breath became a body falling with a rush of air past its mark onto the empty bed. For in the instant of an indrawn breath the daughter had evacuated the intaglio of her own body in the mattress and had gathered herself upon her knees to give the knife-wielding hand its balance.

The stepfather would have to turn himself over to see what had occurred. This much she had planned. Time to draw another breath.

Yes, she well knew that her act must be completed from shoulder to wrist before he could find a way to gain his own knees and use the weight of his upper body to pin her to the bed cushion.

These thoughts hurtled through her brain with a sleekness that gave unrelenting momentum and unerring trajectory to her stroke. For the knife was already in before her eye could burrow through darkness to the place where she had known all along it must go precisely to the mark. She felt the tooth edge of the knife bite down on a taut cord.

She heard a cry gurgle behind her father's clenched teeth and knew that as she pulled the blade free of its incision, she was opening a gash in his hand, in the webbing between the thumb and the index finger. In his attempt to grasp what the searing pain between his legs told him what part of himself was already loosed from its fisted pocket of groin-flesh, her father had seized the withdrawing edge of the knife.

The emboldened little sister licked at the corners of her mouth where the spurted blood dripped from prominent cheekbones. She pulled the hair back from her eyes. She released the knife into the swift running stream of events, wiped her hands on the folds of impenetrable darkness in which everything was still hidden. She stood upon the agonized wave action of the already soaking mattress. Though she could not see the stepfather's face—she imagined it buried in his stomach he was so violently convulsed upon himself—she lifted her own and let her words arc over the invisible scene with the waking authority of a cock crow: "You are not dead. But you are no man either!"

The nurse had not stirred. She did not stir until the first heaving droplet of blood soaked through the mattress to make her blink.

And who had the little sister spoken to in a voice that had to be raised so high, if not the brother, huddled so far away on the other side of the wall? Her ringing words were meant to fall like a hammer upon the imaginary shackle that flexed against the muscle of his leg to keep him a prisoner of the house.

Would the brother have heard?

I ask you, Samaritan, would he have known?

Does he know? And does he know what it is to have such a sister, even if the bond of blood is the barest thread, such as appears to fray from the hacked neck of Holofernes in the paintings that depict our Judith in her moment of heroism? Is she not our sister too? Though we are not Israelites by that admiration, we perhaps have courage enough to honor our kinship with the decisive hand.

Do we, Samaritan? Hand in hand? Isn't that the brotherhood you spoke of, though we could just as well be sisters in that spirit? Do you have the heart for sisterhood? Judith. Jewess. They are the same. Do not fear you denounce yourself in that knowledge. Unless you fear to denounce yourself. Then you would be a weak sister to the virile brotherhood your

sister took up arms with, in the deed that unshackled you from your step-
father's tyranny and gave you the courage to be such a good Samaritan.
You are a hand-holder aren't you?

Well, let me tell you that self-denunciation can be a blessing in
such disguise as strong women and weak men come to appreciate at the
moment of their unmasking.

Consider that your stepfather—having been ministered to by doc-
tors sworn to silence about his condition—gave this manly sister to the
church six weeks later. She took her vows. But he trumpeted the will
that gave her body unto this state of grace. Or so he thought it would
appear when he released her hand that she might step behind the iron
gate. He vowed the celibacy she had thrust upon him to be his own will
and homage to the wife who was recently deceased, that he might leave
his house with his head erect. He thought he regained his manhood by
disavowing it.

He wanted no human kindness. Once he had made such a chival-
rous spectacle of releasing his daughter's hand into the realms of blessed
silence and darkness, he would not accept another hand out.

That leaves you wanting, Samaritan. Does it not?

"Isaac de Zamora?"

"No. I am Osvaldo."

✦ ✦ ✦ ✦ ✦

How often have I been mistaken for my brother? More often than not, the one who asked disguised, with the twitch of a smile, his suspicion that he was being deceived. Now that I am alone, because Isaac is no more, I will come to be known too well. The trick will be worked against me for my sins.

I am standing at the gravelly lip of my brother's grave. I am urged by Cardinal Mendoza to make my peace. I feel his hand on my back. When it alights I am alone. Have I ever been? My doubt is quickened by the appearance of a dwarfish figure in black robes flitting between the yews, in perfect synchrony with the blinking of my eyes. So perhaps I am deceived.

The priest is dead. I would be his ghost. But it is I who am haunted. All my adult life I feared the condemnation of a word, which was no crime: *converso*. Only a word.

Only a word which my brother Isaac would never utter, thereby dragooning his helpless twin into an unwilling partnership with the crime of pretending to be the full-blooded Christian. The blood of Christ himself is impersonated by the priest. Now I remain the bearer of his guilty secret. In the flesh.

To make matters so much worse, I have made invisible criminality all too visible in the lifeless person of the little sister—a thumb in the eye of the Plaza de la Salvación—where I left her: in the place of my pilgrimage to deposit a leg and all the incriminations of fleshly wrongdoing to which it might be attached by a libelous imagination.

What have I done? I do not recognize myself in this deed, and so I am all the more in thrall to my brother's deathly guise. Now, truly, I am the deceived one.

Jew. Converso. Blood of the Christian blood. Murderer. Jew. My guilty self is proved to be the inept impersonator of that ardent innocence that I have clutched to my fearful converso breast since childhood. Until now. Now I am the inescapable Jew.

See me in my secret closet, performing the outlawed rites. I am not a believer in the Kabalah's magic, though perhaps only magic could save me. I am only a believer in my need to practice what I will surely be accused of. The magic hands must occupy themselves with the amulets so that when the knock is upon the door I will have a secret to divulge. The criminal must have a deed to confess or his execution can have no meaning.

Isaac has escaped. In death—at the hands of a horsefly so to speak—he flies upon wings as gossamer as the voice that first lifted him from our stifling courtyard within the Cardinal's remote wine-producing estate into the exalted air of the royal court.

For the King's court rests from its peregrinations back and forth across our expansive country in the Moorishly spired Palacio de Ciudad Real that is also our Cardinal's birthplace. Always anxious to court the King on the occasion of royal visitations, Cardinal Mendoza removed the velvet cloth, so to speak, from the cage in which he kept the rarest bird that had flown to his attention.

Like myself, Isaac was one. I think back.

✦ ✦ ✦ ✦ ✦

"I would say that the child has the voice of an angel, if the comparison were not such an inadequate and foully sweated labor of imagination. No. The child *is* an angel and his wings flutter within the narrow walls of this silvery throat. The very *quidditas* of the voice proves *is*." The Cardinal's encomium was an oozing syrup that he very deliberately licked from his thick lips with the fastidious daubing motions of a grey woolen tongue.

Isaac stood before the elaborately gesticulating figure of Cardinal Mendoza, towering in his ermine collar and sanguinary robes with one hand in the hand of the royal personage. The youth's mouth was still a quavering oval, as if it were the stop of a recorder that one could lay by on a table top and come back to it, pick it up, finger it and produce the identical note, as though it had never ceased to sound. The song was no longer in the air. The musicians had let their hands fall from their instruments. The Cardinal's florid speech had dispersed whatever semblance of music had lingered like smoke from a snuffed candle. But the singer's quavering lips would not desist from conjuring the illusion of a canticle beyond the sensitivity of human ears, as if to confirm the Cardinal's faith in miraculous performance.

The King applauded the child with softly padded palms.

But, of course Isaac was not a child at the time of the Cardinal's annunciation of his angelic nature. Well past puberty at seventeen years, his upper lip and his chin bore the sooty follicles of the most satanic goatee, if one observed with proper cynicism how the seeds of his already widely heralded sexual maturity were planted to the pattern of his lust. The voice however wore the chaste disguise of the castrato.

It was still the delicately blown-glass voice of the six-year-old child, whose small, white almost papery face had long before been pierced, like a butterfly pinned to the collector's cork board by the thrusting tip of the madrigal master's finger. Thus could the eye of Cardinal Mendoza's musical emissary, standing beside the madrigal master, be made to chime with the discriminating ear that had already picked out the special timbre of this most gifted boy in the choir.

✦ ✦ ✦ ✦ ✦

Yes, so many years earlier Isaac had been snagged upon the madrigal master's menacingly hooked fingertip. Isaac found himself drawn up before the three tiers of his brother singers shining in their golden livery. Isaac appeared smaller than he was in the overabundant material of the cassock-like haberdashery still swishing around his slender frame. But he stood perfectly still until the clothing was becalmed upon his straightening shoulders. He was commanded to lift his chin, as pinkly pillowed as a baby's bottom, and coaxed to climb to the summit of the highest scale that would still sustain a human breath.

The fish-belly skin at the base of Isaac's throat began to flutter like a sail catching wind. His mouth ovalled, then broadened at its base. His two front teeth crowned the by now triangular shape of the lips like snow on a mountaintop. One never heard the air pass between his untrembling lips. One noticed a faint inflation of the blushing cheeks. But his eyes, shut as tightly as they were, completely mystified the source of the sound that pealed against the eardrum of the straining listener, as lightly as the scurry of a mouse step across the page of an open book.

The Cardinal's emissary opened his own mouth with such silent exclamation that everyone could see how cavernous ecstasy can be. They say the heart flies up in such exalted spaces. But then his stupefaction was so great that he let his tongue fall out like a bell that has tolled for the last time.

The child's throat continued to quaver, eddying concentric rings of silence from the core of his breathlessness.

"A pure, unblemished voice, I admit. How wistful a portent of the perfection that time will sunder as ruinously as the sturdiest bell. The sturdiest bell in the most mightily mortared bell tower."

So the Cardinal's choir-warden mourned.

This melancholy would have tinged the most enthusiastic appreciation of the child's prodigious gift. But Nature's course couldn't be deflected. The poor larynx must grow. At the age of thirteen, at the furthest extent of the body's generosity, the frog would leap into his throat. The larynx is the voice. The voice the larynx.

In dewy youth there abides a sweetness in the register of the larynx's song that is indistinguishable from cherubic lips and an unstubbled chin. There is a sheen upon the eyes that is innocent of the look of desire for more than what can be seen, because at this age the body and the air that moves through it are one sinew.

But then the larynx sprouts from itself another being. Think of the eye of a potato. See the potato lodged in the child's sweet throat. It has a sound like the first spadeful of black dirt rained over the womb of the gravedigger's labor. A season of such rain follows until the emptiness is filled in. The voice changes. They say it *breaks*. A predictable fall from grace. And so the voice speaks forever more from the grave towards which it hearkens the rest of the body in its weakness for change.

This did not happen to my brother. And, of course, I am no different, though he is dead indeed. Otherwise I am no different. Singing just is not to my taste. It is simply the case that my voice is high.

Which is to say, Isaac's voice never plummeted from its first glorious ascent.

No, his crystalline voice never shattered. And yet one would only believe it if he thought of the surgeon's sharpest knife, insofar as it can serve the artifice of men for whom Nature seems to thwart the ends of art. Did not St. Paul banish the women from the choirs of his church? God, it is said, did sanction the taking of some sons that they might be women to his ears.

Thus to hear the seventeen-year-old Isaac's voice would be to think castration might have served its unnatural purpose.

But it had not.

And so, "Miraculous!" was the word that soared from the lips of those who thrilled to hear him.

So few were permitted.

Isaac was, after all the Cardinal's voice, a property of the realm. He would be audible only to the invited guests and otherwise merely rumored to exist. He could remain, as secret as the divinity of the throne itself which brings the bowels troublingly to mind in the querulous head of the common man.

Isaac was given into the care of the Cardinal's *director de coro* like the most delicate figurine of glass couched in a felt-lined box. A prized possession, he was to be brought out like a sacred charm, a holy bone, a phial of dried saint's blood. Thus was Isaac's voice used to bestow the aura of miracle upon the most special occasions of the King's appearance in the Palacio de Ciudad Real. By the King's most unpredictable and brief manifestations, the palace would be transformed from the Cardinal's mere birthplace into the deathless Court of Royal Succession. How fitting a heavenly sound should herald such an event.

And over time, years following Isaac's selection by the Cardinal's choir-warden, as Isaac's lungs enlarged without a complementary pullulation of the voice-box, the delicacy of the tone that rang from his fully bearded lips acquired an imposing fortitude, as if the wings of a butterfly could resist the fingers that struggled to pull them apart. One stared in disbelief at the man from whose broad shouldered frame issued the filigreed breath of a child standing in a chill air. Child of a woman with the voice of a woman and the breast of a man upon which he could beat the cadences like a drum if he chose to indulge such a display of manly strengths.

And yes, he suffered the indignity of the skeptics who insisted upon physical examination, so arrogant were they in their refusal to be deceived: the dukes of many provinces, their incredulous madrigal masters and their wise doctors. But the world needn't have troubled such expertise. By the date of his twenty first birthday Isaac was the notorious master of a harem of mistresses. It was so public a mockery of the suspicions of his eunuch-hood that it veritably gelded the tongues of gossip. But this was not satisfaction enough.

Isaac goaded the incredulousness of the doubting anatomists by feigning reluctance to be so revealed, despite the protections of the Cardinal's own armed guard on such occasions and the conducting of such examinations behind the iron doors of the most recessed chambers of the palace. The most sacred virginity could not have been more devoutly sequestered. At the approach of the enquiring physician's hand Isaac raised his voice by octaves in shrill impersonation of the most protesting maidenhead. He took mincing steps in one direction and the other, swished his hand back and forth across his blushing cheeks, huffed and puffed, sighed, lamented the fate of one so faint hearted as himself. He raised and lowered the hem of his dressing gown so many times in anticipation of this forcible admittance to his most private nature, that the doctors were dizzied in their attempt to find the object of their focus when it was finally laid bare.

For having so mercilessly teased the doubts of his inquisitors, exciting their resentful hopes to expose a fraud, Isaac
used the molestations of his naked flesh beneath the agitated
dressing gown to produce the evidence of his manhood in a
state of such proud and livid engorgement that the probing
doctors fell violently backwards as if in horror of an unimaginable freak of Nature rather than its most generous endowment. Then Isaac, the true man, upbraided the doubters'
suspicions as such brazen faithlessness that he shamed them
into making more pious devotions to his vocal talents than
even his most ardent admirers within the Cardinal's court.

Thus it was that on Isaac's twenty-first birthday the
Cardinal's gift to him was at last a public performance, that
universal witness might properly enshrine the miracle of the
voice. Once. And then the voice would be ever more sequestered within the precincts of the royal prerogative, a vocal
monasticism to which Isaac would devote himself with the
most uncompromising conviction.

He would become the muse of private audiences for the
King's minions, princes and prelates alone. And he would
use the ever more oracular voice of such private rituals to
enshrine a language that was forbidden by the most public
mouthings of truth. But first he knew that he must give his
voice to the open air in a baptismal spirit. Isaac surmised
that whomever rapturously breathed in the reverberations
of his song would forever carry the taste upon their tongue.

Even the converso gives communion. The thought rest-
ed piously upon his tongue. Did he swallow?

On the day of the promised performance, the Plaza
de la Salvación surged with a crowd as tumultuous as any

assembled whenever the sentences of the Auto da fé were to be publicly executed. The tiered scaffolding upon which the hooded and scarlet robed inquisitors were usually seated when they roiled the blood of the people, whom they could hush with the fate-tinged words of their judgment, was the very dais upon which Isaac was expected to lift up his solo voice.

Yes, yes. On angelic wings.

But for all their heaving motion this audience filled the oval space of the plaza with a silence tighter than an indrawn breath. It was a silence more portentous than any impending announcement of the names of the doomed. Standing with an avuncular stoop at the edge of the platform, the Cardinal stepped forth. He raised his hands to the throng in a gesture of benediction. But he showed them the backs of his hands. Almost imperceptibly the tips of his fingers bent towards his smiling face in a gesture of intimacy more suited to a private chamber. There was room enough for each man, woman and child to take at most a step or two in the direction of the inveigling figure upon the scaffold, until the crowd coagulated against the streams of people still flowing into the plaza from the narrow streets that fed it from behind them.

Now, tugging from his elbows, the Cardinal drew the audience closer still. The invisible strings at the tips of his fingers were as taut as a fishing line in the grip of struggling cartilage and gills. His smile broadened into a crazy leer.

"Venga, Venga…," lisped from his smile.

And then he stepped aside to reveal Isaac standing before three musicians whose instruments might have been mistaken for the tools of mortal torment. None of them were stringed instruments. Each required a human breath to put itself through a maze of tubular contortions before it could gain release in an audible tone. Isaac seemed to stand straighter than he intended by contrast with the slouches of the musicians, burdened as they were by their instruments and the brazen demands upon their lungs that gleamed in the early afternoon light. They appeared to deflate under the stress of the first slow chords that waited ceremoniously upon the soloist's voice.

Isaac touched the beak of his feathered hat in a chivalrous gesture toward his audience. Then he assumed the contraposto stance of a heroic sculpture from the antique world. He swelled his chest. He tilted the point of his goatee like the point of a deftly parried blade, narrowed his eyes. He let his hand fly out from the roost of his right hip. With such a flourish, he released upon those reaching fingers a voice pitched well above the heights of the most soaringly winged falsetto.

The fully grown body of the man appeared to be instantly shucked by its infant soul, there being no visible form in any manner proportionate to the sound that emanated from the rubied orifice of my brother Isaac's mouth.

Well, if the soul could be made so manifest what confusion could the body continue to provoke?

No one who shivered in the heat of the Plaza de la Salvación that day would ever quiet the fibrillating nerve that sounded unto them then as the incontestable presence of soul.

✦　✦　✦　✦　✦

Upon returning from the scene of miraculous witness Isaac begged the Cardinal to conduct him to the family chapel.

It was a sepulchral recess of the Palacio Real that was reserved for the souls of those whose flesh had been conceived within the walls of the familial womb. One would be able to tell by brushing an attentive eye over the retinue of portraits that lined the narrow, whitewashed corridor leading to the massively padlocked chapel door. Different faces perhaps, the vestments of different times, but all concatenations of the same convulsive uterus. And the chapel itself dedicated to the Virgin, whose first brooding motherhood hatched the thought that there could be but one woman after all.

Isaac took it all into account.

Without a doubt his request to Cardinal Mendoza was a scandalous presumption. But it was hallowed in the most propitious of moments. Had Isaac not just birthed himself into an aura of miraculousness credible enough to bestow upon the Cardinal's authority a popular faithfulness beyond mere sacred duty?

Isaac was no caged bird. He was rather the peacock's prize feather.

Therefore my brother Isaac's admittance to the chapel was tentatively granted. The door closing behind him was the conferring of a beatitude Isaac was only just preparing to prove out. Standing alone, facing the altar, motionless in the single aisle of marble benches, he waited the requisite moments before the Cardinal's footsteps could be heard retreating behind him, opening the door once more and closing it. Isaac knew the vantage point from which the Cardinal would espy him and the time it would take for the lumbering prelate to pass through the outside corridor circumambulating the chapel, climb the stairs and arrive at the secret window from which he had already confided to Isaac many times he would *feast* his eyes upon the unsuspecting worshipers. The window was concealed within the barely open mouth of a lion's head medallion stuccoed high upon the altar wall amid a larger circle of lamb's head reliefs.

"In the place of worship," the Cardinal had once whispered into the young man's ear, looking to see how wide he might open his eyes, "the soul is as naked as the body in its bath."

Isaac's eyes were open now as he made what he imagined would appear as a stately procession from the chapel's barrel-vaulted entrance to the altar squatting gnomically at the far end of the aisle. It was a low standing marble block, as one might find in the ruins of a pagan temple if the King's emissaries from the new excavations at Empúries were to be believed.

But the large, square stone, slippery as water to his touch, was immediately recognizable to my brother as fit for the sprawled body of his biblical namesake, struggling under the shadow of the quizzical father's wavering knife blade.

The thought comforted him and gave him confidence to make himself at home at what was, after all, a humble table laid for the business of human hands, though what Isaac intended was far from humility. Knowing that he stood beneath the lion and knowing that the barely open and toothless maw gave the Cardinal a slivered view of his movements—the head of the man dilating in the head of the lion—Isaac addressed the altar wall of the chapel more closely, thus eclipsing himself entirely from view.

When Isaac stepped back from the altar wall into the spectrum of visibility, the Cardinal would have gleaned that in the scant seconds of the young man's transport into the realm of invisibility, he had already trespassed against the sanctuary of the tabernacle. Perhaps peering, at an acute enough angle, the Cardinal could have seen the topmost corner of one of the tabernacle doors swung open into his view. He would have seen the rays of the sun showering from that corner onto a luminously painted scene of the saint sprouting birds from the fingertips of his extended reach into that radiance.

Isaac was of course now clearly embarked upon something. The Cardinal saw that in the fist of his left hand Isaac gripped the fluted stem of a brass ciborium that rose into the shape of a church cupola. In his right hand the cup of a silver chalice shone like sunlit water upon his open palm, balanced between his open fingers from which its crystal stem waveringly dangled. The two or three steps distance to the altar were a tightrope that he walked chary of spilling a drop of the red wine which would have reflected his face in the most unsettling way had he looked into its eddying depth. My face as well, though my face in the wine would be *to my taste* wouldn't you say?

For Isaac there was something else in the wine that he did not wish to see.

He settled both vessels upon the marble. He withdrew from his waistcoat pocket the *corporal* which unfolded into a white square. He placed the ciborium and the chalice one beside the other well within the borders of the square cloth. And from his other pocket he produced the *diskos.* He had plundered the tabernacle of all of its items and was now poised to manipulate them according to an all too scrutable will. No doubt he felt as though the Cardinal's startled eyeballs were laid out smooth and orbicular upon the linen square of the *corporal,* as ready for his impatient hands as any of the other props of the impending ceremony. Perhaps he even paused for a breath, giving the Cardinal's voice a chance to reach out violently from the altar wall before Isaac's hands could desecrate further.

Would the lion speak?

In the absence of the lion's roar Isaac might take confidence in his own predation. And he did.

The unleavened hosts, packed tightly into the dome of the ciborium, were baked the color of failing daylight. Isaac placed a single wafer upon the *diskos*. He waited. Perhaps it occurred to him that his own people fled with only such bread to sustain them through the wilderness. No. He began to scratch the back of his throat for the syllables of the Latin mass that he had swallowed whole in his feat of rote memorization. He coughed them up like crumbs of the body he was about to ingest, as wholly as the impediments of tongue and teeth and saliva would allow.

Then came the realization that he had not draped the chalice with the veil-like cloth. He had dropped something after all in his precarious transit between the tabernacle and the altar. He had not covered the wine. It could therefore not be uncovered. But the host was already simmering on his tongue. There was no time to wonder if the missed step would topple the entirety of the processional he had embarked upon. He grasped the chalice too hastily. Two drops of blood from the wounded certainty of his performance beaded upon the cloth of the *corporal*, the color fading with their transubstantial absorption into the white field. He had been struck a blow. It shuddered through him. He felt the body of Christ breaking upon his tongue into a diasporic mosaic of glistening pieces. He hastened the chalice to his lip as the last hope that the pieces could be reconstituted— if only ephemerally upon the flood tide of his nearly vocal gulping of the wine.

Because he could not therefore speak the sacred words, for the seemingly gluttonous preoccupation of his mouth, Isaac cried.

Blinded at least from the Cardinal's eyes by the substance of his own body, and with his back to the lion's gaze, Isaac conceded the immensity of his folly in a silent but convulsive flow of tears. It fairly choked off the workings of his esophagus. The salted droplets that showered involuntarily over the exposed hosts remaining in the ciborium stimulated a profane osmosis. The breath froze in his throat. The chalice fell from his grasp like the hand of a stone statue sheared off under the sway of a violent hammer. His whole person was seized with a rigidity so brittle that his awareness of tottering was the anticipation of a catastrophic shattering into infinitesimal pieces.

As he fell backwards into a ray of light that incandesced through a small window at the top of the altar wall, Isaac felt himself swallowing leagues of darkness. The window, carved into the shape of a dove, went dead white.

He did not hear the sound of his body falling like a tree in the forest.

✦ ✦ ✦ ✦ ✦

When Isaac opened his eyes again the Cardinal Mendoza's face was upside down and hovering. The Cardinal was kneeling. Their faces were close enough to mingle their breaths. There were words streaming from the Cardinal's mouth but Isaac heard nothing. Nothing entered his consciousness either. Only a ringing in his ears made him present to himself. The sound of the sea in the seashell has as much certainty of its existence.

Much later, when it was ascertained that his voice, not to say his mind, was as intact as the virile body that made the voice so miraculous, Cardinal Mendoza put the proposition to him. If Isaac would submit once more, and this time to the doctors of the papacy itself who must, upon the most scrupulous examination call him miracle, Isaac would be permitted to don the vestments of the priest. He would be given an iron key to the chapel, crooked as any burnished finger from the reliquary and, in the privacy of this place only, he might perform his calling to the priesthood as any actor upon the stage is called to the lines he knows he must speak.

Unlike myself, Isaac had never been known as the child of a converso. For a man who had passed puberty with his voice-box unchanged it was perhaps only too credible that there was nothing to have been converted *from* in his nature. He might remain forever unchanged, which was after all the lesson of the holy spirit as Isaac himself came to preach it from the pulpit on the day of his investiture. Did not every priest who ordained the transfiguration of the bread and the wine appear to the communicant—the communicant's intimate knowledge of digestion is so deeply humbling—to be a figure of the unchangeable?

Thus did my priest-aping brother commit the unpardonable sin: to appear to be the thing which the very idea of conversion confesses to be untrue. Thus did he become the real imposter.

The law of conversion protects the imposter by sanctioning his imitation of the true Christian. Should he be found out, the one who makes an imposture of imposture reminds those who permit the Jew to be the converso that they are such hypocrites. By this impertinence he vehemently calls for himself to be burned at the stake. For the truth of pretense can never be forgiven. The converso is not a version of the Christian the way a twin may be mistaken for a version of himself.

I am that twin.

Isaac dead is all the life left to me. By my visage his priestly masquerade may be discovered. As I have myself committed the criminal deed of murder in the Plaza de la Salvación, I shall be deserving of the punishment I receive for my brother's crime, in ways that my most savage persecutor will never know to relish.

I know, Samaritan, you are not the least bit aghast to hear such a woebegone tale. It takes this much human misery to get your sympathies salivating. When did your heart first heave with those ravenous juices? Who has earned your sympathy lately?

He was such a disappointment was he not? But the true Samaritan suffers the neighbor's betrayal gladly does he not?

✦ ✦ ✦ ✦ ✦

Of course I know. Your own betrayer was the mendicant barber. Lacking a hand, brandishing the stump to passers by with the fervor of a butcher hawking his livid wares, he could not escape your opportunistic notice. The hand that had lost its grip forever lay in a far off battlefield among slain infidels. So read the card that hung from his grizzled neck. Big as a child's slate, the card was still not big enough to accommodate the entirety of the story of how he had lost his hand, crowded as the tale was into an indecipherable mass of letters at the bottom of the card. It was garbled in a script that was surely the work of the hand unused to writing. The remnant hand. Like your own hand in the mirror thrust toward you from the opposite side of your body. You can see it. You can hear it moving through air. You can even feel it clenching. But you cannot use it.

How did you use him, Samaritan?

Did you think he could not speak, could not stand up from his bended knees, could only supplicate with the one good hand fit for a dented cup, though he had only cupped his fingers to make a proper place for you to deposit your moist coin?

You think I was not there! Then how do I know? Look at me and wonder if you would have noticed my stalking presence. I am, to put it bluntly, an unexceptional type. You would have seen right through me, as perhaps you fear I do you. After all who keeps an eye on his own shadow? And yet, the Inquisitor must be the shadow of the accused to know his darkest motives. I must be merely an effect of the light through which he passes if my own testimony is to be trusted.

In any case you were surprised at the strength of the voice that thanked you for your patronage. You had not expected a word of gratitude. Perhaps you had even hesitated to part with your coin where no real commerce of compassion was imaginable. But he gave you back a word. A word plumped with all the liveliness his physical bearing belied.

You could see the ribs blinking through the tears in his shirt, its ruffled front as caked and matted as a filthy fur. The tawny baldpate fairly radiated the light of the sun to which it had been so mercilessly exposed, making the hollows of his eyes as recessive as the empty sockets in a weather burnished skull.

His crouch was deceptive. At first glance he appeared to be a cripple without even a stick to service his affliction. The legs were so artfully folded beneath him you were almost thrown off your own balance when he popped up beside you, almost a head taller, agile as a rabbit, hands flailing, spittle flying, his tongue rattling in his head as frenziedly as a man who, come upon an oasis, dredges the splashing goatskin from the bottom of the well.

The horror—that his first overture was to offer to be your *friend,* your neighbor, *I dare to say—was more than you had bargained for Samaritan. Am I right? It was your coin after all. You had spent it. It was your entitlement to even the most modest self-satisfaction. You wished to claim its value, even as it was being pilfered from what you imagined was a safe pocket of piety. And then to be done with this pathetic beggar.*

But the one-armed barber was in earnest. For your meager generosity, he would do your bidding gladly and without further compensation. He could be a house servant, a gardener, a driver of horses, carrier, a cook, a confidant. He could even hold your head if, sick and alone if, leaning into the void one night, you found yourself vomiting into darkness.

He left you no choice, Samaritan, but to bid him up.

He accepted your offer of a meal more swiftly even than he had raised his wraithlike body from the ground. His speech began to seem mashed, as if he were grinding the words between the uneven rows of blackened teeth. They almost matched the onyx of his dazzled eyes.

He was speaking of food as it happened. And as you listened with better attunement to the mastication of what he was saying, you began to understand that he had gone without nourishment so many times in his life that starvation itself had cast the shadow of death over his teeth.

And then in the very porch shadow of the tavern towards which you were leading your rag man, he urged you to permit him a confession. Curling the fingers of his remaining hand around your forearm—you guided him by a steadfast grip upon the disfigurement of his stump in order to show no revulsion—he wished to pull you close enough to impart a far more intimate squeamishness. Leaning into your ear, close enough that you could feel his tongue beating the air like the heartbeat of a rabbit, he begged your patience. He insisted that before you should spare whatever portion of your generosity remained to satisfy his hunger—and so to foster a brotherhood that binds all men whose bellies can go empty—he wished to confess that once he had partaken of meat from a human bone.

A cannibal. That was the thought which inspired a new fervor in your gestures of friendship. You patted his back as heartily as the rattle of his frame would permit. You would have nuzzled your shoulder into his armpit like a wooden crutch if it would have reached. Instead you merely bumped him and had to catch him back into the balance of your bracing arms.

"Sit, sit," you implored him, holding the chair back from the inn-keeper's table as if you were the host yourself. "An honor," you smirked to yourself, "to host a man whose appetite has been so mistreated by the hardships of the most desolate reaches of the earth. There survival itself is the only God who can condone such guilty necessity as eating one's brother."

"Nothing less than a feast will do," you announced to the true host of the establishment, who approached, his portliness smeared with the fruits of his fire. You blared the command that all might hear it: "This man must be fed to the hilt, my good steward."

The host spat upon his own floor. He shook the whole obesity of his person like the intimation of a fist coming to blows. The squirming features of his face were as red and as grainy as the skin of a sausage stuffed to bursting. The man's eyes exhibited such a violent distaste for the ragged skeleton that had just been propped before his table that you feared the worst. You could see how he was about to use his livid tongue like the clapper of a bell. But, just as abruptly, he honored your request. He even bowed fancifully, risking an inadvertent squat—as deep as the bottomless pit for a man of such uncontrollable girth—before he heaved himself in the direction of the kitchen.

The broadness of your smile, Samaritan, has such a milky and pacifying effect, I will admit. And you offer it as readily as the wet nurse does her ample bosom. Could you cajole a cannibal to suckle?

You waited for him to fill his stomach. You imagined it hanging from one of his visible ribs like an empty stocking. How much leg would it swallow before it held the shape of a living organism? Your patience stood by for the passage of a loaf of oat bread, a greasy rack of ribs from a goat's kid, a honey basted rabbit on a skewer, a clay pot brimming with the toasted orange bodies of tiny birds swimming in a green oil, a curded caramel custard stuck with raisins and cherries. You waited for him to draw his thin lips together and smear the back of his hand with the excrescences of this appetite.

A convincing enough cannibal.

Then you offered him, as you so unappetizingly put it, a supper for his soul. But how to make it succulent enough you wondered.

"I have a favor," you broke the smeary silence.

"I have a father," you said, belying your own blood. "You will know him by his black cloak, black stockings, black doublet, the black ribbon oozing redness at his throat, the black and blacker eye, the black and dusty shadow he drags behind him in his daily transit between the front door of his town mansion and the steps of the cathedral of this ciudad, always at midday when the streets are molten. Or you will know him by the hunch of his shoulders. He has suffered an injury to the groin. The hand of God couldn't have pressed harder to snap the prideful bone that once held him so haughtily erect above other men. And yes, above children. Such a fisted heart!

"It is his hand upon children that he wishes to disavow in the kneeling box of the old cathedral's confessional, close with the fetor of dirty feet. He spreads the five fingers in a mutilated spider walk across the lattice work of the screen where the priest's words are still throbbing like the fat pulse of a fly baiting the spider with his own trap.

"My friend, you must see this in your mind as I am telling you now. Wherever a man secrets himself for confession he is vulnerable to eavesdropping."

You were candid indeed, Samaritan, with your inveigling will.

"See me. See him. This very morning I, like him was kneeling, with my ear pressed hot as a branding iron to the back panel of the confessional I speak of. For the cramped sinner who recoils from the monstrosity of his own words that wall is already a scalding reproach to the backbone. The bruised bone striking the unyielding grain of the wood in such cramped quarters is a portent of more demonic persecutions to come, if the sinner does not persevere in regurgitating the most molten curds in the stream of his sickened conscience.

"Hear me. Hear him speak from within the confessional where I eavesdropped. I was a quaking shadow in the shadow of the trembling wooden box in which the sinner could not be still for the peristaltic action of his words. And though I knew the worst already, the sound of his confessed guilt scratching at the priest's window was worse yet.

"Did my revulsion at the thought of his ultimate forgiveness make me finally an avenging angel?"

You noticed the graying pallor and distant gaze of your captive, did you not, Samaritan? Hence your ever more beseeching tone. "I beg your attention, friend. I speak of a father, speaking of his worst deeds." Your voice only caused the beggar to blink.

"In the wheedling voice, the whining solicitousness, I detected the grating teeth, the ravenous maw of his monstrosity. And then I heard the terms of his penance as he dictated them himself to the invisible priest whose body was suddenly audible as the dropping of a weight upon the boards of an already unstable floor. Surely at such moments the avenging angel is meant to leap up! How else does he know that he has wings?

"But does the avenging angel not tarnish his halo by the deed itself?"

Well, I heard it all, Samaritan. I was the still shadow of your shadow in the shadow of that bouncing confessional.

And this was the inspiration for imagining what use you could make of a one-handed barber. You knew you must trump any forgiveness the priest might wager against the arrogance of such an inveterate sinner as the stepfather confessed himself to be.

So you pressed on.

"Follow me. I will lead you to him. Once you have him, you must hold on to him. Everything he does from the moment he descends the steps of the old cathedral this eventide leads in one direction." You stretched the barber's ragged cuff over the leathery stump, Samaritan. You yanked the barber closer still, tightening the leash of his cuff around your reddening fist.

"For tonight, this very night, I know that he plans to take his own life. He plans to take his own life as though it were a fair exchange for what he's taken from others. Is this not what we heard through the planks of the confessional? Did you not hear the words with which he had battered the priest, who was no doubt collapsed behind the screen of the confessional? Have you not heard me say these things, carrying his voice to your conscience like an offering to the altar?

"But you, you'll thwart his profit and earn your own. You'll do what I implore of you. For, like the villainous father, you owe a penance do you not?

"To me you have confessed your sin on an empty stomach. I know you were in earnest. Your full stomach was my proof of your desire to make amends for the toes and fingers you have tasted of your unfortunate fellows. Their strength was the greater for you, the less it was for them. Am I not right?

"And of course you want your forgiveness too.

"Well, my good barber, it is here in my hand. Let me lead you to the steps of the old Cathedral this minute. I will point him out to you. My father. I will repeat again the words he offered up to the priest only this morning as if he were giving sacrifice or instruction. Then you will know the meaning of our meeting, yours and mine. You will even know what to do because I will tell you, though if I am judging you correctly, you will not need to be told. You will understand how I am asking you to save yourself."

Well, Samaritan, you were already employing the empty end of the barber's sleeve as a leash, tugging the added weight of him from the seat of the chair. You needed him to use the very legs you had imagined he lacked when you first saw him begging rescue in the street. A look of agitation spread across his face as if he were not convinced himself of the power of his legs to support the meal he had just hefted to his belly.

Or was it really a snarl?

Then you repeated to him the words that you had collected in the coiled chamber of your ear, kneeling in the dank shadow of the confessional, suffering the posture of one milking a cow. Now the words were frothing on your lips as if you yourself had drunk from the milk maid's pail.

Was your beggar barber imagining the lather that he would have prepared before he cut your throat? What was it you saw in his face that so subtly pulled the drawstring of your lips around the words as you blurted them, that made them all the more propulsive?

"Tonight," you tell him again, "this night, my father promises to go to his home for the last time. To his hearth, so he confessed to the priest. To the hearth room heaving with light and heat. When my father spoke to the priest he said that he was already exhaling the breath of the fire that he vowed would consume him tonight. He promised to sit before the blaze meditating the act that—so he assured the priest—would effect his purification.

"Let me advise you, that for anyone who would peer through the window of the emblazoned hearth room, with the same foreknowledge that my father whisperingly disclosed within the walls of the confessional—I trumpet the words to you now—this would be the moment to strike. This would be the moment to calculate the distance that is mazed between the front door of the town mansion and this simmering chamber several passageways removed from the narrow corridor by which a

stranger could enter the house. Such bravura timing is required to effect a rescue.

"What else would I be imploring of you?

"When the father's thought is crisp with purpose he vows to rise from the chair that warms to the flame. He will take three steps. He will make a fist of his right hand. With the fleetest of fingers he will open the fist to capture a single incandescing coal from the bevy of golden eggs brewing in the hearth's nest. The torch length of his arm will ignite the whole of his person. Then will this person become a torch to the whole of the house, perhaps to the whole of this quarter of Ciudad Real.

"Except, except, except, for your merciful intercession. I beseech you!"

And you had him, Samaritan. You had yanked him across the tavern's threshold, even if your grip on the shred of his sleeve made it little more than the useless lead that is worn thin against the stubbornness of a halting mule. You had him up and leaning in your direction.

But this meant your words were audible to the rabble who had been drawn with such rowdy excitement out into the street by the spectacle you made, as well as to those who were already milling about the street without a tickle of purpose. They were as happy to make room for such a spectacle as farm animals eager to drink from a filthy pool of water in a cracked and desolate yard.

"Your intercession, I pray you." The words, Samaritan, might have been spit in the one-handed barber's eye for the menacing glare it produced, had you wherewithal to notice anything but the purpose you plied him with.

Indeed, you seemed intent only upon making the words into more of a halter for your ever more vigorous grip, weaving your own sense of them tighter and tighter about his head as if by so lassoing his thoughts you could lead him wither.

The swelling gaggle of oglers found your next words worthy of even self-confounding laughter. One looked furtively to the other for a sign of its appropriateness.

And yet you persisted, unashamed of your own confessional.

"How could I do what I implore you to do?" you choked without the excuse of laughter. "I have known the back of my father's hand, the force of his knee in the small of my back, the bitter drop of hatred that forms on the tip of the tongue after it has swallowed all pride. My cause is too vengeful if I lift my own finger to dislodge the coal from his flaming hand, to save his sinful life for the holy inferno.

"Be my intercessor and save yourself by the kindly deed I may not kindle myself."

With shaggy heads and wagging bellies ringing round you, Samaritan, the swaying rabble made idiotic mugs and laughed the louder to see you tugging still on the empty sleeve. I could see how assiduously you were shaking the absent hand in the hope that your one-handed barber might realize how important it might be to let the stepfather go so far in his stratagem as to disfigure himself, to lose a hand. But you were amazed that he could resist the offer—a one-handed man himself—to be divine intervention. How could the one-handed barber resist the opportunity to come between a sinner and his sin, with the one good, now better hand? How could he resist the opportunity to burst upon the would-be-suicide with a fervor hotter than the flaming coal, in order to extinguish the misguided act of contrition? A spark against God's heart, so you exhorted him, scars all humanity.

The mangy crowd was enthused to see even such obtuse entertainment presented for their benefit as if there was some dignity of their being that deserved more honor than they ever knew to expect. Only the barber seemed eager to put a stop to the proceedings.

But your eagerness to have him see himself in the role you had cast him in carried more momentum.

The tether of your voice, stretched to the breaking point, had dredged him from the clouds of dust kicked up by his resisting feet into the very center of the street where he stood visible to all like the fully dilated pupil boggling in the whiteness of a skittish eye.

"Follow my words. Let the father live on, a one-handed man forever mindful that a stronger hand than his prevailed. Then the father will have the charred nub to contemplate for the term of his penance. He will be like you if you save him.

"But you will no longer be like him, carrying the conscience of your cannibalism. Be the instrument of the mercy I cannot render without God's displeasure at my vengeance. And, by heeding my instruction, wipe your own sin from the lips through which you guzzled your brother's flesh.

"Even if, I admit, I have never known your distant desert or deserted sea more empty than my most fasting stomach, which drove you to such an act, the circumstance fills my mind with the mercy of God's understanding: to think of it as mortal necessity. And yet I know the deed needs forgiveness. It was and is a sin. But God is only too brimming to quench your spiritual thirst, if you will only let your tongue soak up the waters of that well. Be the willing instrument of my own inadmissible hunger for revenge and by that dutiful willingness reap the virtue that I would have to call myself selfish to claim.

"Were I to pluck the father from an earthly conflagration, the stridency of such a prideful act would be as unforgivable as the father's intended suicide. Let my sacrifice do your penance for you."

Well, the quizzical expressions flickered about you, Samaritan, until the crowd went completely silent. The fall of darkness could not have been more sepulchral.

Almost tottering in your efforts to move him, you had by this time drawn the barber's head within the frantic grip of your two hands—in the manner of one who clutches the sides of his own face to howl his foreboding of what will happen next without falling to pieces himself.

Perhaps the deepening hush of the mob gave the resonance of a mighty bell to his stroke when the clapper of your barber's brutally foreshortened right arm struck the side of your naked skull. Not a shiver of impact could be seen to vibrate along the bone of his forearm as it swung metronomically back to deliver an even more clamorous knell.

His eyes seemed to bare teeth by their bulging whiteness, the pupils gone as suddenly as if they had been swallowed in a single gulp. The lips seemed to be torn away from the teeth by their lividness. They bore the snarl of the bestial gnawing through which a bloody mastication might have been apparent.

The unhanded arm continued to strike its blows against the side of your head.

But the sound echoed not from the ghastliness of your agape mouth. It came back to you from the human encirclement like a sudden loss of balance. The mob could have been singing to the rhythm of those blows, a drunken chorus of bobbling heads, lit with flickering smiles and becoming more brazenly raucous with each assault.

The wet pig snout that kissed your cheek with the sudden passion of the butcher boy's arm caught your eye only when you saw his filthy hand reaching back for another into the slop bucket that was slung across his chest. You realized that none of the ogglers was empty handed however idle their recreation. A one-eyed crone hurled her overripe tomato, its seeds spraying the air before the pith of it pulsed inside your open shirt. A mouse with its neck wrung fell at your feet like a lock of hair.

And then you fell too. The rutted clay of the street rushed toward you as precipitously as a ceiling collapsing upon your head fracturing upon impact into the spittled syllables of your barber's final declaration as he turned away from you:

"I owe no penance. It was a taste I'd never savored. I am a man possessed of an exceptional palate. It was only the taste I wanted. And now I know."

And now, Samaritan, I know that what you begged of your barber was more gluttonous than any sin you have let me imagine you were capable of before this.

You were coveting the virtue of forgiveness for yourself. The violent crimes the furious stepfather had hurled against your childish physique—dwarfed as you had been by the cast iron shadow of his open hand, fingers spread the width of two faces—would be rendered smaller by your generous Christian heart. Saving the suicide by surrogate means. Saving him for God's more punitive ends would have been the really blessed feat. It would absorb the remembered blows like a pillow feathered with blood, that you might rest your head more lightly upon the clouds of eternity. There the body sleeps, like a dream of itself, that it might no longer be a drag upon the etherea of one's airiest dreams.

If I know this how could God not? God knows the self-server, especially when such a mortal is proffering the gift that he most longs to receive himself. You thought your barber would have cherished the opportunity to be the recipient soul. You thought he was like you. The Good Samaritan.

How good is the Good Samaritan? He thinks the other must be like himself or the world would not be useful. Who would not use a selfless samaritanism to buy a place in heaven? But to imagine your barber's conscience to be so delirious with hunger for redemption, to be so famished of divine forgiveness, was just the deviousness of you imagining that God's beneficent witness to the barber's good deed—had he accepted to be your missionary—would redound to you, as if you hadn't solicited it.

That is the trick of it after all. Is it not? To be blessed for foregoing the allure of the heinous act because you know it is so alluring. If your

barber's good hand had done the good deed with which you wished to
burnish your own halo, you would have been good indeed.

    Or so you thought.

"Exposing the truth of pretense can never be forgiven," I have said before. Look, for example, into the tolerant eye of my *Christian* brother when he appraises the act of his converso wine merchant at the moment of the sale. You will see the patron struggle with his knowledge that Jewish blood squeezes even the most generous heart dry. The last thing he wants to be reminded of is that the hand that strikes the legal bargain is a Jewish paw. Exposing the truth of pretense can never be forgiven.

But I have never pretended to appraise the truth of taste. Let's say that taste itself is beyond appraisal.

There is no pretense to my vocation. My tongue is, rather, the proper mate of the fruit that suckles it so incestuously. I have eyes to see the color of the fruit bulging in its glass belly, looking back at me. But the eye is always at a distance from the sheen of the world that reflects its own intensity with such focus. If I were not a taster perhaps I would be a painter. But I have no patience for that distance. Blessedly, I am a taster and I use my tongue. It is what it beholds without the ambiguity of wondering what that is.

I lift the goblet to my lip and my lip is already bursting with flavor as if I were my own elixir. Is there a difference between my taste and what I taste? Not in the buds of my tongue where this knowledge is secreted. Unlockable and keyless. These are the privileges of taste. I say it again. There is no pretense to my vocation.

✦ ✦ ✦ ✦ ✦

As for pretense consider my twin. He too served and was served by the grape. Or so it would have appeared through the brittle glaze of the painter's eye should the priest's devotions have solicited the easel and the palette. But the grail cup lifted above the pristine altar cloth proffers nothing that can be seen. The palate after all, was never the relevant canvas upon which Isaac's spectacular illuminations were revealed. The priest boasts ever so humbly that in his throat the wine undergoes a second fermentation when it is swallowed. It is a more severe decoction than the wine maker ever knew. And yet, whoever has suffered a crackling blow to the nose has tasted it. There are no corpuscular refinements to be discerned in the taste of blood.

There is only its salty sting. Like seawater. The taste of the divine. For the sea is like the bleeding God's father. The father is like the sea's reflection of the sky. Like, like, like, like…. I could go on. It is an invitation to climb the ladder rung by rung. Isaac inveigled the mumbling worshippers in the tiny chapel to take the first rung, to sip. It was his first giving of the communion.

For me wine is wine. Blood is blood.

I think perhaps too palpably of the little nun's blood.

It shone so radiantly in her cheeks when the Cardinal's pages wrestled her from her throne-like seat. As it happened, the baptism of the little nun's body in hymeneal blood was the eve of Isaac's baptismal tasting of the most rancid wine from the communion cup.

Her eyes glinted a tincture of what looked like the bloody ferocity of murder at the moment when she was seized. Though she struggled wordlessly, she knew what she kicked at between the legs of the most burly of her attackers, as he sought to pry her hands loose from their grip upon the chair arms. But even he was reluctant to touch any part of her that might have moved without her volition. He knew all the soft places beneath her novitiate's habit where the offending hand, despite the Cardinal's stern edict, might feel his own soul slip from its grip. Which made him so much more vulnerable to her tenacity. She reddened the nails of one hand with the flesh of his cheek, like some piece of harlotry. He thought he heard the rasp of a serpent's tongue in her throat when arching her back away from the back of the chair to better secure her grip upon it she caused him to catch his hand in the looseness of her garment and pulled him off balance so that he tumbled into the seat with her.

The sudden colliding fraternization with breasts, and belly, and groin hollow released him from his soul's inhibition. It was like an unbuckling, letting the white knuckled fist extruding from its ruffled cuff spring violently upon the tender gash of her open mouth.

The blood splashed as if over the brimming rim of a wooden bucket carried in too much haste.

And then, in as much haste, she was gone, a prisoner of stronger arms than even those of the chair that remained in her grip when they pried her from the refuge of this fortress-like furniture. She had flailed so tempestuously in the net of her abductors the rest of us were left swaying with precarious balance in her wake, as if trying to keep our footing on the deck of a storm tossed vessel. By contrast, the empty wooden seat of the chair was so stilled with the tortuously tight fit of its intarsied pieces that it seemed to emit a silence indistinguishable in its intensity from a shriek. Surely the blood that would flow from the vent of the little nun's defiled holiness—upon delivery into the hands of the winning bettor—would be as thick with grief as the tears she had rained upon us as she was flown above our heads by the stiff-armed pages who whisked her to her doom. Of course I could imagine that the hymeneal blood would bead with the same force of gravity as teardrops pendant from the salt-scarred ducts of the most grievously livid eye. I wiped her tear from my own cheek and lowered my face to meet the others in the room who had been so watered. The silence that flooded from the empty chair engulfed us all. Perhaps it muffled our cries. Were they drunken huzzas or were they pleas for mercy? The faces would not tell me. The gaudy guests only stared at me as if I were naked. Naked stares.

I would see her again. Perhaps they knew.

The blood that heaved to the rim of my brother's chalice, when I saw him perform his mass the next morning, would dry up all the world's tears. Or so did Isaac preach to the lonely worshippers who stood with me within the narrow and chaste marble walls of the chapel where only full-blooded members of Cardinal Mendoza's family were meant to take communion.

We were another family. There were two ragged sculleries, a stable boy who was already well into manhood, a footman sporting an overly burnished pair of boots, a famished cook with a sunken belly and a humped back, a stooped crone who had no doubt been a servant to the family from an early orphanhood and a wooden-shoed orphan whose livery was yet to be cut for him. We each stood with our tongues dangling before us like hungry dogs to receive the wafer, which burned upon my tongue with a fire that I was convinced, as the chalice was passed to me, could only be extinguished if the wine were changed to water.

The passing of it gave me cause to peer at the other end of the short line of communicants which terminated in my own irrepressibly curious self. For I knew I would be able to reckon the face of the one whose footsteps had just trod so daintily upon my ears as I awaited the chalice. The unshod soles had made a wavering haste, a hastening patter from the back of the chapel. They had sounded an embarrassed urgency to catch up with the ritual before the last drop of blood quenched our holy thirst. Alas, the body was already a clog in the throat. I thought of the mash of a deformed foot entangling the narrow passageway of a finely knit stocking.

I could barely find a crook of the neck crooked enough to spy angularly beyond the tips of the noses that ranked in single file to my right in order to recognize the little nun when she appeared in line with the others. There, as if balanced on the tips of those noses, her face bobbled, so much like a bright red ball, a bubble of blood ready to burst. Who had smashed the shame into her face?

Who would know better than I? Would the droplets of wine that gave a sheen to my knuckles be noticed as I took the stem of the chalice into my trembling grip? The one who passed it might have imagined that the transubstantial incubus had splashed over the rim in some flailing attempt to manifest itself. I felt the blame. But I indulged no such illusions. Wine is wine. What shone with equal lividness in the little nun's cheeks was no less her own blood than the droplets that could be observed like rubies scattered at her feet when I dropped my shameful gaze to the floor.

I could see her bare feet dancing beneath the hem of what was, after all, only a chemise, and dribbled with the roughly squeezed juices of her person. The more she danced the more strewn the stone floor was with incarnadine pearls.

Her knees punched at the thin shroud of her chemise from within, the more frantically her dance revealed itself to be her rage against the realization that all the ritual portions of the body and the blood had already been distributed. And I, the last of the slurpers, held the cup of emptiness in my hand like a bird alighting to the parched rim of the birdbath. Though she might have been mashing the grapes, she was too late for the wine.

Isaac neither looked up nor down but stood before us with eyes as white as peeled eggs. He awaited the return of the chalice with open hands upraised at his sides, a man gesturing too late to ward off a devastating blow because he did not see it coming.

I saw it. Because my eyes were already fallen to the darkly veined marble floor I saw it in the whitening tips of the little nun's toes. They were purged of the blood, blanched by the weight of the whole body as it abruptly sprung off them, soared to the dais of the altar, landed upon the soles of both feet, and then leapt upon Isaac's erect form as if to the rungs of a ladder. The frenzy of the white chemise was a wave breaking over him. The only sound was the rough entanglement of the limbs, the sighing ropes of a small boat being drawn taut against a bluster of wind in the sail. And then came the sound of her salivating lips. Water. The vessel capsizing? Or drinking? Kissing?

Kissing!

We stunned communicants, standing in our regimental line, could not see that the suckling motions of her mouth upon his mouth bared teeth. Not kissing so much as the sound of her biting his lip. Is there a sound of the hook tearing the mouth of the fish? Until we saw the blood we could not tell that her intent was so atavistic. Did I discern the tiny grinding of tooth upon tooth where the sheen of dianthian flesh was bitten through? Could the nails of her toes be so sharp—or the razor-like hoof be so violently planted—as to rent the hem of Isaac's vestment even as the fingernails could be seen to shred the vellum of his blenching neck? With her knees firmly dug into my brother's rib cage she was riding a runaway horse, the horse itself oblivious of direction or whatever obstacles might obstruct the path of its thunder. Isaac writhed beneath her, though still standing and trying to unbuckle the cinching grip of her flanks with violent thrusts of his pelvis. Trying to pull his face beyond the increasingly near reach of her claws to his eyes, he was exposing his throat ever more perilously. We saw the exhausted hauling of the chin above the waterline by a man who knows he is drowning. Or perhaps he was only offering his throat before he would offer his eyes to her ravenous maw.

All of this in relative silence, the barely swishing silence of a maiden disrobing in her private chamber.

Bare and white as it was, Isaac's throat broke the silence with a vellum surge of invisible strength. The threads of blood that ran from her fingertips where she was fastened upon the back of his neck made the sudden bob of his adam's apple pulse all the more whiteningly like a bubble in the wooden bucket after the first splash of cream is churned from a bursting teat. The whiteness of his throat darkened the whiteness of her chemise.

Then the whiteness was so dulcet that each one of us felt we were seeing blindly into the coiling depths of our own ears where a bloodless membrane quavered under the tendril touch of the unexpectedly sounded note.

Song.

We heard it and we did not see how. Our eyes were shut with sound. Blind men. Blind women. All the blood gone to our ears, we were no doubt rendered as white faced as the dead under the timeless spell of our listening. The tone extruded from what could only have been Isaac's thick lipped grimace, rounded itself against the yielding silence, bellied like a tear drop. Its resonance filled the air until the air heaved with the tautness of the vocal chord strained to its fullest extension. And that vocal chord did not break. The song was its own gravitational pull against the firmness of our footing, we weak-kneed communicants. It lifted us up. It made us weightless upon our toes, until the sensation of rolling was as much ours as it was the lilt of the song. It carried the little nun off.

Or at least she dropped to the floor.

Pendant as a teardrop, her body, lower back and buttocks, had seemed to swell with the unceasing surge of the song. The agitation of her limbs, so pacified, succumbed to their dead weight and fell out of the corner of my eye.

Weeping? Singing? Praying.

Praying. Though the little nun had fallen with rhythmic aplomb into a kneeling posture at Isaac's feet there was still a slender thread of connection between his quavering lips and her joined fingers, as iridescent at their cuticle tips, as if she held the wheel upon which a thread of his saliva paid out the ever more glistening vocables of the song that would be spun into gold.

Her eyes were so wet with the sheen of such magic that we did not notice the corpuscular bloom of her virginity unfurling in the porous white weave of her chemise. It had become caught up like a tourniquet between the bowed trunk of her body and the heels of her dirty feet.

Only when the words of the little nun's prayer were audible enough to shatter the tremulous glass of Isaac's song—they were coughed up like stones thrown at windows—did my brother himself look down. The prayer was a rumbling of words that were at once begging forgiveness and molten with such a profane rage that we feared another eruption of the body that had only just been quelled by the spirit of song.

But she remained prostrate. She was now so blossoming with blood she would not have had any but a wilting strength to raise herself from the marble slab which she no doubt would have preferred to be encrypted beneath than to be panting upon it as she was when the feigning priest knelt softly beside her.

When he was low enough to be a man dredging a well, the little nun lifted her face to him. As swiftly as the outspread wings of a bird ruffle against the wind to hover above a watery surface, she dipped her hands into her lap. Just as swiftly did she flap them into the air again. The blood rose upon the priest's cheeks just barely ahead of the fingers of her two hands now smearing his face with her most intimate gore.

The priest released a harrowed breath. But his lips weren't torn to grimace by it. Nor did he fling his head back with repugnance.

Then, because he raised his upper lip with the slow ceremony of a curtain lifted to reveal the most toothsome smile, I realized that the priest could not be defiled by the blood. No more than any other actor prating upon the creaky floorboards of a stage could be defiled by the sword that does not pierce him at the lips of the open wound, however lavishly it weeps blood.

The stage hero will bare his breast again and again to be so admired for his courage.

And so it was unmistakably true. This tiny chapel, secreted within the innermost wall of the Cardinal's fortressed palace, and sacred only to the full-blooded members of the Cardinal's family when they were in attendance, was of course in no way consecrated by the histrionics of my brother making the sign of the cross, blessing the chalice, purveying the host. It was rather rendered, by his presence, a private theatre. It was a space in which Isaac had begged the Cardinal to let his voice resonate a different miracle than what Cardinal Mendoza himself had purveyed in the Plaza de la Salvación. Here, in this chapel, my brother was no less robed in glory than when he rounded his lips to suckle the first notes of the sacred music at a lavish spectacle for the court.

Playing the priest's part Isaac would of course understand the use of face paint and by reaching into the sop of the little nun's chemise—taut and still dribbling between her firmly planted knees—Isaac made the act of taking her face into his anointing hands. The induction of another player into his repertory cosmos. Now they were face-to-face, both of them dripping, both of them radiant with the crimson fervor of the moment. They might have been feasting together on the flesh of some fallen prey that lay between them like any gruesome prop for theatrical entertainment meant to curdle the blood of the audience in the theaters of our ciudad. Two cannibals.

It was as strange to the eyes of we wet lipped communicants, who could not cease to stare drop-jawed, at the most crudely enacted *tableau vivant*: one that might arrest one's passage along the street during carnival. What could it mean? A man and a woman. Their sudden embrace was no less compellingly a part of the spectacle which was, after all, what my brother lived for and was, in this instant, the transubstantiation of his yearning to make the priestly image of himself a full-blooded illusion.

And do we not all hunger for it in our way? Moths to the stage lights whether the stage be as grand as the gilded opera house when it rumbles with applause against the abutted walls of the Cardinal's palace, or as humble as the stones of the Plaza de la Salvación when the Auto da fé is in session. The insensible wafers that the priest had placed so ceremoniously upon our tongues only moments before had been nothing but whetting for the appetite which we now seemed to gag upon in our stuporous state.

Isaac clutched the little nun's fluttering shoulders as a man holds his own belly in a fit of laughter. Self-possessed. Were the little nun's audible sobs a savvy mask for that laughter? Was she as fervent a player as my brother, impetuous to elaborate whatever action upon the creaking floorboards of the stage might make the audience stir the pot of their heated emotions, make them squirm in their shoes, feel the tightness of their clothes, sniff the spices of their last meal in the expulsion of breath that thrills to the spectacle of the protagonist's last gasp? We put our hands upon our hearts do we not, when all appears to be lost?

Or was she only weeping upon the hard edge of my brother's collarbone?

In any case it was there and upon the altar of that place, so to say, that the forlorn little nun found a perch for her sorrow. And there it was that she roosted.

From that day she became my brother Isaac's faithful lover. The willful impersonator of the priest was compassionately wedded to this involuntary impersonation of the nun whose virginity had been proved too brutally real. They were semblances to one another as though standing face-to-face with the imperturbable mirror of their thwarted desires.

So they lived together. Isaac took her into the private chambers of the palace which the Cardinal had provided to sanctify his Godly gift. In that cloister of fervid imagination they married their fancies. The little nun was an impassioned wife to the compassionate priest. He, in his turn, was grateful to consubstantiate the body and the blood in the ardor of a physical embrace. Twice a day he performed the rite of this communion upon the little nun's ecstatic person. In that sanctuary of mutual mindedness the little nun was permitted to preserve her virginity against the opinion of the world. In that sanctuary of mutual mindedness Isaac was permitted to carry the priest's raiment upon his person and pass the day performing the rites of the faith with tedious diligence until such time as he would be called to perform his official miracle for an elect audience of eager ears.

Thus was he used by the Cardinal. An instrument of the faith to be sure.

Over time and under the aura of Isaac's voice the priestly robe seemed a more and more apt mantle for his piety. Over time he was permitted to walk the streets openly undisguised as an ordinary gentleman. When my brother Isaac became the priest out of doors he finally closed the doors upon himself. He was the priest. It was taken on faith. To all the faithful his rooms came to be regarded as inviolable as a monastery.

Or a nunnery. The little nun found the godly man's refuge from the world to be fit for herself. After all, faith in her ravished purity could only be sustained away from the society in whose glaring eye it was otherwise a shimmer of knowing light, as wrigglingly captive as a gilded fish in a marble pond.

Perhaps the little nun countenanced it as a shard of the looking glass world in which she felt herself becoming ever more urgently illusory: knowing that the purity of her sister sisters of the purple habit was secured by the thick walls of the Convent of St. Iris, which no eye could penetrate.

But there is more to this story that might explain how convoluted a path we have already traveled. Did the little nun believe her own eyes when they dilated upon the fact that this priest was a double for the wine taster, whose lascivious tongue had, only hours before the scene in the chapel, as good as denounced her to the most severe tribunal? That calamitous day in the Cardinal's family chapel, as Isaac turned the little sister in his arms the better to cradle her swoon, her gaze, gently winging over my brother's shoulder, and then hovering over the motley gaggle of communicants, incredulously met the identical face whose kindly expression she still felt shining upon her like the sun upon the back of a bird.

But now her recognition was a glint of the distance the bird might fall into the blackest sea. For it was myself staring back at her that met her gaze. We communicants huddled speechlessly before the abandoned altar of the little sanctuary, struck dumb by the ever so convincingly priestly word that had become such unimaginable flesh before our eyes.

I see it now myself. I see her seeing myself, if such a thing existed. The question mark that surely formed in her mind at that instant, though it was only a scribbling wrinkle upon her brow, as she frenziedly fit together the features—eyes, nose, mouth—to my puzzle face, was already the portent of the severed leg which I would discover, years later, upon the threshold of my personal chamber as querulous punctuation to the knowledge that my brother was dead. Did I not always think of the leg, bent at the knee, as a question mark? Have I not said so? At that moment was I already becoming the twin of my brother's death in the darkening glass of her vengeful mind? Was she already the answer to the question?

"Who are your leg? Who are your leg?"

Now I see that it was she. Now I pick out the puzzle features of the little nun's face with the same trembling finger motions of the brain that solved her recognition of me as the priest's twin when, on the blood-tide of that Sunday morning in the Cardinal's chapel, among a rabble of subaltern communicants, she realized that her newly won sanctuary with the kind priest would never be entirely safe. The Cardinal's priest and the Cardinal's devil were one.

Only now my memory unflinchingly touches the roughly incised portraiture of the girl I left strangled on the luminous stones of the Plaza de la Salvación.

One and the same as Isaac's sisterly concubine.

It was she who, so many vengeful years later, had laid a trap for the dead priest's twin. It was she who had laid the leg upon my doorstep. It was she who waited in the shadow of my door until I made the discovery, observing so frantically the water rising in my own legs. It was she who shadowed my footstep as I made pilgrimage with the leg. Perhaps it would be better if I, myself, were to offer up the evidence of a crime to the tribunal that daily sits in wait of the accusations— they flow from the mouths of so many rivers of hatred into the Plaza de la Salvación—than to deny the guilt to which a severed leg must inevitably be attached. Did I (who?), leg in hand, imagine myself presenting the most guilty evidence as evidence of my own innocence? I do confess it.

Was it not the vengeful little nun who stood in wait, in the black disguise of a gypsy crone? Was it not she who raised a voice in the silent blare of noontide on the miraculously deserted stones of the Plaza de la Salvación.

"Who are your leg?"

She was the demoness in black who unshriveled herself of the shadow disguise, in league with the dilating light of the sun itself, whose shining nakedness illuminated me all the more starkly against the dark stones. It was she whose tumultuous writhings and pummeling of my person made the spectacle, as I saw it in my own scrambling mind, visible to the blindest eye.

"Who are your leg? Who are your leg?"

Only now I comprehended the full portent of her question. At the time when I wrestled her onto the scalding stones of the Plaza de la Salvación I had believed its meaning was nothing more than the furtive prodding of my identity by the invisible hand of a fate that I had been awaiting all of my life. The converso ceaselessly awaits his exposure. Yes, only now do I recognize the demonic crone in the Plaza de la Salvación to be identical to my brother's lover—the priest's wife, the little nun, the unholy holy. She had been made most unholy by my impetuous love for myself. She was, after all, the perverse issue of the wedding of myself to myself, which was my giving way to the licentiousness of the tasting tongue. So I realized that the hobbled grammar of her question nonetheless had more than one leg to stand upon.

I now see what she undoubtedly saw so long ago, aswoon in the arms of the priest, peering out at the line of communicants still chewing their holy cud. At that very moment the little nun had resolved to incriminate me to the Inquisition.

She already saw the spectacle of the man carrying the leg into the full view of the Plaza de la Salvación for all to see! In the most scandalous illumination of the Plaza de la Salvación I would be recognized as the unimaginably monstrous being who would covet the leg of a victim of the Auto da fé, as if to make the arm of God's justice serve the most criminal appetite. I, Osvaldo Alonzo de Zamora, would be such a perverter of the law that breaks a man to pieces, as to scavenge one of the pieces for my own all too vividly imaginable cannibalistic purposes. Can abomination be so abominated? But the leg was only the lure and the assurance that I would be taken into custody.

How did she know that I would walk the leg to the place of its dismemberment?

It does not matter. More momentously, more exquisitely, she meant for the ensuing investigation into my hideous crime—that would open like a palpable wound upon my person—to reveal upon the public stage of the Plaza de la Salvación, and before the full tribunal of the Auto da fé, what would be for her the more loathsome knowledge: that I was the living image of my dead brother, her soul and savior.

For the innocent priest to be dead was that much more insupportable if the criminal brother could bear his visage abroad in the world where she herself must remain all the more invisible. She who had possessed herself most buoyantly in the deep waters of the priest's compassionate gaze.

Surely this is what she thought. What else would she have thought, but that the eyes of the man who had rendered her invisible must be put out?

So first she would accuse me of the pilfering and cannibalism of a body part. And then she would disembody me altogether. She would see me pulled to pieces upon the slick stones of the Plaza de la Salvación.

For she possessed even more testimony to heap upon the pyre of my condemnation. What more perfect revenge could there be but the revelation that he who bore the face of the priest could be exposed for that priest's own forgery of a Christian soul? My dead brother's travesty of the priesthood would be proved upon the features of my own face. When the accusatory finger would be pointed in my direction, I would be converted into the communicant of my brother's denial that we were a family of conversos, which no priest of the Inquisition could countenance if he were really a priest. For the Christian to wear the beneficent face of tolerance most self-satisfiedly, the converso must remain the converso. As I am well aware, reminding those who permit the Jew to be the converso, reminding them that they are such hypocrites, appearing to be the thing which the very idea of conversion confesses to be untrue—that is the truly unpardonable sin. That was my brother's crime. The little nun would see me suffer the punishment. The crime of the self-disguising Jew would be revealed as the disguising motive for the crime of the severed leg.

To her alone Isaac had confessed the secret identity that only his twin brother could deny. For what reason? However unwillingly, I would produce the body in whose image the otherwise frustrated and frowning law could find its most austere and flattering reflection.

I would be known for the criminal she took me to be. I would be unmasked by the face of my dead brother. I would stand before the unrelenting tribunal finally revealed in the radiantly yellow shame of the sanbenito, answering for crimes I did not commit and for one that I did. I would be executed. The crystalline spectacle of my quartering might leave me another leg, its meaning as clear a fact as anything in the Christian God's creation.

Because I was the victim of her inquisition in the burning illumination of the Plaza de Salvación, before I imagined my victimization at the hands of the holy See's official Inquisitor, I alone could have grasped the full deviousness of the little nun's revenge, when it uncoiled in the snakelike logic of her question. Had it echoed in another's ears, the little nun's interrogative would certainly have been misunderstood, however incriminating it would have been nonetheless for any man cradling the disjointed leg.

Yes. I have unraveled the logic of our inquisitional entanglement. I am a student of my own catechism.

"Who are your leg?" The knowledge of her ingenious vendetta, secreted as it was in the ill-fitted words of her question, demanded the answer that only I could mouth. I, the brother of the brother.

My *leg* makes a pair. *Are.*

Yes.

Who is my brother?

You are your brother.

Then who am I?

What *are you?*

A leg upon which my brother could stand.

Your brother is dead.

Am? Are?

Is, not are.

My brother is dead. I should be dead. I understand. We are dead.

You are your leg.

Or, so I am convinced, she would have answered any man cradling the ever more inflexibly jointed limb.

Or perhaps it was no such labyrinthine riddle at all.

Who can say her disjointed question was not some incidental madness, a spasm of her grief manifesting itself in a nonsense of speech for whom no one could bear responsibility because they were the words of no one who would say such things repeatedly with good cause?

But it is all such seeming sense.

After all, if the intricacy of the revenge that I have plotted for the little nun here were a perfect decipherment of her provocative question, I would have had to kill her anyway, and with all the due deliberation that I have exacted in my making it a question for me to ponder so fatefully as I seem to have done.

Such conundra are enough to make me wonder if it is the intricacy of some mind, even more devious than what I have attributed to the little nun, that I traced out in the very act of killing her. Is not my fate now the legacy of that deed, just as she would have plotted it herself, according to my divination of her plan? Now, by virtue of being her accidental murderer, I realize I am the very necessary criminal she meant for me to become in the all-seeing eye of a law whose mercilessness she would certainly have counted upon.

What have I revealed by following the twisted pathway of these thoughts but myself?

She is nothing but the proof of my criminal act, if it were only to be known by someone other than myself.

So I must wonder, half in fear and half excitedly: who has already discovered the evidence of my crime upon the naked stones of the Plaza de la Salvación. Who is staggering with as much perplexity as hobbled my own step that morning when I discovered the leg upon my doorstep?

✦ ✦ ✦ ✦ ✦

Ah, but to have tasted the wine and to have wrung the name of the grape from the same tongue without a dribbling droplet of doubt!

What *have you learned, Samaritan? I have turned the page.*
The next is blank. It gives us pause to think, as though the author's need
to interrupt the story coincided with our silent thoughts.

Or perhaps the wine taster is merely smacking his lips to savor the
fleeting salubriousness of the moment.

After all, what can you learn from the wine taster when his tongue
is what it tastes, an indissoluble truth? The corpuscle of grape's juice—
indiscernible from the bubble of life's blood—makes the tasting follicle
sprout from a deceptively smooth muscle, if the curious eye inspects it
closely enough. Nothing that is inside will not be outside and visa versa
if the taster exercises his powers deftly enough. His tongue is the scepter
that holds sway over one world, indivisible, forever. Such is the wine
taster's domain.

Quite right. I speak of something more than the capacity to enjoy
the flavors. It is the power to divine what can come out in one's own
nature if it is squeezed with an adept enough hand. The wine is the
skinless grape. Just so, the taster's perfect judgment is something beneath
the skin.

Like your stepfather. Isn't that your complaint? It feels like he is
inside you? Remember the grape-hued bruises that ripened under your
skin? He was there, mashing your existence, imbuing such intimacy. In-
side and out. You can't keep him out any longer because you can't stay in.

Now that the stepfather is repentant enough to take his own life—
let us not expect the crudity of his conscience to comprehend his con-
founding the sin of suicide with the sacrament of sacrifice—you can no
longer remain a passive eavesdropper on his fate. You must break out of

the rigid shadow of that confessional where you first overheard the plot he hatched against himself: like a dog licking his raw parts you might have thought. The priest of the confessional no doubt attempted to elucidate the contradiction festering within the moist piety of the stepfather's declaration, the self-ordination of his new found faith. You will remember his words, do you not, Samaritan?

"I will murder myself!"

"To take one's hand against one's own body is the sin of sins!"

You heard the priest exerting a force upon the stepfather's logic as fruitless as a wooden lever prying the iron bars of a prison cell. But you, Samaritan, were already too agitated in your cage-like shadow to think of anything but your own escape.

How could you remain so docile within the confinement of this knowledge that the stepfather would make a bid to free his soul, even and especially by his own hand? It is the hand that still holds you by the scruff. You remember your life as a creature of that hand, less than a dog yourself perhaps. Only hunted. Never the trusting hunter's nose loosed to other prey. Never the son.

Well, you were never the proper son, not even to the real parent. But we've wrung out the last droplets of that grief already have we not?

Better to renew the strength of your hatred by remembering the stepfather's grip, feeling the imprint of the bloodless knuckles where the stepfather still has a purchase on your brain, as surely as if it were nothing more than a fistful of cloth gathered about your poor neck. Yelp if it will harden the muscles in your neck. Make a fierce spittle in your throat if it will bring your rage to a boil. Let your tongue become a shrieking flame to the fuse of your vengefulness.

And then you may be able to tell me what it was like to be a child and know nothing of forgiveness.

+ + + + +

You do remember. He put you in a room that was little more than the hollowed out interior of a stone. No doors or windows. One entered through the floor of the room above it, so that once the prisoner was forced to descend the lashing rope ladder, prodded from above by the menacing tines of an enormous iron pitchfork, your keeper could replace the marble stopper. The muffled clink of its perfect fit was a kind of suffocation to your ears. But even in the absolute darkness that seemed to suck your eyeballs from their sockets, you knew where you were. Your prison was once the wine merchant's secret cellar. When he lived. The most rare and valuable wines could not be exposed to the glare of a shop front open to the traffic of the street. Where better to hoard the most treasured vintages but beneath the stone floor of the wine merchant's bedroom?

It was a dark and humid chamber wombed by expert masons beneath the matrimonial bed.

Now of course the wine merchant was no longer the master of the house.

Now the wine merchant's widow was no longer mistress of her own body. Now the stepfather slept above the secret cellar undisturbed by the restless movements of his stepson reaching out in pitch-blackness to pound the walls of his confinement, one after the other. The stepson was tireless in the belief that when he had found the right spot it would fall beneath his fist.

But the stepfather did not sleep alone.

The pillow of the stepson's fist thwacking against the chamber wall was no match for the sounds that were made to resonate through the stones of the bedroom floor by the dancing feet of the enormous bed, so ingeniously carved in the shape of a bucking bull. Only perhaps the bucking spirit of the animal itself could belie the immoveable weight of the oak.

The delicately horned head of the bull was lowered in the massive base of the headboard. The footboard reared up, on perfectly straight hocks, the rippling haunch of the true Tundaca. The animus of the line, from one end of the bed to the other, gave such snap to the whip end of the tail one felt the impossible brittleness in the wood where it flew free of the hulking beam of the bed. As nakedly exposed as the rapier horns by the intricate vehemence of the woodcarver's blade, the tail was something that might easily break off.

In this violently sculpted bed the stepfather heaved himself upon the pinned body of your sister, as mercilessly as if she were thrown beneath the hooves of the bull.

The stepfather knew the sounds would be muffled. They would be efflorescences of the blackness that blocked your eyes and made you see that much more luridly.

The stepson breathed the cork mold though it had been a long time since the flagons of wine were hauled from this cellar space. The mold spore clenched the fruitiness of the grape. The stepson knew it would never be released, for all his vehement inhalation. This was all he could do to distract himself from the sounds of the bed.

The sister did not emit cries that might beat more faintly, but more shatteringly against his ears. She knew her brother was close. The stepfather had arranged it all. She would not cooperate with his plan. She had already been destroyed. She could only show him that his efforts were fruitless. She could show him that she could not be more crushed. She too thought of the grape.

Or did she?

Thus did the stepson come to his provocative thought. He had been sealed in this chamber before. The stepfather gave the order and the stepson was brought forth, forced to descend into the vault. Of course the stepson needed no further physical confinement to know himself as *an absolute prisoner of the stepfather's will. But to see ten of the most brawny servants of the house straining to shift the bull-bed, so that the stopper stone of the dungeon could be revealed as promise of what the stepson was meant to suffer, always impressed upon him the elaborate artifice of the stepfather's design. The purpose was plain. The stepson must be both witness and witness to his witness of the violence that would be meted out to the sister. This was some slowly extending shadow of the blows that the stepfather would have already landed upon the stepson's own person at some earlier hour of the ever-waning day.*

It was part of the stepfather's design. The stepson must see that the stepfather knew in advance all that the stepson would not be able to see with his own eyes, but what would be no less sharply etched upon his mind's eye.

And so on this day the stepson was alert to something amiss. A provocative thought. For on this day he recalled the stepfather had not been present at the ceremony of the stepson's interment in the bedroom's marble vault. The bed had been moved in advance of the stepson's arrival. Thus was it acknowledged to be a mere chore rather than the hostile theatricality usually orchestrated among the servants of the household. The look on the face of the valet wielding the pitchfork had not been as illuminated with malice as the stepson was accustomed to see it.

Then, Samaritan, your submissive descent.

Now fully acclimated to the pitch-black—so that you were beginning to see the halos of light that seemed to eddy from your pupils but were in fact the stubborn flickering of the brain which refused to accept such blindness—you were aware of the absolute silence. You did not hear the stamping hooves of the bull, however muted by the stones above your head. Your ears were as stoppered as your eyes. And yet there was a sound. It was a sound above the sound of your own breathing which ordinarily you would not notice under the rain of blows from the bed which concentrated your attention into an inertness as damping of the sound as the walls against which you sometimes pounded your impotent fist.

There was a sound in the darkness that was also the sound of breath, drawn faster and crouching smaller than your own, but somehow extending and retracting a talon that scraped against the stone floor, incising a mark you imagined. You felt an itch in your forearm. Your ears prickled. It was as you thought. Something was amiss. And it was present in the darkness. It was waiting for you to move.

Yes, something was amiss. That night the darkness was not a bell chamber for the clamoring of the bull above your head. That night there was no ceremony of the descent into the stone cell that was intended by your natural father as a safe haven for his most prized vintages. Though there was not even the sound of a footstep echoing into the abyss of your imprisonment, that night you were not alone.

And then it was scuttling towards you.

You could not resist the savagery of the moment. You leapt as violently as you imagined you could into the dark, knowing that without claws you would have to use your teeth against the furred muscle of whatever feral entity was about to spring upon you fully fleshed with the atavistic instinct that confinement in the dark only enraged more.

How does the short and bristling snout of a rabidly fibrillating mongoose make itself identifiable to the unseeing victim in time for the larger and more slothful prey to improvise a suitable parry?

You opened your mouth.

As effortlessly as breathing in, you closed your jaw over the projectile snout before it could bare its own teeth. With your hands cinched around the savagely convulsing upper body, your fingers deep in the bristle of its fur, you could feel the animal's hurtling heart brake against its rib cage like the wings of a bird thrashing in the meshes of an iron captivity. Its helpless talons rasped the air. You could taste the bore of its nostrils as you forced your tongue against these stops of its frantic respiration. You knew that this most vulnerable organ of your own mouth must now flex itself with as much strength as the muscles in your jaw would muster to bear down upon the rows of the mongoose's unnaturally clenched teeth, if you were to successfully stifle its life with your own. The jaws of the mongoose were torqued against the pressure of your bite. A moment's loss of control and all would be reversed. The efforts of your tongue would be overmastered by the razor meshes of the trap sprung within the mongoose's own jaws. As long as you did not relent, the mongoose's bite would be only a shrieking of its civet breath against your bristling taste buds. And so you pressed harder with your tongue. You knew it to be a muscle unequivocally. You plugged the nostrils of the mongoose with the tongue's exertions and pushed beyond the sensation of a probing nodule that was the muddy imprint of the animal's snout upon your unblemished lick.

You felt the suction of the vehement rodent's last breath searing the tip of your tongue. A ladle of scalding soup brought too hastily to the pouting lips would not have been so scarring.

Hours afterward the light emanated from the dead eye of the mongoose as sharp as the bevel on the looking glass in which your image was frozen by the lack of recognition. The stepfather's ungainly servants had to pry your rigid fingertips from the animal's neck after they had removed the stopper stone, after they set it upon the slabs of marble flooring from which it was indistinguishable, after they had stepped down into the chamber where you lay as inert as the stone itself if it had been carved in your likeness for a tomb. They kneeled down to do their work.

They groaned with the weight of your body upon their shoulders. They heaved. They raised you to the floor.

They left the bristling pelt of the mongoose in the well of the chamber, until the master could be summoned to bear witness.

From that day—you marked it I know—the stepfather lost interest entirely in punishing the son. Never again was the stepson mustered from his private rooms to be imprisoned in the stone chamber, to feel the pressure of full immersion in his ears when the stopper stone was fitted into its place by the heaving strength of four men. Never again was the stepson to feel the pulse of the darkness driven like the stabbing tips of his own fingers into the core of his hearing by the clattering hooves of the wooden bed.

Instead, idleness was yours. The disturbing peace that comes with the knowledge that one is no longer the purpose of another person's thought. You became acquainted with the boredom that is cobwebbed with the guilt of being elsewhere than where one knows one's suffering goes on without one.

Sitting upon the end of your own bed, dangling a leg, an unstockinged foot, into the stagnant air where the sunlight from a high barred window pooled upon the brick floor, you felt a shimmer of the warmth that you knew was burning more brightly upon your sister's skin where the stepfather exerted himself with the most vigorous punishment his frustration could devise. Your sister's old nurse kept you informed of what you could have expected. The skin above her eyes seemed to rend itself with worry as she uttered the words. If the stepfather now realized he could no longer finger the nerves of your pain, he could make you contemplate your sister's suffering, like a cloying melody which no stoppering of the ears can expunge from the brain.

So, Samaritan, hatred is yours again. Feel the hard knuckle of rage in your clenched fist, burning like a septic tooth. Bite down to ease the pain. Bite down to release the poison. Bite down and strike a blow against your enemy.

It is as easy as your wine taster's piercing the skin of the grape to certify his faith that the sugars are at their peak.

Bite down, Samaritan. The moment is ripe. If your one-handed proxy will not serve your purpose, you must be yourself to the deed. Or the stepfather escapes.

Bite down.

I had been summoned. It was the season. The honeyed warmth of the harvest sun bled through our skins under the press of long afternoons.

But this time I had to wonder if the summons came for my tongue or for my head? For myself or for my brother? For my service or for my crime? Why did my brain, protuberant as it felt with the budding quest of these questions, not serve as well as my tongue to taste the meaning of the moment?

Who would have stumbled upon the heap of my victim's naked limbs in the Plaza de la Salvación by now? Someone.

Run or run away?

My choice was a false one. My fealty to the Cardinal's vineyards is absolute. To fail the call would only be the confession of another crime. I lacked the legs for it in any case. They were water running beneath me, a flood tide beyond my powers to dam it up. Thus was I swept to the marble threshold of the Cardinal's Great Room, as cold I imagined, as my own gravestone. And the silence beyond the massive oaken door rang as ominously in my ears as the funeral prayer.

When the door creaked open the sunlight fell from the narrowly arched windows, like so many molten shields cast upon the brick floor. The audience that gathered itself around the perimeter of the long hall—perhaps a hundred souls—seemed to inhale one voluminous breath at my entrance. If they breathed out I might be blown back through the portal. Even my fearfulness to attend upon my summons had not conjured so devouring a beast as seemed to crouch here.

So many eyes. What did they see?

Cardinal Mendoza gathered himself from the ample seat of a porphyry throne at the far end of the radiant hall. It shone white as the filament of a flame in the flicker of his scarlet robes. It gave vehemence to his stride, only to be snuffed out entirely as his shadow wafted upon me with wide arms and a scalding breath of roasted garlic. I felt the smear of his painted lips upon my cheek like wax running from the wick of a candle.

"Beloved servant! My taste, my tongue!"

I felt the devil's goatee slash both cheeks. When I lifted my face, I saw the color of my blood flooding from the brim of the Cardinal's *Galero*, illuminated as it was by the invading sunlight. The glare blistered my thought that, so nakedly exposed to the sun as I was now, I could well have been standing again in the meridian of the Plaza de la Salvación, at the very moment when I was accosted by the black crone, when she turned herself inside out to reveal the vellum skin of my brother's little consort.

Black and white. The colors of the habit that I had stripped from her virginal body, so long before with nothing more than the parting of my lips to declare the name of the grape for which she then bled.

At this moment my own breathing had become so shallow it might have been the ghostly echo of Isaac's membranous tremolo when it had first brought the ever-suffusive light of this very shimmering hall to a pitch of clarity, as brittle as a bubble of glass blown to gossamer thinness. Isaac had given his first royal recital in this hall.

I found myself peering into the Cardinal's acherontic nostrils where I had hoped to meet his eyes. The fierce luminosity of his eyes would at least let me see his purpose however slitted and sharp-edged they might be against the whetting sunlight. A person of my stature finds himself forever looking up and never seeing what he wishes to see.

But I could see that he meant to take me kindly in his arms. It was a patronizing affection, not the wrathful blow I imagined he should have known me to deserve.

And how many more smiles surrounded me there! I saw their teeth and understood I was, at least on this occasion, safe from the venomous bite that is always coiled within the ceremonious poise of this society. And then a shower of applause. I heard bells. The brittle sheen of sunlight itself tinkled. A glass raised in my honor? A toast to me? In the blaring arena of my exposure I was alone. The milky limbs of the little nun sprawled upon the stones of the Plaza de la Salvación evaporated in the glare of so many smiles. Surely I was an innocent.

Or at least I was forgiven. I wanted to make my gratitude for such innocence bend at the knee. I spread my arms, as if the hem of an invisible robe were pinched between the thumb and forefinger of each hand, signifying my intent to genuflect. Thus did the twinge of recognition in my knee tell me how was I about to founder upon the very question mark of the severed leg which I still carried so guiltily in my mind and which I was now threatening to etch in space, the very tableau vivant of my self-incriminating conscience.

The Cardinal himself saved me from my tumble into that abyss. His hands plucked at my shoulders lifting me upon reluctant wings from the descent toward which my leg was unquestioningly bound, before my knee could make contact with the livid floor. I cast my eye upon the sheen of lavishly lacquered brick. It was shimmering with the image of my fall like something fluttering into air. So at the same instant that I saw the leg forming its question in that sunbaked mirror I answered the mandate to stand up. I submitted to the force of Cardinal Mendoza's muscular hands, the fingers dug graspingly into my shoulders, the straightening embrace. Were these not, after all, the impatient fingers of the puppeteer untangling my strings, loosening the limbs into the grip of some more zealous dance?

The open palm of his hand waved brusquely before my blinking eyes was spell enough for him to cast over the otherwise unruly motions of my body. I froze like any dead weight hanging on a taut string.

We were waiting for something.

I had a moment to focus upon my audience, for I realized that was what they were about. All were masked. I had not noticed it before. The sculpted faces splashed the still torrential luminosity of the room back in my eyes. The human expressions did not flicker. The brittle, needlepoint noses, the leaping cheekbones, the smiles licked with a glassy sheen, the foreheads chiseled smooth as masonry, the hard chins blunt as hammerheads, all mocked the amiable sociability of such a gathering with their outrageously extroverted immobility. But the colors! Did I imagine it? The colors were all too recognizably shades of vinous derivation.

Pigments decocted from the grape, and goaded by the excess of illumination which the hall was still brimming with, exuded the intoxication of their most perfect fermentation. Cheeks shining with the mealy whiteness of peach flesh that is the soul of Rías Bajas. Lips gashed with the deep vermillion that pumps from the robust heart of Valdepeñas. Eyes highlighted with the blush of Navarre Rosada, where pinkness eludes itself in the sparkle of light from the River Ebor. The deep river brightens the goblet and quenches the darkest roots of the vines.

Not a tint scintillating from any of those stony faces—behind which I now realized a silence was growing ever more weighty—was one that I could not taste.

I was reminded, by the salubriousness of this thought, that all of the Cardinal's dabblings with my magical tasting wand—none undertaken without a human fate being wagered—led inevitably into the labyrinthine corridors of a kind of drunkenness, where one leans and sways to keep one's balance. One tries to keep one's head though in the end one is left holding it haplessly aloft of a puddle of vomit, like any spilled vessel.

Now I began to understand my predicament. I enjoyed a vision through the vent that opened in the folds of the Cardinal's ermine-trimmed robe. He had already crooked his arm, signaling one of his minions to march forward from a diminutive door that had creaked at the far end of the hall. The arm launched a brittle snap of the Cardinal's fingertips into the air. Through the livid aperture of velvet I watched his erstwhile servant hurrying my own tasting coat onto the stage of this ever more dramatic scene, as if that fluttering garment were a reluctant actor whose limbs had slackened in a moment of uncontrollable nerves.

The Cardinal squared the loose shoulders of the garment with a single brusque tug of the brocaded vermillion and gold fabric that made it seem to stand stiffly before me like any human nemesis. The spinning balls of my feet had already comprehended the demand for me to turn upon them, with my arms stretched out behind me into enfeebled wings. I understood my duty. My hands must fly to the armholes like pigeons to their roost. All of this in a single unconscious movement no more alive than the empty raiment itself when it was bustled into our midst in the nervous grip of the servant who now stood by to witness its miraculous embodiment by my personage.

Who?

Indeed, I had reason to ask.

Because in mid-arabesque I saw myself undone. My consciousness of this fate was a thudding blow to the mindless torso and gravity-borne limbs and appendages that were about to find their repose in the fully fleshed contours of the marvelously tailored tasting coat. After all, it had been fitted to every inch of my being by the Cardinal's microscopically exacting sartors.

But now I espied a stranger in my mirror, an enemy of my ever more vulnerably bulging eye.

The coat was turned inside out.

Inside the coat, unseen by anyone who was not wearing it, I recognized the intricate golden threaded tracings of bunches of grapes whose weave was meant to deceive the eye. Where the fascinated focus followed the outline of the pear-shaped clusters of vermillion fruit it discovered along the same sinuous line, the very shape of the goblet in which the ripened nectar will bubble and roll as it is raised to the expectant lip. It was a painter's ruse that had pricked the ambition of a deftly fingered seamstress in the Cardinal's employ. But at this moment an unexpected trick of the eye revealed how the richly imagined skin, in which my tasting feats were typically cloaked, had become the lining of the coat. Outside was inside. And inside was so outside the bounds of my comprehension that, as I tucked my shoulder into the eagerly proffered armhole, I was as toppled from my footing in the world as the intoxicated imbiber who knows nothing of the grape but his appetite for oblivion.

For the inspired seamstress had been employed to a far more devious purpose than the playful visual illusion revealing the grape through the goblet, a mirage as clear and breakable as the glass itself. When the Cardinal finally drew the long narrow lapels of the coat taut across my chest I looked down to see myself trussed in the vermillion and white and purple vestments of a cardinal's priest. The fit of the coat was my familiar, the taster's second skin. Within its tautness I imagined myself the bearer of juices as succulent as anything crushed from the grape itself. But the skin of this grape was unrecognizable. What would be squeezed from its body suddenly surged behind my eardrums, a flood tide of cold fear in which I already felt myself drowning. At my wrists a bit of lace frothed over my hands. Vermillion pleats hung from my waist like iron weights. The hem of the garment bore an unreadable inscription in characters cut from thick velvet and sheened with what at first appeared to be a contrasting shade of the same color that shrouded me from head to toe. As my eye adjusted to it I recognized the blacker blood that palpitates in the heart of the deepest ruby rioja, when the belly of the glass is raised to the light: *Verbi Dei Minister. Hic sepultus.*

Hic spultus. Isaac himself would not have doubted his resurrection had he peered through my eyes.

Was there anyone assembled in the hall who did not see what I did?

But I needn't have worried. Nothing I had done had anything to do with what I was looking at.

I was not seeing the inquisition of the surviving brother. I was not seeing the indictment of the converso priest, the pretender pretending to be more than his pretense of the Christian soul: Isaac's double deceit. I was not seeing the brother punished for the sins of the brother. I was not seeing the misprision of those who would never have been able to tell one brother from the other, let alone the converso from the converter. I was not seeing my own incrimination by resemblance to the priest's heretical charade. Nor was I seeing myself, the criminal of the Plaza de la Salvación, discovered in the fermenting depths of his brother's desecrated grave.

No. I was safe.

My refuge was the Cardinal's own irrepressible delight in the power of illusion.

It was not my brother's incriminating disguise that the Cardinal meant to cloak me with, anymore than with the flowing sanbenito, which would have swept over me like an erasing tide, rendering the crude scribble of my existence in the yellow sand invisible to the most searching eye.

No. The game was more complicated, soliciting a more subtle mind than can be titillated by mere retribution, mere recognition of the victim. It was *himself* and his guests whom the Cardinal wished to render unrecognizable to themselves. They would be transfigured by disbelief: a transubstantiation of the soul—he promised—that would be visible to even the most muscular eye bulging into empty space.

✦ ✦ ✦ ✦ ✦

"Miracle of miracles," Cardinal Mendoza smiled, lofting his white hand in my direction as if he were releasing a dove into the air.

He assured the company, in whose midst we were now more closely encircled, that for this feat he required the offices of a far more robust priest than the one who typically presided over only the thinnest of wines and who feebly coughed crumbs of the holy cracker upon the altar of blood.

"We lose our appetite for the antics of the daily mass do we not? Can we savor the miracle if it is not savory?"

Cardinal Mendoza let his tongue drop from his mouth, a slobbering dog-pant to taunt the cloth upon my shoulders.

"We shall have truly Godly deeds!"

He licked the corners of his mouth with the crudity of a greedy communicant, then swallowed strenuously enough that the pale skin of his throat blushed as he started to pace a circle within the circle where we had stood together, now making me the perfect center of everyone's attention.

Why had he requested the company to don masks for this gathering? I felt the nakedness of my face all the more vulnerably for the sacerdotal disguise of the body hanging like a dead man from the straining sinew that straightened my shoulders. Had they sewed lead weights into the hem of the garment so that its folds would be as stiff as these plaster noses, lips, foreheads, cheeks ringing me round?

There was no time even to pose the question. No doubt the answer would have been as unwelcome as an unrecognizable face in the mirror.

I fleetingly caught sight of mine in the steep cheekbone of one of the revelers suddenly turned against me, blocking my view, but sheened with a glaze a painter would envy. It was blood red, my face-mask face.

My reflected features were no less rubied than the gem colored vintage whose mysterious facets I knew awaited my discriminating eye and tongue on the other side of the obstructing mask. For I knew that in a moment, the faceless companions would open the barrier in which their garish retinue cordoned me. Then I would see what was in store for the wine taster.

Immediately the papier-mâché devil turned violently away, like a crimson shard of himself flung off into the air by a shattering blow. The would-be revelers loosed one another's hands, breaking my enclosure. The returning intensity of the midday sun seared the moment with expectation. The blindfold was lifted. The shadows flew faster than harrowed ghosts. My challenge was revealed.

I had thought I knew what I would behold. As fitted as I was to the sartorial form of the tasting coat, so the occasion of my wearing it was fitted to the appearance of the tasting table. That claw-footed mahogany beast, its smoothly hewn legs stretched to the impossible stride that made its beastliness all the more imaginable—for these events I seemed to exist in the magical time of that stride—lunged into view. Upon its straight back, so stretched was it toward its equally magical prey, the gleamingly waxed, black-veined beast bore into our midst the implements of the trade. It was, for all its heft and violently carved grain, a domesticated beast.

The tasting table, my familiar, bore upon its back all of the tremulously blown crystal globes into which the wine was decanted from flagons. The crystal globes which were irregularly formed only at their collared tops where they were open to receive a pouring, were susceptible to rolling. For that reason each sat in an iron frame no different from that which held the rolling map of the world that turns upon the inquiring fingers of the scholars in the Cardinal's library. The glass globes were also meant to be turned with a guiding hand: the better to display the color of the wine even unto its most distant hues.

There were phials as well, ranked vertically beside one another in wooden racks, each containing samples from the must vats, taken at variously measured intervals in the process—another long stride—of fermentation. One in my position must guess the time marked upon that faceless clock.

And then there were the vessels themselves, a fleet of them: leather vested litre bottles, carafes of water, retinues of goblets ranging from thimble droplets to the size of a man's bruised fist still empurpled with fight.

Upon the boards of that table the grape would be crushed and by that destruction, known.

So I had thought I knew what I would behold. But I was held first, and more firmly than my own grip upon the moment. My first clear look through the unlacing limbs of the Cardinal's retainers had been pre-emptively met. Though she was caged in a wooden frame with bars that still held their bark, and though I realized that the cage had been lowered from the rafters above my head—I now understood that she had been suspended there like an unforthcoming thought the whole time that I had fretted my fate in the Cardinal's advancing shadow—the girl threw her gaze over me like a net.

I recognized her by the color of her nudity. It was all of the grape that appears to the naked eye. She was my fellow swimmer against the vintage tide of our youth. It had dyed through her as evenly as if she were a linen vestment. She was no less brilliantly vermillioned than the sleeves and robes of the vestments in which my own immobilized person was then so stringently bound.

As bound as she was by her bars perhaps. Though I could take nearly weightless steps in the direction of the tasting table—for it was there, after all, in full stride between us—I was not unconsciousness of the hands levering into my lower back, or the tug of her eyes, as strong as the hands upon the rope that must have made the wheel of the pulley cry out from the rafters when they lowered her cage. The rough timbered cage had been lowered to the clatterous tiles on the other side of the tasting table.

I was blocked. And yet I knew a way was open.

I waited for the parting of Cardinal Mendoza's lips to show me the path. And as he drew in a black velvet breath I saw his tongue find livid footing upon it.

The Cardinal ascended onto a porphyry dais, the better

to point downward at the caged specimen and across the expanse of the table.

The girl's gaze squeezed through her bars seeming to have sloughed the body behind. It hung from its iron grip upon the bars as limply as anything flayed and nailed upon a wooden board to dry in an arid wind. The Cardinal might well have been pointing at me since her eyes were so fixed upon mine that I could see nothing else. I was her spectacle. I was bespectacled by her.

Then the Cardinal's needle-sharp finger soared, making one deft stitch in the air, bringing everyone's eye to its point, pulling the silence taut.

His own voice was the proverbial pin dropping.

"Who has not pondered the miraculous transubstantiation of the soul? I have preached it myself. Do I not believe? I do. But my eyes, my eyes. They have wished, so to speak, to peck the nearly invisible mustard seeds of this truth. They are such hungry organs. Not unlike your own I suspect.

"Today we have the proper priest. Today we have the perfect specimen. So shall we commence the experiment?" The Cardinal merely turned his head in direction of the lifeless cage. His face waned into profile as a lengthening ray of sunlight lit the corner of his mouth with a smile.

"We will not dally with bread. The far from illusory flesh of this young woman will furnish substance enough for our lubricious eyes. I do not deny they are such organs. We will not blink to see a miracle. We will behold what we can hold."

The girl seemed to let her nudity cloak the Cardinal's words with credulity. She stood within the cage presenting a posture that made no concessions to modesty. I alone knew that her shamelessness was explicable by the fact that her most vivid person had already leapt from that body through the windows of those eyes. They now opened an abyss to my powers of concentration. I caught my balance on the lip of that precipice, knowing that I must remain behind the bars of my own corporeal cage. For, as Cardinal Mendoza continued to speak, I understood what it must be within my powers to do.

"The substance of this girl will pass from one state to another before our eyes. And this priestly navigator of the vinous tides will guide us through the changes."

Then he turned his face away from the caged girl, full faced to us. And now I could see the far corner of his smile, waxing with an expression as alien as the other side of the moon.

"Here is my brother." Cardinal Mendoza rotated on one foot to cradle the shoulders of the figurine standing stiffly on his left flank, with a long reach and the ostensible brother's far shoulder-joint socketed in the palm of Mendoza's hand. The ample drapery of the Cardinal's robe, hanging loosely under his raised arm, swished against the statue's straight back as if blown by a vagrant gust through an open window.

The brother's body was a match for the sculpted immobility of the mask still adorning his face. But in his erect stature, straightened by a wooden crutch under one arm, in the caved-in chest deep as a buried hump under the lattice work of his tightly stitched bodice, in the bow of his gold-stockinged calves, and even in the inverted triangle of the russet goatee that tickled the porcelain cleft of the mask, his whole person revolted against the youthful vibrancy of the papier-mâché facade. There were lake-blue tears in the garishly iridescent corners of the eyes, though the extravagant lashes curled back above the gleaming brow bone with the unabashed freedom of an undisguised artist's brush. The rose-rouged cheeks and the deeper blood of the enormous lips, gashed to evoke the moans of an ecstatic smile, were all so coquettishly primped that one didn't notice the brown baldpate rising mountainously over the luminous alabaster of a finely chiseled forehead.

The Cardinal's speech blew harder.

"My brother here would be the girl's stately groom. If… if he is lucky enough I tell him." Mendoza let his free arm flourish balletically in the direction of the motionless cage.

"My brother Fortunato's ministry to the wretched despoilers of our faith who await their pyres in the gaols of the Secadora, has been smitten by one of his sinners. He declares his love, however shrouded in the ample folds of his missionary robes.

"How? You must imagine my brother dungeoned under a barrel-vaulted chamber of the Secadora, with the multitude of desperate petitioners eddying around him. The barrel is full of their cries. It is the sound of birds shorn of their wings. Or imagine my poor Fortunato, bent in his prideful humility over the soup ladle. Feeder of a forlorn flock indeed. His hand trembles to their lips, feeble as the parishioners of hope might be in the city's well of despair. Only imagine the glint of the ladle in the darkest corridor of the Secadora where my brother serves. It shows us what a bejeweled spirit he possesses.

"So how is it that this peerer through the stone-stockaded darkness, guided only by the light of his haloed ego, how is it he is drawn to this girl whose cursed skin bears the color of the grape, as if she had ripened on the vine herself? In the radiance of this hall today we can see clearly how dusky is the hue that in the roiling dusk of the cells of the Secadora, would have been nearly invisible. How did my brother Fortunato envision her where she would not have been apparent?

"Some transubstantiation of the soul you might surmise. Perhaps her soul is the curious stain upon her skin. We imagine our souling bleached to a whiteness that defies all ocular cravings.

"No. We are wrong. 'Darkness visible,' my brother Fortunato retorts. That's how my Fortunato must have fallen into his confusion. He has a weakness for miracles. Not to mention his affiliation with the grape, whose rarest of juices this girl mocks with her shameless pulchritude. My brother you see—you do see don't you, he is no less palpably visible than the girl herself—is the proprietor of the vineyards of *Sola Sol*. I think our avid priest here might attest that the fruit of the *Sola Sol* is as much beyond compare with the Cariñena, the Monastrell, the Macabeo, the Parellada, the Tempranillo, or the Graciano, as any soul is beyond compare with even the most ephemeral flesh. Are not the most labile parts of the body, in its state of arousal, the most fleeting flesh after all? It could almost make you forget that pleasure belongs to flesh at all. No doubt, the girl has convinced him of the purity of her purple stain. She convinced my brother as fervently as the grapes of *Sola Sol*, crushed against our palates, would convince any of us of the perfection of our taste. Poor Fortunato!

"So it is against the grape of the *Sola Sol* that I wager the skills of my miraculous taster tonight. The fruit of the girl shall be her fate. It bobs in the balance with my taster's powers, a cargo adrift upon uncertain seas. Not so different after all than the rudderless hold of the grape in its wave-bound passage from the vine to the flagon. This is what I propose.

"Transubstantiation of the soul. Let's see whether this girl's soul will pass into the bridaling embrace of my brother's estate, into the kingdom of the *Sola Sol*. Can she pass from the pitch cells of the Secadora, where until a day ago she languished by self-accusation, into the forgiving sun of my father's younger son? He would be her loving savior, without whom she must face a tribunal that would strive to enlighten the darkness in which her body is cloaked, with a flickering torch. If the hue of her is an intoxicating wetness, the tip of the flame would lick her dry. Can she pass the dusky boundary of her own skin without a light shining?

"Or can my taster pass even more miraculously through the skin of the grape itself and into the earth which suckled it?

"So here is the wager. Here at the end of the table are flagons from three different vineyards of the *Sola Sol*. All the same grape. All the same wine.

"So seemingly. So deliciously. So sameness always is.

"But different plots of earth tell themselves differently. To distinguish the three draughts would be to sift the very grains of soil from the tannic grit of the taste that is their common sprout. We will not make it easy for our taster. We are lovers of the miraculous are we not? We will press upon the taster's tongue to make him tell us one plot of earth from another.

"Transubstantiation. *Trans. Sub. Stand. Station.* We will know the meaning of these sounds in their communion. If he can find the way, my taster will give us transport from one substance to another. Not just the three draughts of the same seeming wine. But for each draught, he will lead us through the stations of the cross that bleed their sacred juices from the root of the vine. He must taste three wines three times each: first the freshly uncorked wine, then the curdled must, then the long shriveled grape.

"'Tell us taster,' we will command him. 'Which is the wine from the vineyard of the Sorrowful Donkey? Which is the wine from the vineyard of the Happy Cactus? Which is the wine from the vineyard of the Obdurate Rock?'

"But we will not light his path by sorting the specimens for him. They are disarranged on the table. Each a glassed relic to be marveled over. For each wine he will be obliged to follow the tip of his tongue to align the decanted fermentation with its proper must, with its improbable raisin. Only then will he make a path for his soul to follow through the tortures of diverse embodiments. Only then will he taste the earth differently enough that he will be able to tell us how to walk from one vineyard of the *Sola Sol* to the other, as confidently as if his tongue could put roots into the soil for his own fructification.

"By this success we will know him to be miraculously transported beyond this near shore of our savoring senses. The girl will be instantly transported to the bed of coals.

"And then, alas, my brother's bed will be cold indeed.

"Unless my taster fails. And then Osvaldo Alonzo de Zamora will know what a prison his own person can be. He will devoutly wish for the transubstantiation of his soul that we pray him to show us now.

"Ha! Am I not a jester at heart?"

Then, as if they had arranged it in advance, the entire costume party drew off their masks and spilled the viniferously colored robes upon the floor. All except for the girl, whose costume was tattooed to her skin, though, as I have stated, the skin had already been cast aside where it still hung from the bars of her cage like the merest drapery. The nudity of her eyes however, still fixed upon me, made we want to shield my gaze.

So now Osvaldo was the only one disguised by the mask of his naturally born face, a face frozen with an indecision that could kill the finest vintage at the root. Underneath their intoxicated colorations the other guests were all swathed in black. All of them were suddenly thrown into the ominous shadow of something unseen but felt in the chill of my mounting pulse. Because I could not look upon them except through the girl's eyes, I could not find the light that had so darkened the scene.

That something unseen was myself. A man cannot stand in his own shadow after all.

Cardinal Mendoza extended his hand to me. It was the gesture that commences a partnership in dance. His foot, the toe coyly dipping into the sheen of the floor, was already tapping the beat of a *chaconne*. I needed the tempo of an *allemande*. His hand was open. But he did not expect me to take it. Rather, it proffered what he expected me to take from him: the beaker of juice that I must follow back to its root with the gossamer glide of a specter passing through masonry.

My focus was blurred by the wetness of the girl's eye through which I realized I was still obliged to see everything.

Staring, still. Weeping? Her gaze might have been a goblet englobing my purpose, liquid as it seemed to become in the trembling of the moment. I could not raise my arm, or lift my chin to take what was proffered to me for fear of jostling my fate to the point of spilling.

"Osvaldo," I might have called to myself.

Two rivulets forked across my forehead just beneath the hairline where I had been doused. Since I had not taken it to commence the theatrics, Cardinal Mendoza had emptied the proffered beaker upon my head. The snarl of his impatience struggled with the smile he wished to turn upon his expectant audience, especially upon the dour face of his brother Fortunato still standing beside him, but now with the grit of a grin masticating between the rows of his teeth.

"Osvaldo!" he finally cried out, as though smashing a fist through the invisible pane of glass behind which the waxen face of the poor narcoleptic stares out like an effigy of itself.

I said nothing.

I took the empty beaker into the palm of my hand. We all heard the crackle that sounds before the magician's puff of smoke. I made the brimming vessel seem to disappear into my grip. Only the stream of what could have been taken for something other than blood belied the illusion. But, when I unfisted my fingers all could see how I was impaled upon the transparent knife blades sharded in the heel of my palm. Light sprouted like extra fingers, or the reddening rays of a sunset as I raised the garish monstrance before them.

But the fiery blood streaming to the brick floor had ignited Cardinal Mendoza's face. And the wild corona of his rage outshown my own weak flame.

In the same moment I realized that the girl's flesh took on the color of the Cardinal's howling cheeks and blistering lips, as if he'd dropped a torch at her feet. With her hands fanning the anatomy between her breasts and her pubis, she was consumed in the blush of a shamefulness that had been lacking from her person when her eyes were all I could behold, when she seemed to have leapt from the voluptuous sheath of her mortality into the ethereal whorl of my thoughts.

She no longer looked in my direction. I could see. She might have been a leech plucked from my eye sockets, wriggling back into the warm vitality of its own bloodstream. My gaze was liberated. I looked out through my own eyes again and felt myself within.

Though, I must say, if "I" is the right word, the feeling is deceptive.

The wine taster dwells within the buds of his tongue. He knows what it feels like to be what he feels. He does not have to think about it.

But I had already thought about the girl, however fleetingly in the brittle moment of the shattering beaker. It had been a kind of slipperiness in my grasp of the reality I otherwise mastered in the routines of my service to the grape. I felt myself slipping from the purchase upon my body, which is all I can claim for mine, when the flavor of my life unfurls from the violently crushed fruit. Having lost my freedom from thinking about myself, because I had given an uncontrollable thought to the girl, I realized that now the taster was barely a vapor of that purple elixir.

Nothing could happen now, I imagined.

Then the body of the girl, came preternaturally alive

in the cage. She rocked the rickety structure on the perilous axis of its floor edge by throwing herself high on the wooden bars, from which perch she then released the celestially pitched shrieks of an hysterical castrato, raising a clamor as high as the flames of the Cardinal's wrath. Their two furies mounted together.

Because I wavered between them I might be consumed by both. Unless I moved. But how can a person move in two directions at once without being perfectly still?

"Still myself?" The thought flickered in a high window of my mind before the imposing façade went black.

No. Not myself now anymore than then. *Now and then.* The words were clouds of smoke scattering over the roof of my mind in a tempestuous midnight wind. Nothing. Nought. I did not need me. I did not need to know.

I am the taster. I am what my tongue tells me.

Listen. Listen. Only listen.

Instead I heard the Cardinal's simmering words. They were the tip of a rapier blade barely slitting his lips with whisper so only I would know the menace that he meant for me to comprehend.

"Do you wish to know how you will die?"

He had swallowed his apoplexy to preserve what decorum he thought was expected of him. Flame swallower. No doubt it had fired those bladed words. The hilt of it must have been tight in the fist of his gut for me to know the glint of its metal as if he had flourished it an inch from my nose.

In truth I needed no other goading than the spindly arousal that stiffened unexpectedly at the root of my tongue.

And then I heard the long swish of a sword-stroke knock the still keening girl from where she had knotted her arms and legs atop the bars of the cage. When I felt the dazzling glare of its silvered hilt stab the corner of my eye, as the Cardinal no doubt lowered his swatting arm from the distraction, I realized the point of the sword was real.

But I had already stepped forward, even though my bold footfall was muffled by the thump of the girl's body upon the floor of the cage. I heard the low-throated recognition of my initiative rumble approvingly in the crowd that enclosed me should I imagine an escape was possible.

On the contrary, I was already at my post, casting a winged shadow across the top of the tasting table. I had already thrust my bloody hand into the maze of preferences that I was meant to negotiate by blind turns, this way and that, until all of the phials upon the tasting table should be arrayed according to the vaporous ascent of their decanted spirits, harrowed each from its unique ground. I understood my charge.

Yes, I was immersed, and swimming, despite the throttled echoes of the girl's despair lapping at my ears.

Cardinal Mendoza stepped back and smiled. The eyes glistened with emotion. The jagged edges of broken glass smoothed over his grimaced lips to a mirror sheen, though shards still bristled out of the palm of my hand. For my hand was raised vigorously into the air above my bowed head. It was the ceremonious flourish of a toast rendered to a patron by a loving servant, who now grasped the symbol of his fealty between two strong fingers: the first phial. My own lips pulled themselves back to give the tongue its maximum extension into the narrow barrel of the delicately fluted glass. It was expressly designed to cajole a feathery action from the budding muscle so that only its livid tip would be titillated by the drop of elixir that was fairly perspired from the deep and slippery recess of the vessel.

The organ was not capable of imposture. It was itself, in a way that I could only admire. I was like a man standing behind himself, a silent ghostliness clinging to his corporeal semblance. But the first tingle of sensation out of the glass shook off the ectoplasmic worry of identity. The sound of it being dispelled was indistinguishable from a vaporous sigh escaping the deflated form of the girl where she lay crumpled in a shadowy corner of the cage. The tongue was its own man now.

The juices that sluiced between the nodules of that probing muscle soaked into fertile ground. Root and stalk germinated at once, in the two directions of a salivating intuition. Each new probe of the tongue decided the placement of the empty phial in its transubstantial order: juice, must, fruit. *Must. Must. Must.* I must end with three rows. Three phials each. I must follow the footprint of the vinous spirit passing from body to body, from vineyard to vineyard.

By the time I had drained the fifth phial, my hushed audience could already relish how my placement of it among the other vessels that had been lit with emptiness was already fitted to the puzzle pattern of the girl's fate. The black shade crowded more closely about the tasting table. A murmur of blood seemed to have raised the spectators' pulse to match the pace of my deliberations. As the zig zag configuration of the empty phials standing against the broken rows of the still untasted phials took on the appearance of an ever shrewder game of *chaturanga*, the taster's whole body swung with new momentum onto the game board.

The taster rolled up a too-generous sleeve of his sacerdotal robe. His placement of each newly emptied phial became more precarious for their gathering proximity to one another, each phial all the more fragile for its vacuity.

If one had looked, one would have seen that for a brief, tingling moment, the taster peered at a protuberant bone glistening under the skin of his naked wrist, as it torqued and turned, approached and retreated from the glossy allure of one shade of crimson fruit to another. Perhaps he marveled that he possessed a body that did not only lunge from his mouth. He would not say "I."

Just three phials remained.

One was brilliantly rouged with the fully fermented juices of the justly prized vintage. One was clotted with a purple impasto of must. One would rattle with a brittle stick end to which its puckered berry, black as a pit, was attached like the scab of a wizened virginity. The final pieces of the puzzle. The last strategic moves of the game. The opening of the transubstantial pathways of the grape upon which human soles must trod now, if Cardinal Mendoza should have his winding way.

And so I noticed through the bars of her cage how the soles of the poor girl's feet were turned up to me, tucked beneath her buttocks. She was curled up behind her rough hewn bars, humped with shadow, her head lost to a deeper darkness, facing away from the spectacle around which I had gathered all the other eyes in the room.

So I am he after all. And she my shade.

Three vineyards. Nine phials. I had aligned the fruit and the must of one to the left of me. The juice and must of one to the right of me. The fruit and the juice waited directly beneath my gaze for their kindred must. *Must!* Was it not already ordained? I let my hand hover. But the workings of the body were too obviously a charade in the final working out of our mystery. What each of us already knew no longer depended upon a labor of my palate. No substance was required to substantiate the truth of what I had accomplished. Certainly the Cardinal himself was quivering with impatience to upend the last of the glass phials. For each was scored upon its bottom with the code of its provenance. Invisible from the drinking rim. But all already known without a sense to quibble with.

And yet I still extended my hand, in the manner of a benediction, over the yet unsorted phials. I felt a gentle heave of the audience against my back. An exhaled breath. Though I faced away from them, it was as though I held a full congregation immobilized under the spell of the Holy Spirit, until the word "Amen" should be pronounced.

But something inside of me was already speaking a contrary word. Gurgling. An acid bubble. A gaseous word. Annunciation of a rebellion coiled in my gut. I felt that it was fanged and about to strike—a single snapping action unleashed from the serpent's tail. My mouth was already a mummy's rictus.

Was I seized? Was I therefore I?

Or was one part of my anatomy merely the obedient servant to another? Before I could stopper my mouth, the head of the snake wriggled through me and burst upon the air in poisonous gouts. My vomit hung upon the crimson folds of Cardinal Mendoza's robes in roseate, roiling tentacles. The space around him gaped as his retinue recoiled to a safer distance. His holiness's taster, shaken from the knees and now doubled up at his patron's feet heaved a final splatter of mash from the bottom of the vat onto the crocheted lilies crowning the toes of the Cardinal's velvet slippers.

The sound of a bird fallen to hard ground accompanied my split second sight of the girl standing upright in her cage. Barely a flutter of my eyelid kept the image aloft. Then my eyes were struck wide open by the expression on the Cardinal's face and she was gone.

Again it was his mouth that menaced most. The livid sheathe of his lips was pulled back so violently, his face might have disgorged the gleaming white skull. But instead Cardinal Mendoza turned. Tearing the mucoid threads from the pillar of stifling air that stood between us and pressing the hot glue of himself against the front of his brother's body, he planted his lips upon the other's gaping mouth.

Had the mouth been turned down before the kiss? Yes. It was still the sculpted form of the papier-mâché shield that had adorned the entirety of our assembled company. But brother Fortunato's mask was the only one blemished with a frown and the only one that had not been removed at the commencement of our ceremony.

Brother Fortunato pried his body away from the fetid embrace. Raising both hands in the air, he pulled at his ears to disengage the mask from his face. The gesture of one gasping for breath revealed what appeared to be a visage encrusted with hundreds of tiny hard and brittle growths, grey as a shoal of miniature oysters, pulling at the weak flesh so that the slightest motion gave the impression that it might be torn from the bone.

I saw it all now. They had been all masked to conceal the necessity of concealing the brother's face, in whose honor this whole event had been cursed. It was the 23rd of October after all. The hideous brother's birthday. Always in the season of the harvest. Who in the court did not know? Who did not remember the annual spite perpetrated by Cardinal Mendoza upon this day? Who would not understand how the motif of transubstantiation of the soul was only this year's felicitous malice against the shame of his family? Brother Fortunato. Was there another soul in the court that would have wished more passionately to be shucked of his body?

Released from the Cardinal's grip and now unmasked as well, brother Fortunato, whose gilded crutch had come unsocketed from the sweltering armpit, swayed and toppled sideways. It was as if the whole of his body were but another clattering prop for the person whose embarrassment, like the fine dust of a smashed plaster cast of himself, settled over the entire room.

Cardinal Mendoza's finger, raised in the air, seemed to signal the necessary silence as if an admonishment to preserve it stood upon his lips. But he did not speak then. Instead, he daubed a taut roseate curd of besmearchment standing up on his collar. He dandled the offal-tipped finger before his dropping jaw. Though the tip of his finger seemed to sear his tongue with its touch the gesture caused his whole person to wheel upon the gaping spectators elongating the word he would not otherwise have even thought to say:

"*Consubstantation,* my angels! Is it not upon us?"

The Cardinal's open palms, flanking the front of his splattered vestment like the tabernacle doors flung open for the Eucharist, were suddenly drawn to inspect the design of such filth upon his excitedly heaving breast. Whatever held his fascination there had bowed his head into an attitude of mysterious sanctimony. When he lifted his face, lit with a perverse radiance, the smile upon his lips all but masticated the jubilant voice.

He gestured towards the befouled front of his vestment.

"Is it not the face of our savior son? Unmasked." With the illuminating flourish of a dazzling scribe, the Cardinal peering down upon himself, used his stabbing finger to conjure the outline of a shape that shimmered in and out of focus where his own hastening breath stiffened upon the already crusting front of his vestment.

"Who does not behold it?

"More importantly, who will deny it if he does not taste the body that is proffered here?" Again he turned in a foul wafting circle to address his audience. In the passage from his brother's face to the girl's silent cage something flickered in his eyes.

I knew at once, from the rise in the Cardinal's voice that the girl might be saved, though her sad visage, drawn so mournfully to this new arena of action, wore an aspect of stupefied concentration.

Cardinal Mendoza turned brusquely from her. "We promised the miracle of transubstantiation." Cardinal Mendoza nearly shrieked the words as if his voice had caught a spark from the look in his eye.

"We wished to walk the road that leads out of this world did we not..." he shrilled even more piercingly as he let his eyes rise and fall upon the surrounding congregants, "...perhaps the better to find our way back. Was not the grape sifted from the stone? The stone was sifted from the soil. But our most priestly taster has taken us one step further along the thrilling road. Look! The consubstantial being of the grape, the stone, the soil, is hosted here upon my very suckling breast, if you understand me well enough."

Cardinal Mendoza let his eyes fall upon the brother's upturned face.

"So this is what I wager now. Whomever would save the body of the girl from the vaporizing flames would take the body of our King upon the tip of your finger. Commune with Him. And then we will have come full circle from the body wagered as an idea in transit, to the body won as a heavy, muscle-bound, gagging fact."

The dead weight of brother Fortunato seemed to be made somewhat buoyant where he lay astride of the splintered crutch.

Now with his finger pointed heavenward brother Fortunato smiled, giving the facial warts the animus of a hive of bees, swarming the honeycomb. Cardinal Mendoza then knelt, the better for a fallen pilgrim to reach the bespattered vestment, however pictorially it was proffered to him. Fortunato's finger scraped the plush weave of the fabric with the finesse of the painter's spatula. With the impassioned gesture of an artist applying the finishing touch to the canvas,

Fortunato smeared a shadowy raisin-hued gout of my digestion upon the brilliant amethyst background of his protruded tongue. A feral grimace sealed his lips. Even the entire weight of his collapsed self could not hold down a rabbit-sized leap of the gurge from its sour depth.

The Cardinal's long fingers made a soundless friction above his head. The minions had heard something. They came as quickly as skipping children. The multi-colored feathers in their helmets were veritably shaved by the axe-blades that tilted back and forth over their armored shoulders. They ran not to us, who still stood side by side, nor to the aid of Fortunato where he still lay helplessly, but to the purple girl's cage.

She was re-animated within it. Denuded again of all shame she stretched her naked body. The deep hue of her skin fairly eddied. She had become an animal in her captivity. As she stretched her remarkably relaxed and limber limbs and torso she licked her vegetable lips, more darkly infused with the taint of the vats than all the rest of her, except the nipples. They seemed to stare at me the more intently for all the sudden self-absorption she so surprisingly displayed as she waited for the iron key to be inserted into the clanking cavity of the lock.

The tallest of the minions, whom I recognized by the fingernail traces of scar tissue upon his cheek as one who once had once carried another young woman off to her fate, had flourished the key, as big as anyone's hand, for the Cardinal's approval.

The motion of the key turning in the lock was synchronous with the gingerly effort of three guests—chary of the

fetid paste stirred into the air of their strenuous breathing—
to raise brother Fortunato to his brother's shoulder. The Cardinal bowed to be his brother's new crutch!

The turn of the lock barrel under the pressure of the
enormous iron tongue seemed to produce the blurring of the
purple form between the rustic bars of the cage. No longer
a captive, the girl seemed even less a gravitational body. She
was the swimmer once more whose body I remembered as
all unseen titillation. So she still moved.

A deft, brightly finned undulation between the Cardinal's eager body guards propelled her beyond their reach.
The ermine cloak one of them, held out to cover her shame,
fell to the pavement.

Because the girl herself had left the earth beneath her.
She was already upon me, as heavily as a cloak of chain male,
her arms dragging at my shoulders, her legs tight around my
hips.

Her lips burrowing for my tongue told me of my predicament.

All of the warts upon Brother Fortunato's coruscated visage seemed to pull more forcefully against the fragile frame
of the skull as he realized what had transpired. Cardinal
Mendoza was forced to stoop as his brother slipped from the
crooked arm that engirdled his waist, all that a one-legged
man might depend on for the illusion of manly vigor. The
ungainliness of the movement was clearly an offense to the
staggering figure who had expected to let the body fall into
the arms of the girl herself and be done with it.

And then the Cardinal's eyes caught my notice like the
gnashing teeth of a salivating dog snagging the hem of a

garment, though it flies above the heels of its earth-pounding prey.

Only the girl's tongue in my ear deafened the imaginable roar. She roiled over me in an oily sweat.

I saw however how the Cardinal used his poniard finger again. This time its signal to two henchman who stood gaping into the open and swaying door of the abandoned cage, was the tightening of an invisible noose that drew their heads together with the force of a violent blow. A crooking of the same finger then snapped the length of the invisible tether taut so that the two wobbling figures were yanked in my direction. The blades of their axes, swung more purposefully than ever over their shoulders, glinted with recognition of what I so clearly saw to be my immediate fate.

The girl's heated undulations intensified into an inescapable memory of her younger self promising my younger self that one day she would be delivered up to the itinerant priest of our village and, in all the accusable pulchritude of her purple skin, be transported over the mountains to the Plaza de la Salvación, where a denunciation would issue from her own mouth to feed the flames. She never said that the maniacal flickerings of her enflamed body would hold me to the stake as well.

I was seized. I was taken. I was certain that Cardinal Mendoza imagined that all of my tortured behavior this afternoon, so seemingly evasive of his purposes, was cunningly plotted to achieve the girl's captivity in my own arms.

Thus he dispatched me to the dismal cells of the Secadora. There perhaps I would have to await the light of Fortunato's charity before I would escape the blinding conflagration of my proper end.

*S*o, Samaritan, now you know what it is to be caught. But don't let the wine taster teach you to be too cautious. You're already tangled in that net. You've tasted too timidly of the cup of vengeance have you not? Sate your thirst with a more guzzling draught.

If the guilty party goes free, who is guilty?

Remember. When you leant your ear to the tremor of the confessional wall, overhearing the stepfather's vow, you agreed with him that he should die. Then you thought twice. But if it is to be by his own sworn hand, the sinner will possess the deed of forgiveness itself. The priest preached against this profane will with a scolding fervor.

"*Only the Divine* possesses!"

But could the priest be wrong?

The stepfather knows too well that sin is something clenched in the sweating palm of one's own hand, as resolutely as the hilt of the sword. He only knows the strength of his own grip, as you might agree. Is it any wonder that he thinks he can thrust redemption upon himself as he thrust himself upon your little sister?

Not even your one-handed barber would thrust himself between those fates.

Ah yes. That would have spared you the preoccupation that tenses like a fraying rope between your ears now, as we face each other in this dismal light of day. No the sun does not shine. And the stepson?

He must illuminate the moment before the stepfather gives it his own meaning.

And are you in time? Where does the stepfather wander in the maze of his thoughts that you could be confident enough to follow? There is no *time even to answer the question. You must be in pursuit of him before you can contemplate the movements of your body that would be sinuous enough to track him around the blindest corner.*

What was it the stepfather swore to the holy confessor? Remember the words exactly. "I know how to stay the hand of a divine vengeance before you can tell me that it is a sin.

"Hear me father!"

You heard him clap his hand upon the confession grill.

"'When I spread my fingers across the lattice you will hear the wings of the dove spreading beneath me."

You had already listened to him confess his sin, Samaritan, breathing harder with every word that pulsed in your ear, feeling the wavering of the wooden panel where you knelt against it, your whole person reddening in the shadow cast from the high windows of the cathedral. He left no detail untouched, so that your own fingers flinched from the crannies of your sister's body.

You were shocked to hear everything you already knew. The step-father's candor was exceptional. Because he had wreaked himself upon the stepdaughter's body he would not let it loose from the carnality of his words. He left nothing to the chastened imagination, knowing the scrawny confessor to be naked inside the heavy cloth of his cassock and so vulnerable to its movements—the details of his crimes were meant to coax the discomfiture of an involuntary tumescence inside the roughly woven garment. And you thought: he, the sinner, is no longer capable himself of the crimes he is describing. But he would demonically possess the unimaginable organ, which lay as lifeless in an anonymous fold of the confessor's cassock, as the pupa in its frozen chrysalis. Thus would the stepfather strike the priestly father between the legs, the very place where the little sister had taken her vengeance on the sinner himself. Think of the stepfather coaxing sin from the spirit, with the wetness of his confessional mouth. What daring piety!

Could one really blaspheme against blasphemy?

And then, Samaritan, you heard the blacker blasphemy.

The stepfather ordained his own repentance. The impassivity of the priest had enflamed him even more. Standing, tossing the heft of his body from one wall to the other, the stepfather rocked the confessional box. He could not hear the body on the other side of the lattice be dislodged from its silence.

The stepfather repeated himself, like a man stomping the floor with an irate foot: "When I spread my fingers across the lattice, you will hear the wings of the dove spreading beneath me.

"I promise you my life. But just as the Son promised his to the ethereal Father. Was it not the bargain that he would die, if not by his own hand, by his own words? And, if I am wrong about the words that sealed the bargain, he had power over other hands: the hands that seized him in the garden were beckoned by him. I have only my hand. I will use it. Like pulling fruit from a heavy bough."

You detected a change in the voice then didn't you, Samaritan? Like something squeezed by the hand itself. A wet cry? A throttled wind in the throat? Some seepage from the declamatory convulsion of a moment before?

You knew what it was immediately: the sound of the encircling grip, thumb and fingers mashed together to choke off the respiration of the argument that hung between the sinner and the confessor. It was the sound of the fist that would be the fulfillment of the stepfather's promise. The stepfather's fist was closing around his own throat. He was turning his speech into prophecy.

And then, Samaritan, you thought the worst. He could be right! *If the Son had the power of words over strangulating hands, did he need his own? Was his death not an assent? Was it not a bond? A handshake? How could the Father have acted by himself?*

Then the Father would have been himself a son of Cain.

But if He needed the cooperation of the Son, then did the Son not act himself? And was the act not needed? Doesn't one act in the absence of what one needs? What is absent to the Father is present to the Son.

Did the Son not know he must act, despite the appearance that it would be a sin? Did he not open his hand to receive the iron nail?

By what other appearance would the sin against him be known?

The stepfather's relentless reasoning gripped you, Samaritan, did it not? It would appear you cannot escape his grip. Now you see there is only one way to pry the fingers loose: one by one. You must do what he would do before he can take the initiative. Take his life before he can give it up to the exalted Father by his own hand. It must be by your hand not his. Or he might escape his inferno.

Imagine yourself to be the barber's missing hand, if that fancy helps you to raise your hand up.

One by one, Samaritan, you must take the steps yourself, though you commit a crime punishable under many laws. If you do not commit the crime, worse crimes may be expunged. By the stepfather's hand wiped clean. Lest you wipe the knife clean upon your own pristine garment—no, alas, you shall never wear such whiteness again, Samaritan!—the stepfather may be washed of his deeds. He may stand drenched in golden light. He may rise like dew into a crystalline dawn.

Only the dross of your violent deed can bring the stepfather down!

So you must follow him, Samaritan. Enter the cobblestone courtyard where you felt the first blow of his shadow upon your smiling face. Cross diagonally, pirouetting around the central fountain, to the carved granite doorway at the opposite corner of the cobbled yard. Push. The door, despite its oaken mass, will open to the pressure of one hand. Climb the spiraling steps to the resonant chamber that you always imagined was the place where he held his head between his hands until the livid cries faded into the silent corners where they hung on like dusty cobwebs. Pry open the door of his darkened room. By the light of the fire that you have already foretold would illuminate the scene, see him tangled in the intricacy of the rope that he means to knot about his neck. He will have forsaken the more fearsome punishment of the flaming coal!

But there he stands, crooking his neck to concentrate upon the iron hook which claws at his inquisitive eye from the ceiling above his head. He will be startled by the creak of the door, the sudden footfall of your advancing specter.

He will turn.

At first his face will appear to be a puddle of perplexity as if a pebble had been tossed into it. He will face you. The lengths of rope drooping from the tight fists will coil at his feet. But you will step closer. You will make haste. Though your arm hangs loosely at your side, you pinch between thumb and forefinger of your right hand the glistening shaft of a long needle, sheathed in the ample sleeve of your gown. It is a needle milled for the mysterious inner workings of the massive clockworks that ticked and tocked the advancement of the hours and days of your father's work life in the cellar of the old shop, when you were too young to tell the time.

You will have required a brass forceps to extract the pin from its deep bore in the noiseless machinery.

Now the point of the needle glistens in your mind. The light from the fire glistens in the stepfather's twitching eye. The yellow pupil emits a ray of amusement. The corners of his mouth are pulling at the roots of a smile that you can imagine will erupt into maniacal laughter.

You must believe the explosion of laughter is imminent, bursting instantly, leaving you almost no time at all to pinch the grip of your fingertips tighter against the needle's shaft. Then you must leap up and flex the bowstring of your elbow with enough torque to plunge the point of the needle into the prematurely gleeful pupil of the stepfather's golden eye. The tip will be imperceptible when it lodges in the molten center of the stepfather's brain. You will have to wiggle the smallest bones in the avenging wrist to convince yourself that the deed is done.

When you believe what you have done, of course, you will not elude the prick of the deed in your own head.

Say the poultice words now so you will remember them when they are needed. "Innocence for innocence."

So you pin the stepfather to the yellow card upon which his sin is inscribed. Now the unblemished gown of innocence may never flutter about his ankles in the weightless luminosity of heaven.

But, yes, you purchase the stepfather's conviction with the innocence of your now murderous hand.

With bloodied hand you will pass the incriminating yellow card into the hands of the priest who, with as much trembling, took the stepfather's blaspheming confession. When the priest burns the incriminating card in the cinerary bowl, the smoke will be an acrid spirit to inhale. You may not hold your nose against it. The judgmental eye of the priest who performs the rite falls upon you like you like a black cassock. You must wear it to the grave. The darkness of that grave will fill every footstep you take until the last one.

Innocence for Innocence. It seems a desolating bargain, one which only a devil could council. But perhaps not.

Innocence for innocence. Say it again.

✦ ✦ ✦ ✦ ✦

Now let me teach you how to pronounce the words with a different meaning.

Guilt for guilt. Can you not see the solution to your problem? The hand that wears the stepfather's blood might be disrobed of its crime.

A white soul might yet step cleansed from the sullied body as if it were merely fallen about your ankles. You might still walk unfettered in a shimmering white skin where the light of forgiveness lifts you from the ground like your reflection from a pool of tears.

There is, after all another guilty party, against whose fate you might wager your patricide. I use the word deliberately. Your murderous deed makes the stepfather a blood relation after all! This is only to show you the precariousness of your situation. If I led you to the espadaña of the Catedral de San Salvador and we ascended to the top of the bell tower, into the shadow of its swaying bell, if I urged you to take one more step to the sill of the balustrade and there dared you to lift yourself upon the tips of your toes, you would not know your situation more fearfully.

What if I asked you to jump? What if I swore the air would catch you? Yes, a leap of faith.

I ask you to think of this. You have heard Osvaldo Alonzo de Zamora's story, but not to its end. The end is yet to be written. I hand you the inky quill. You might write down the name of the nun whose body he confessed to ravish of her young life in the Plaza de la Salvación. Now think. I ask you. Think and say what is most useful to our colloquy.

Is it inconceivable that the victim sprawled upon the stones of the Plaza de la Salvación was your own sister?

Surely you have thought it might be true. Or do you imagine your sister safely sequestered behind the walls of the convento where the stepfather pressed her into the iron embrace of the Mother Superior as if he were sealing her up in the stone cellar where you yourself spent so many solitary hours beneath the trampling hooves of the wooden bull?

Osvaldo Alonzo de Zamora's confession is heartfelt. I know you admire the sentiment, Samaritan. You covet it. Here is your chance.

Chance makes us good or bad after all. You do not accept the point. But I know it pricks you.

We may not know who the little nun is, flickering in the glare of the stones upon which Osvaldo tells us her body broils in the naked view opened by the Plaza de la Salvación. If she broils is it a double crime: that her death mocks the just and purifying flames of the stake that would be erected according to the dictate of the Auto da fé? Perhaps not, if nothing is illuminated. For we have not discovered the little nun's body. We see nothing where Osvaldo tells us to look.

And yet Osvaldo confesses the crime. And what if Osvaldo's crime is the savage sister to your murderous ardor, bright as the point of the pin you will have lodged in the stepfather's brain? What if it is? You could say so.

The Inquisition waits upon the word. Is it not an expiation to serve the Auto da fé? Does it not give you courage to do what I am urging? In killing the stepfather you are saving his soul for damnation. But I will not lie. You risk becoming entangled in the gyrations of his fall through smoldering air once you have pushed him from the precipice of his attempted redemption. Still in his grip.

Break the grip. Pry the stepfather's burnishing arms from your shoulders. Fly upward from the sulpherous vortex where his carrion flesh plummets. Fly upward upon the words of an accusation: that Osvaldo Alonzo de Zamora has murdered a girl, a blood sister, upon the well-trodden stones of the Plaza de la Salvación where the footsteps of the murderer now must be traced.

Your guilt for his.

It is a fair exchange, Samaritan. It is possible. Guilt is like the blood under the skin. Think of the purple bruise on your arm. That it fades. It fades.

...

You fear the blemish of the lie?

...

It is not a lie if the girl whose limbs are no longer splayed across the stones of the Plaza de la Salvación is unidentifiable by virtue of her absence.

...

But Osvaldo has confessed.

...

If Osvaldo cannot tell us who she was, perhaps you *can.*

...

A nun. A sister. Your *sister.*

...

You needn't doubt it. It is a wonder only.

...

A lie depends upon what you know for certain.

...

A mark, Samaritan? You fear a black mark? Mark Osvaldo's confession and the soot from your own murderous hand will go up in smoke.

...

The stepfather's flame, of course.

...

Remember, Samaritan, none of this has happened yet. We wait upon you.

The darkness of the Secadora lurks in the pith of every quavering mind.

I waited for my eyes to adjust without satisfactory illumination. Though everything became visible in a dozen swift heartbeats after my transporters removed the sweltering worsted hood from my head, the scene materialized as if I were viewing the barely incised lines on a copper plate before it is inked. You have seen the engravings no doubt. An enormous barreled roof belching out the smoke of the close and distant fires that give the most convincing impression of how vast was this prison. The furthest sparks of light were nearly stars to the fluttering eye. Fires to heat the iron poker. Fires to scourge the fur of the rat on the spit. Walls festooned with the same smoke raised themselves around me at different distances as the firelight heaved against them. My nostrils slithered with an unshakeable stench of singed lice.

Human forms pulsated against the walls, flickered blackly, were huddled in groups and strung out in islets of immobility. A low, tidal roar washed over the spaces to be traversed. Between the echoing pavement and the belching vaults twisting and towering staircases communicated vertically. Or did they sway? Were they only other wavering columns of smoke burning my eyes to tears?

My hands were bound with iron cuffs. My arms were cinched into the small of my back. I was still tethered with a slack rope to the erratic jostling of my transporters, bunched and blurting laughter behind me. They seemed to be alternately prodding me forward with the tines of a pitchfork and yanking me off the heels of my boots so that my forward steps were hobbled by my backward steps. But forward I was meant to go, whatever the amusement such a drunken jig afforded my transporters in the process.

The reason was apparent at a short distance when a looming construction of wooden beams came obscurely into view. A kind of gibbet, surmounted by a pulley, from which the hangman's greased and thickly braided rope could be raised and lowered. But what pleasure could be drawn from hanging the hanged man again?

The pulley was a fist hardening itself at the fullest extension of that wooden arm. The rigid grooves worn into the curved wooden roller were fingers strengthened by the most violent exercise. I could imagine the rapier index finger of that fist mercilessly extended and parrying my gaze. I knew. I knew. This towering form, rearing up before me, expressionless without a head, but authoritatively robed in billowing smoke, this mercilessly erected power was surely intended to be my judge. Now with the accusatory finger sticking in my eye I expected nothing less than the blindness of pain.

As if out of that impenetrable darkness, another prisoner, bound and goaded forward with the cudgels of his gaolers, emerged before my scintillant eyes. The real victim? My surrogate? Indeed, I had already asked my queasy self if I were to become the victim. But why I had not been stripped in readiness for the apparatus? The body does not suffer fully except in a state of nakedness. Surprisingly the face is a poor mirror of torment. My progress toward the roughly beamed monster had been halted only steps from the shallow pit gouged beneath the pulley by myriad victims' naked feet scratching the earth to keep their footing. But I was still shod and still fully cloaked in the taster's vestment.

Then I realized. Turned inside out as it was, I would have been recognizable to any stranger's eye only as the priest. The officiating priest of the Cardinal's charade to be sure. But, fully dressed as I was, I appeared to be the priest no less than my brother, the false priest. Perhaps the criminal.

Surprisingly, the victim was fully clothed as well. Both of us driven to the gibbet. Both of us fully robed. And yet, there was no ambiguity that it was he who was to be trussed to the wooden brute. Nor did he struggle in his voluminous garments that would have magnified the struggle were it in him. If he was in them. For however present his person, he remained invisible to me, hooded, shrouded in black robes.

The mysterious victim was cudgeled into position beneath the wooden arm and pulley by his gaolers. But he neither cried out nor gave any sign of resistance. And the tormenters might have been striking at an elusive mosquito. Their victim seemed a veritable incubus eerily animating his featureless garb. The excessive robes appeared to float in the air, absented by the physical weight of the body upon which everything would now seem to depend.

The proof of the victim's fleshly existence came with the brusque attachment of the rope to the suddenly flapping black wing of his already tightly bound arms, yanked out behind him and now cinched at the wrists by an unforgiving noose. The folds of loose fabric sounded the feathery ascent of a bird into blue sky. But the twisted metal crank, already in the industrious grip of a gaoler's enormous palms, and beginning to turn, made another sound. The victim was to be hoisted by those wrists.

My own gaoler seized my dropped jaw in a grip—as strong as his grip upon the onion that he must have grasped as proprietarily at his lunch—so that I would not be permitted to turn away from the sight of the victim's arms. Now their pale mortal being was exposed where the voluminous sleeves receded against the slow ascent of the two hands, pressed ever more prayerfully together by the tightening cincture of the wrists. And now the victim was winged.

The victim's teetering toes pointed haplessly at the gouged earth that had been yanked out from under him.

Only the breath of the onion held me aloft of the same ground. For my legs had become vaporous with fear. The more palpable the weight of the hauled body the lighter was my head in the cloud of onion fetor.

Did not the sight before my eyes deserve a foul odor?

I observed how the declining angle of the now swaying body—the bound wrists gradually rising to the median point of its horizontality—would cause the head to fall from its black hood as the meat of a cracked nut is popped from its shell. This would happen. Unless the shoulder joints should crack open first, releasing the ball of the upper arm into the violent slackness of torn muscle and distended skin, and causing the whole anatomy to fall slackly into a straight line again.

But the head emerged, emblazoned with blood. The eyes were shut with the force of a facial tremor that affected the mouth most noticeably.

I thought I had been deafened by the sight. The lips peeling away from the prominent teeth, the jaw, virtually unhinged by the tongue-forced gaping, surely made way for a great bellowing. Does the fetus emerge any less tormentedly from the pelvic girdle?

I heard nothing. The paralysis of those facial muscles prying the jaws so far apart seemed to stop time altogether. Until the face slowly turned in my direction, the eyes open now and bejeweled with glee.

Then I heard the sound of the unstoppered bottle.

A burst of rollicking breath, with a flow of hilarity behind it that would have choked any ordinary gullet. The face of Cardinal Mendoza poured forth a torrent of merriment to see me so stricken. The fit of his laughter loosened the invisible halter that had no doubt been hidden in the voluminous disguise of the robes. For they shriveled about the shackled apparatus of the feigned arms. Those marionette arms were still swinging loosely in the air above him, pendulous from an equally swaying shoulder-harness hoisted higher yet, as the Cardinal's feet struck earth with a surfeit of aplomb. Cardinal Mendoza bowed with his real and elegantly jointed arms generously thrown out to me, the gesture of an actor marking the arena in which he stands fully accomplished of his role.

"You have been tasted!" was what I heard.

You assure me that the glint of the needle's point has been quenched in the moist and gruel-like tissue of the stepfather's brain.

But I notice the sorely pricked finger pad of your left, less favored hand, Samaritan.

Do not make me doubt you. Tell me that the stepfather struggled to make you perforate your own skin. He stood taller than you by almost a head. He had the leverage of his own enraged arm. But you are elusive are you not, Samaritan? Wiry enough to parry that arm with the whole of your wriggling torso, from shoulders to hips. You slipped out from the noose of his grasp. You bent your knees. Hunched your shoulders. Out of the posture of prayer, we might say, you sprang up again, this time with the long gleam of the needle brandished with such violence that the stepfather snapped his head back. All the better for you to see how to point the needle. All the more suited to the angle of your wrist. Tell me that you seized the momentary advantage given to you by the virtual flight of yourself, fully sprung, now looking down, now glaring into the astonishment of that unblinking eye.

I believe you did.

Cardinal Mendoza's imitation of torture was meant to be its own scourging liturgy. Such titillations of human frailty are known to induce a conversion. But can the converso have a conversion experience? Or is all experience already denied to that bereaved spirit by the first conversion? The conversion from what one never knows.

Cardinal Mendoza's laughter shivered the limbs of his bent-over frame as convincingly as would have the final snap of pate-bone against the gibbet's full and unbending height.

It was the spectacle of my own collapsed self—a man cannot stand without legs—for which the Cardinal brayed.

On my knees I still trembled. Still trammeled by the illusion of a physical sundering. I, the transubstantiating priest of the grape, was rendered of those vital juices that keep the stalk of the self planted firmly in the ray of the sun.

I wept before the Cardinal's most cruel forgiveness.

✦ ✦ ✦ ✦ ✦

The shrieking daylight into which I was exposed—it was like the unhooding of the reprieved prisoner who is already kneeling at the block—as the bronze doors of the Secadora murmured shut behind me, told the full injustice of my standing there: a free man in a street filled with the pristine silence of a just-broken dawn.

And so I had earned my forgiveness. I had been forgiven

for the crime I did not commit. The regurgitation of the grape was as involuntary as the flow of blood. The impetuosity of the girl, flown from the opened cage, was a spasm of her own recondite being. What had I to do with brother Fortunato's fall? No stain of these acts did I wear.

But the nude girl lying like a white glare upon the stones of the Plaza de la Salvación burned painfully in my eye, beyond any power of my chafing knuckle to ease its pricking. Because she was my own work.

✦ ✦ ✦ ✦ ✦

The leg. I thought of the severed leg. How questioningly it had lain before me when I first opened the door of my chambers onto the pathway of these events. What is the answer?

Now I must think. Was it, as I have already thought, the little nun whose fate fell from my tongue into my brother's arms? Was she the one who laid the questioning leg before me, knowing that I would bear it out of the shadow of my doorway into the glare of the Plaza de la Salvación because I cannot but bring things to light? Must I think again?

The taster gives himself up to the taste.

And now I must think again. Was the caged girl, whose skin I tasted in the vats of an earlier acquaintance with the grape that stains her purple skin to very the cuticles of fingers and toes, somehow a familiar of the little nun? The caged girl thrust upon me an embrace that was a mirror image to the little nun's entwinement with my brother's priestly limbs, long ago in the theater of the little chapel where Isaac performed his ritual feats.

Does transubstantiation happen like a thought? I think that I have sinned against them both the same, the blood-blemished nun, the girl of grapey hue. They are united in my contemplation of the act. The taster acts no less than any other laborer, even he who toils under the brunt of the sun to harvest the fruit of the vine before the sugars quicken. Both women, or do I ripen them precipitously by that word choice, have been ravished by my tongue. So my choice of words is the least of insults.

The one, the little nun would have drained her body of its blood by virginal devotion to the ray of light that blossoms heavenward in the high window of the Church of the Hermanos. Though she was old enough to bleed according to a calendar of worldly days, she vowed a scab against that hymeneal flow.

The other, the purple swimmer, possessed a body that just as willfully shut out the light. The darkness that dimmed her mortal sheathe might have been an emanation of the darkness to which the innermost organs of the body cleaved like barnacles to the deepest shoal. She was so immersed.

The one casts a bloodless shadow, like nothing so much as a pool of blood, upon the stones of the Plaza de la Salvación.

The other is soon to radiate the heat of the brightest coal stirring among the pyres set by decree of the Auto da fé.

Through me their fates have been joined.

The mystery of taste is that it is always itself and always different. Through me the two distinct bodies suffer the same disembodiment. In me they taste the same. It is a sourness above all. A yeasty spore of something that might be called an unacceptable aftertaste, if I were tasting for Cardinal Mendoza's audience of ship owners and merchant bankers, cloistered for their deliberations in a candle-lit cellar. As an unseasonable chill and wetness in the air will knit its woolen mold about the fevered grape, irreversibly altering its destiny upon the palate, I wonder if the pall upon my tongue portends some permanent alteration of the tasting follicles that will cork the vintage of my days. No. The taste is always itself. It is always different. Always.

I think, what is substance in these two women, these changeable bodies? And I think only I am substantial. Through me they have passed and will pass to nothing. I ask what is it to be so porous?

Perhaps that is the meaning of the question posed by the severed leg.

✦ ✦ ✦ ✦ ✦

I tense the muscles of my leg to feel the animus of two female bodies that seemed to weigh so solidly upon the ground. Upon this leg one could carry another body fast and far.

But I limp back to my beginning. Thus I think of another condemned man in the Plaza de la Salvación who attempted to flee from the thunderous massing of equine hindquarters gathered like a noose around his person. Demonic hostlers alternately lashed the rump end of the horses and reined them violently at the bit. Thus they would heighten the animal fury into a maelstrom. It might have carried off the entire mob of spectators surging upon them with reddening faces and glistening teeth.

The prisoner was momentarily loosed from his shackles, that he might be fastened, hands and feet, to the four rope ends harnessing the horses. There he stood amid the roiling hooves and glistening buttocks as if he were up to his neck in a cauldron coming rapidly to boil.

From the staged daises upon which the full tribunal of the Auto da fé presented itself—the robed and black-hatted clerics and judges on the first tier, the retinues of richly liveried servants and more roughly groomed henchman on the second and third tiers—the privileged view of the prisoner slipping his wrists free in the space between clanking iron chains and hovering rope loops gave rise to a unanimous cry of alarm.

From the daises all could see how one of the grooms, startled by the unexpected hoof beat of the prisoner's rebellion, lost his grip on the rope and leather leads tethering his snorting beast to the high protocol of these proceedings. The rearing forelegs of the white-eyed apparition struck right though the bridling chests of two brawny spectators who had bullied for greater proximity to the site of execution. This was seen only a breath-beat before the flexing hindquarters of the horse propelled the equine head like a black musket-ball—mane afire with the wind, the flanks shuddering against the prospect of illimitable freedom—into the heaving throng that surrounded the executioner's arena.

The trodden flesh bore the spouting hoof prints like a string of tiny geysers erupting from the ruts of a muddy carriage road.

Shrieks, caterwauls, and more keening vocalizations of terror broke open a wider pathway of escape before the unstoppable stallion, in his stampede to unfettered pastures.

It was this tumultuous confusion, seeming to rupture the very stones of the Plaza de la Salvación, that distracted all but four eye-witnesses in that vast and seething throng, from the comparatively tranquil miracle of the prisoner's flight.

"Into the air!

"The sky!"

"A bird!"

"A miracle!"

Later, only after the prisoner was unfurled from the collapsed canopy that had been held aloft on black and green striped poles by the Inquisitor's lackadaisical footmen for his protection from the sun, and which seemed to have foiled the prisoner's escape, only then did the four eye-witnesses point out that the prisoner's fall had been broken by the roof of billowing silk. It had not fallen upon him. The prisoner had flown.

When the white-faced witnesses to the reputed miracle of the prisoner's skyward ascent were summoned separately before Cardinal Mendoza's high bench to give testimonial of the vision, they were in meticulous agreement.

They agreed upon the amazement of their vision. Once free of his metal constraints, the prisoner took only one step. He cast his liberated hands into the air as if releasing message-bearing pigeons into a spiriting wind. Instead, the hands carried him aloft. The arms flapped. He suddenly hovered, more a butterfly than a bird, above the melee that had been stirred up in the Plaza de la Salvación by the escaping hooves of the maddened horse. Hovering. Floating. Peering down. The witnesses each recalled the prisoner's smile, aloft of the bloody scene where they had to have shaded their eyes to see.

They swore oaths that the prisoner's smile was as iridescent as the artisanship of a master goldsmith. The molten beam of the prisoner's smile melted the eyes of the witnesses who were still passionately tearful the sixth and seventh and eighth time they were implored to conjure the prisoner's miraculous ascent into the blank and skyless minds of their tireless interrogators.

"The wings of an angel might be invisible to the blinking eye," was Cardinal Mendoza's blunt retort. "A man does not fly, though the fluttering eyelid of the excitable witness may lift him upon wings of illusion. The angel, after all, is not the man. Nor is the man himself, if he *can* fly. Well, there are other tests than the eye's witness.

"We can taste a man's mortality, can we not?"

The dagger of the Cardinal's goatee stabbed the mystification that seemed to envelope his nodding head no less than a cloud of incense billowing from a swaying thurible. The vociferousness of the Cardinal's assent to his own words seemed to give the motion of his head the weight of a bastinado beneath which the four eye-witnesses were manifestly enfeebled. Each was now swooning upon the slumped shoulders of his fellow as if they had just raised one another from hard ground.

But the blow fell most forcefully upon my consciousness of the Cardinal's intent. The taster's ear is attuned to all the nuances of the word itself. Taste.

As I observed the notion forming on the tip of Cardinal Mendoza's tongue, I could not deafen myself to the pendulous doom chiming in my head.

"A man's mortality is no doubt a flavor of the blood," the Cardinal dispassionately sermonized. "We are well aware how cunningly it must course through miraculous flesh, whose blush we are meant to take as a sign and a wonder. And yet, angelic blood must taste differently enough for the discriminating tongue to tell us about what we are so wondrous." His eyes fell upon me like the wings of the arrow-pierced crow.

"Tell us Osvaldo."

Blood is blood. Wine is wine. I said nothing.

I was the inquisitor's tongue after all. I might have commanded myself, if such an I—atavistic homunculus that I would have devoutly wished him to be—existed to contend with the lingual organ, wielding its irresistible powers of speech and of song, and of taste, but, most unexpectedly of touch.

Such is taster's secret knowledge. The taste buds themselves will bear no eye-witness. They are invisible. They steal embodiment from the fungi-form papillae. These words do not form easily. They are the goose bumps of the tasting flesh. They muscle the surface area of the slender appendage to its maximum nudity. Thus is the exposure to whatever stimulus arouses the organ to its passionate vocation made most labile.

Now, I thought to myself, blood will be wine.

More than one man from the corrida-like stockade behind the Plaza de la Salvación, where the testimonial proceedings had been convened, now clamored to be bled. The whitest arms were proffered from even the most refined and ermine-trimmed sleeves. They volunteered to prove out the miracle by comparison with their mere mortal blood. By that communion with the already sworn to be exalted prisoner, they sought to earn perhaps a precious droplet of blessedness for themselves. Only the prisoner, himself now splayed and shackled to a standing wooden lattice, as lucid as a figure drawn upon the gridded field of a draftsman's folio page, seemed to hold his lungs against the imminent breathing of the vein in his reputedly miraculous limb.

The tourniquets and the wooden handled *scarificato* had been summoned along with the one-handed barber who possessed them, and to whom the Cardinal and his entire retinue showed an inexplicable deference. A glass chalice, inverted and seemingly capped with a leather suction bulb, then appeared mysteriously from some secret fold of the barber's red and white vestments. Using the circular and empty motions of his stump arm to balance the delicate work of the good hand, the barber set this vessel beside the other implements of the ceremony whose commencement I, among all, awaited most patiently.

I was seated at the table laid by the gaudily trimmed barber. The prisoner in his bonds stood at my back. Before I turned my gaze away from him, and toward the bustling ministrations of the barber, the prisoner had appeared a young man who was so suitably flushed with enthusiasm that I thought he might *pour* all the more easily. He had peered at the table without comprehension, a lonely vessel.

I, even more alone, understood the additional setting of two goblets before my place.

The goblets were etched with the official court poisoner's insignia, the hollow skull, the broken bones crossed beneath it. But the goblets were purposed otherwise. I knew it was simply that no other glass was ready to the grasping hand of such improvisational urgency. The taster would have to ignore the signs.

I had only once witnessed a public poisoning. It was administered to the victim strapped head down upon a board slanted off the fulcrum of a wine barrique. Once the venomous draught was assuredly swallowed, the board was seesawed to give the audience a comprehending view. The poisoning, after all, was meant to display the most feral churning of the bowels upon the face of the prisoner. His sin, being the pride of Reason, smirking its vehement denunciation of all fanatical superstitions, required the most severe effacement. Thus was the boastfully rational prisoner obliged, by the poisoner's stronger argument, to turn all that can be expressed by sparking eyes, soaring cheekbones, the most aquiline nose and the most sensuous mouth, into an irresistible confession of human fetor.

Today would be different. Today the deadly serpent's tongue would slither from between my lips.

I waited for the blood to be decanted from the opened veins. First from the prisoner. Then from the selected volunteer who was now seated across from me. As I waited my mouth dried to a confusing astringency, something usually stimulated by the sting of tannins flooding the palate. This time there was nothing to suckle but the unnerving thought that the pallid and breathless face of the foolish volunteer upon which I gazed mirrored the fact that behind my back the forearm of the prisoner was about to give up a morsel of flesh to the single-toothed blade of the Scarificato. And then

I watched the young volunteer squirming across the table from me lose his appetite to the same ravenous incision in his own limb. At the last moment, the brawny elbow of one of the disgraced grooms from the Plaza de la Salvación, was required to lock the innocent's head against reflexes that might have permitted his body the unbridled spasm of a creaturely flinch.

No. The creaturely flinch must belong to the taster, for whom no choice now presented itself but that between the two goblets, filled to two identical brims. Of course, the taster does not want a full goblet of wine. It risks inebriation, overstimulation of the carefully shortened flex of the tongue against the palate that is required to tell the grains of tannin and sugar that have been sifted from the skin, the stem, the earth in which the vine flourishes. Blood, the less intoxicating elixir, should require a longer tongue, more tightly fastened to the palate to staunch the ingestion, I might have thought. But I did not think.

I have said the taster does not think. Tasting is an act. An action.

I pinched the stem of the first goblet between two fingers. I knew nothing of its provenance. It had been poured from an anonymous flagon. There was a whiff of sweat-roughened animal hide. The snort of a bull came to mind. The color of the liquid was uninflected by the light. Its redness would not separate into hues. The density was not quite an embodiment. There was a skein of particulates dragging through it when I curled my tongue against the roof of my mouth. It was like all things that can be tasted: itself.

The other goblet tasted the same.

Thus the prisoner's fate was divined.

The only *flight* to which his existence would testify now would be that of the sparks crackling aloft of the bed of coals upon which he would most certainly be put to sleep.

✦ ✦ ✦ ✦ ✦

And the grape girl will flicker in the same flame.

Transubstantiation.

My regurgitation upon the Cardinal's finery was no recanting of the miracle upon which Cardinal Mendoza had wagered the life of the empurpled girl, whose skin mocks the inwardness of my powers, which cannot therefore be called *mine*.

The sentence of the Auto da fé will nonetheless be carried out, as if by *my* will. Now the girl, whose incestuous sisterhood I once fancied in the fever of a youthful fermentation, and who is so closely filiated in my mind—my mind?—with the little sister whose blood stained my hands after it stained my tongue, and whose carnal affiliation with my brother Isaac makes her a sister of mine as well, however profanely ordained by such tortured logic, will suffer a new and transfiguring substantiality at the stake.

Transubstantiation *is* a thought if there is a thinker. Bodies pass through me. Fates, I think. *I think*. No. *I* do not think.

I am only the taster. The lascivious tissue itself, the taster's tongue, tumesces in the mouth to tell of the body that possesses him, as if he were some untouchable plasma of the seeded juices that are clutched within the skin of an uncrushable grape. Who is the taster to say "I think," even if a leg crooked in the shape of a question mark tells me that it might be so?

Well, where there is a question, one thinks there is an answer.

*A*nd so, Samaritan, can you not give out a sigh of relief to think how, by invidious comparison, the rayless guilt of Osvaldo, our once heroic character, bleaches out some of the blackness of your own besmirching deed? Which is not to say, by any means, that it is bleached to whiteness. Such luminosity could be blinding after all. Nor is it what either of us bargained for. We must reckon with what is before us.

You are still the murderer of the stepfather whom I grant you was thereby saved, for us, from murdering himself. Or should I say, we were, by your deed, saved from his curious belief in the expiating authority of the human hand, had he proved it by a logic that surpasses our logical belief in the infallibility of a Divine hand. That hand, I assure you, does not bargain with squeezing fingers and a sweating palm.

The deed was your doing, Samaritan.

A good deed, Samaritan. A good deed.

And we will not forget that you have strived, since your boyhood, troubled by two fathers, to be the Samaritan whose blamelessness does not suffer the need to take succor from another's hand. The good deed. Your own doing. It is something that can be proven to oneself. This is how you say "I."

Of course we must scruple the thought that the blameless self is perfectly selfless.

You will be the first to admit that you are not selfless. Or perfect. Empathy, you need not point out, has been the sodden rag with which you've blotted the accidental stains upon your soul. Dribbles of envy, covetousness, sloth, greed, avarice, lust.

Yes, lust. Now think how murder and lust embrace one another. When you plunged the gleaming point of the needle into the glint of the

stepfather's eye didn't something rise up within the stalk of your be-
ing that was as irresistibly pleasing as the breast of the young woman
against whom you crushed yourself with one toe still teetering on the
wooden ladder, the ladder itself trembling against the threshold beam of
her wooden loft? Can you remember what I witnessed?

What was that sensation tickling the unsteadiness of your body at
the top of the ladder?

"Empathy," you wish to say.

But not so fast, Samaritan. It was the sensation of falling without
fear. The sinning fall is bottomless. But does that make it all the more
exhilarating? The needle in the eye. The spear in the side, though it was
not the young lady's side you sought to penetrate. My point is, they are
not dissimilar thrusts.

The murder of the stepfather then is the involuntary memory of
your capacity for arousal. Even if I must remember for you. How will
you become the blameless sinner except by rising to the moment of arous-
al?

Let me tell you: by extending wings into the ominously calefacient
air of your fall. By becoming useful.

✦　✦　✦　✦　✦

I will now say something about myself, which I proffer to you as a
kind of hand to take hold of though I am well aware you do not wish
to be solicitous of the empathy of others. You know nothing of me but
my manner of forming the questions. Now you may hear an answer for
which the question has not yet been formed.

I will share my knowledge of a virtuous murderer.

I will confide to you my knowledge of a devout sister among your
brothel's sorority. You would not recognize her. She is nested at an ob-
scure distance from the roosting place of your own "plump chickadee"

as I overheard you covet her in the ever dimming vaults of that smoking basilica. But if you saw Doña Fernandina, unveiled in a ray of sunlight, you would know a regal bearing in the brusquely canted hips and narrow shoulders upon which the head and neck are balanced like a plate upon a stick.

Doña Fernandina is indeed someone's sister. She is the sister of Cardinal Mendoza. I have known her from her childhood, if it may be spoken of so. She was an adept at needlework. Even in her youth she was capable of using the tip of the needle as if it were a paintbrush. She suffused white fabrics with color. Doña Fernandina belied the prick of the needle's point with finger strokes that were polished to such silvery smoothness that the design fairly seeped into the unrippling linen cloth where it was pulled taut in a halo-like brass frame resting upon her lap.

A scattering of rose petals that begged to be picked one by one from a snowy field. A livid and winged unicorn lathered with its emergence from a billowing white cloud. A shower of pinkish raindrops pooling into deeper red footprints that one could follow by observing the meticulously articulated tips of the toes. The remarkable trait of all these images was their rebellion against the dominion of the eye. It was the sense of touch that they aroused most fervently, at the free edge of the fingernail where the itch to scratch is always hiving. No sooner did she unframe a finished piece of work than the nearest hand, that of a child, a nurse, a man, a woman, needed to caress it between rough fingers, impassioned by such elusive tactility.

There was nothing to feel. She made even the vision illusory by tightening the threads until they were part of the weave of what they penetrated.

Well, I must tell you, Samaritan, Doña Fernandina's confessor did not know the meaning of the word Samaritan.

*He was a small man with pinched features that seemed to minia-
turize his facial expressions, though his corpulence, in the short arms and
stubby calves, not to mention the pendant belly of his person, made him
more conspicuous than he wished to be in the Cardinal's court. His baldpate did not gleam with perspiration from the exertions of his obescient
bending toward every rank of the palace's dignitaries. It wore instead
the dull patina of a pewter salt shaker. Nor was he bald. What shone
upon his skull was the stubbly shadow of a full head of hair, albeit grey,
which he had razored every other day in the belief that a bald skull is a
sign of one's distance from the vanities of the world.*

*Doña Fernandina was remanded to the chastening chaperonage of
her confessor three times a week in the grey hour before dawn. She would
be conducted by a sleepy page into the intimate family chapel that was
secreted in the foundation of the palace's ancient edifice like a tomb. The
privacy of the chapel was immaculate. Here only the blood relations were
permitted to take communion, privately, purified of the ceremoniousness
of public places of worship where their official robes made them effigies
of worldly power. The chapel was a vault resounding from floor to ceiling
with the solemnity of white marble slabs fitted seamlessly against one
another. Smoothness persisted as hardness. Like a bone in a reliquary, the
tiny chapel solicited the touch of those pious members of the family who
sought spiritual revival from the weight of their world-weary footsteps,
which in this place became the sound of an easy exhalation of breath.*

*Here the young lady's confessor had supplied a crimson velvet pil-
low to soften the marble ledge where his pupil was meant to kneel in
readiness for giving up her sins into the turgid shadow he cast over her,
squat as he was. You can easily imagine the scene, Samaritan. But you
cannot see what is most apparent.*

*The confessor, Fraile Benito, did not ask for a verbal litany of her
sins from her tongue: an unkindness toward a cat with her foot, cross*

words with her nurse, a lie to her tutor? No, it was the tongue itself that he solicited, an embodiment of sin to which he would lend the support of his own flesh and from which he might take the added pleasure of knowing the sin without having to be told.

To be a girl of fourteen years is already too little means of defense against the passionate tremors of male adulthood, however dwarfed in the figure of her confessor, Fraile Benito, whose virtues otherwise towered in the opinions of her family.

I ask you, Samaritan, what manner of incomprehension is needed to contemplate the young girl's encounter with the feral animality of her confessor's exposed manhood? To what remote outpost of our own imaginations must we make pilgrimage in order to countenance Fraile Benito's command that she fill her mouth, already brimming with well rehearsed and themselves purely imaginary sins intended to satisfy the ceremony of confession, with the livid engorgement of his pulsing maleficence? Is it not true that only the most feverish imagination of the adult is adequate to the lived experience of the child?

And yet, Fernandina was possessed of an imagination.

This profanation of the girl was repeated three times.

At the next time of her deliverance to the confessor she bore the means of her revenge as invisibly as a thread of the enveloping and bouffanted ropa in which she imagined he would want to find the smallest, most delicate parts of her person like some preciousness wrapped for a gift. The needle pierced the inner lining of the fabric in two places that it might lie flat in its readiness to her fleet hand.

When Fraile Benito reached for her she bowed lower than courtesy demanded. When he tried to lift her head with a stiffened finger under her chin, she sank the chin bone like a nail into her breast. When he reached for the scruff of her neck, she went flat against the marble floor, her arms spread out so that the ropa flourished like a cape to the aroused *bull in the arena. When Fraile Benito stooped to turn her sprawled self over, his eyes were wide with the expectation of what she was hiding.*

All the better, she thought.

When she was sure that Fraile Benito was stooped low enough to be unbalanced upon the balls of his feet, his eyes bobbling white above her, she rolled over herself, and out from under his tumbling shadow. Reaching into the lining of the ropa with the same liquefying speed and deftness that could make the needle dart in and out of the fabrics she tattooed with her designs, her fingers thrust the point of the needle upward to meet Benito's toppling incredulity. It was a stroke so precisely angled that the child could let go of the metal nub and observe how the impact of the Confessor's face against the blunt pavement drove the needle's apogee so deeply into the brain that its penetration would not be apparent upon anyone's first inspection of the corpse.

But Doña Fernandina had no intention of disguising the deed or of denying her guilt, if guilt was due. What do you think, Samaritan? A virtuous murder, as I have advertised it?

But I promised that I would say something about myself as well.

Fraile Benito's stiffened body had to be removed by a pair of burly pages using leather halters slung over their shoulders. There might have been a ballast of river stones in the bulge of the confessor's belly.

I am only saying that the physical evidence of a murder was not easily disposed of. Nor was the family's problem helped by the fact that Doña Fernandina confessed the deed to everyone she met—servant, counselor, cleric, page, courier, captain of the guards—as she wound her labyrinthine way from the depths of the chapel back to the domestic apartments that were perched in the highest towers of the palace.

Cardinal Mendoza, the older brother of Doña Fernandina, by enough years that he could stand officially for the father, whose death had coincided with the birth of this first daughter, was already assured of the authenticity of my good counsel. I could tell you why. No one would be surprised that in his capacity as ambassador of his family's shame he should seek me out. For knowing what to do in such circumstances I could be trusted not to have to think.

The sin was undeniable, notwithstanding the sinfulness of the victim. It was of the flesh and for the flesh. It was, above all, in the flesh that the steel needle was lodged and so rendered forever bereft of the silvery gleam that was its scintillating affinity with soulfulness.

Because Doña Fernandina's murder of the confessor was the defense of a womanly virtue, the brooding sisterhood within Cardinal Mendoza's family wombed around the girl's vulnerability. They implored me, through him, to substantiate the girl's blamelessness. Her blamelessness was more palpable than the victim's corpse, which otherwise just presented the mortally weighful evidence of a crime. I concurred with that opinion.

But I am not a worker of miracles.

Instead I imagined for them a way of converting the corporeal manifestation of their dilemma into a holy sacrament. I merely asked a question: did the girl not feel the ripening of her own flesh as palpably as a bud disfigures the bark of the branching tree? I merely made a suggestion: the perishability of the flesh might be something to trade in as every blameless soul is inveigled to believe.

Where better to nurture that belief than in a brothel?

I proposed it. Doña Fernandina could take up a roost in the Palacio de la Salvación. Her disappearance would be no violation of law. I did not joke to say that her disappearance would be indistinguishable from the vocation of the sacred sisters who sequester themselves from our streets, from our noisy mortal midst, to reside in sepulchral silence. Fernandina's disappearance from the world would be as indistinguishable from the soul's absenting itself from the body. Such is the vow of that holy sisterhood, without which they must see themselves as the bucktoothed, faintly mustachioed, mole-sprouting, ungainly and luster-less corporeal presences they are.

But invisibility is invisible.

So it is with the soul. So it might be for the girl whose act must otherwise come under the scrutiny of unforgiving judges. Their eyes unduly influence what they know. Better that Doña Fernandina dispose of the burdens of her small and still developing body as if it were the beloved pet, the dog, the cat, even the ferret on the leash, which can be given into the hands of others. The affection remains, unencumbered by the acrid smells, the claws, the teeth, the licking and scratching, the bleeding. In the Palacio de la Salvación Doña Fernandina would give away her body like that.

Nor was I hampered by the fetters of practical reasoning to persuade Cardinal Mendoza that, as his sister grew up within the walls of the Palacio de la Salvación, her physical existence, by its careless usage, would come to matter less and less in any case. So would she attain the exaltation of that spirituality, which depends, after all, upon abjection of the body.

Such, after all, is the vocation of the nun is it not?

And is the fortress-like edifice of the Palacio de la Salvación so different from the imposing wall of the Convento de la Concepción Immaculata? The only difference is that the little sisters who contemplate their bodies with earnest revulsion within the implacable silence of the Convento beat their thoughts against the hymeneal wall, which they know to be more formidable than mere mortar and stone. The little sisters of the Palacio de la Salvación know the substance of the world to be such an unformidable illusion, because its permeability is the condition of their beating hearts. Who enjoys greater proximity to heaven? Invisibility is invisible.

Certainly the kingdom of heaven is no walled city.

✦ ✦ ✦ ✦ ✦

Which brings us back to your conundrum, Samaritan.

Innocence for innocence. Your first bargain tendered your innocence, as you would call it, to redeem your sister's blamelessness. I have already inveigled you to make a brother bargain: guilt for guilt. Now you may pay in the coinage of the stepfather's murder for that much coveted blamelessness by which the true Samaritan is duly recognized.

Now redeem your own blamelessness, if it can be said to have been what you believed it was. There is a way.

Do as I say. Revile your sin against the stepfather by a public denunciation of Osvaldo Alonso da Zamora, wine taster to the court of the Auto da fé and murderer of the denuded innocent of the Plaza de la Salvación, whose sisterhood I now invite you to lay claim to, stoking your guilty conscience to more feverish action. Make your denunciation vehement in proportion with your capacity for self-recrimination and I believe that you will do justice even to the criminal de Zamora, who surely begs his recognition as eagerly as you do yours.

A virtuous murder. Would you not call it so? Find the empathy.

*I*t thinks to me that the girl will perish at the stake, my tongue does.

Me? My?

Nothing else will answer. Not I. Not Osvaldo. Nor Osvaldo's brother who is dead, except for the semblance frowning back at me in the mirror. Me? Him?

Perhaps one could say the feat of sifting the three *tierre* of the *Sola Sol* spoke for itself, my glumly inarticulate regurgitation notwithstanding. And thus does the priestly visage, glower out of the reflective glass as if he knows how the empurpled girl's fate tastes, as well as I. I? We. We? Two tongues. One voiced. The other mute, but voluble with consequence. Always two. Always one. And the girl too. Not just herself. Not even when she will breathe fire from her incinerating mouth.

She will. The Plaza de la Salvación heralds the conflagration. The spectacle of industriousness already brings a flush to my face. When I walked out upon the stones of the Plaza de la Salvación this very morning, I stood amidst a clamor of industriousness. The sight of bare-chested laborers erecting the wooden stage upon which the tribunal of the Auto da fé will be enthroned siphoned a droplet from my heart. For my memory shimmered with the long ago image of my brother Isaac standing upon such planks. I was reminded of the buzzing within my breast that day when my brother's tongue was a tuning fork to which all our ciudad's ears turned, like bees to the hive of the Plaza de la Salvación. Then song was the tremor that melded the hundreds of bodies jostling for a view of the man through whom the voice of the child flickered with molten luminosity.

What I see for the girl is different. I see her dancing in the flame. A reluctant dancer to a tuneless compunction.

She has been taken into the iron custody of the Secadora that was mocked, in my case, by Cardinal Mendoza's wish to show me my own frailty. As if I had never submitted an inch of my gooseflesh to the icy waters of that mirror.

I do recall that the girl was a strenuous swimmer. But I do not imagine she possesses the strength to break the clanging chains that will drag her to the depths of these waters. She has been shackled. She has been barred. Iron bars now. She dwells in a darkness of which the prisoner is herself the very pith of the oblivion that she imagines could be discovered by pacing the stone cell in concentric circles. How else does one map the space of one's invisibility? And she must be famished. Not even the watery paste of oats left over from the horse feedings is permitted to pass the threshold of the enclosure in which she sits upon her hands to gather warmth to herself. The prisoner is always naked. The tufa blocks against which she feels the segments of her spine chattering to one another are seeping a colder current of darkness into the abyss. Here indeed the swimmer's frantic motions, arms and legs flying, would be the most buoyant relief from the cold, though there will be no coming up for air from these depths. And when the leaping flame at last provides a cloak of warmth it will rob the victim of the very breath from which the sigh of relief sought to escape.

She is my prisoner no less than Cardinal Mendoza's because she is no less a creature of the tasting than I. That she wears the pulp of the offending fruit upon her skin makes her imprisonment that much more cruel a conceit of fate. And I am a prisoner of the conceit, if "I" may be so conceived.

Who then will know that when the girl is led into the cauldron of the Plaza de la Salvación, when the shallow dish of the plaza is perfectly aligned with the dilating pupil of noontide, the earth is eye to eye with the cosmos, the flame ready to the straw, who then will know that this execution of the judgment of the Auto da fé is clutched at the root of Osvaldo Alonzo de Zamora's tongue?

Cluck, cluck.

*A*nd so, Samaritan, you are contemplating the culpabilities of our once virtuous wine taster? You are considering the bargain that for the moment whispers like a taut rope between us. You know his dilemmas as calculably as you understand the terms I am teasing to you here. Osvaldo Alonso de Zamora is the agent of a murder committed under the same exposing sun to which the empurpled girl has been sentenced to become spectacularly luminous.

Two girls. Two deaths. Are they not twinned as Osvaldo is with his own brother?

Osvaldo and Isaac. Are they are not doubly twinned in the guilt of the converso? But Isaac is dead. Isaac, the priest, whose angelic voice was the soul that consecrated the liberties he took with his sacerdotally garbed person. Who will be recognized as the priest now and, soon enough, unmasked as the masquerader in priestly vestment, though Osvaldo does not adorn himself with his brother's apparel? Osvaldo does not wish to be seen. Yet people see what they will. Soon enough a denouncer will come forward.

Well, will this denouncer come forward in your place, Samaritan? Would you forego the chance to be so useful to the Auto da fé?

But you are skeptical, Samaritan. You say the denouncer is nobody's neighbor. The denouncer and the true Samaritan do not speak, any more than the Levite spoke to the man from Jerusalem. The denouncer is the neighbor's betrayer. Is this what you fear of me? That I will betray you? And yet we are speaking openly are we not, as neighbors should?

✦　✦　✦　✦　✦

May I share my own parable of neighborliness with you? Only three days ago, a man stepped timidly into the silent noontide of the Plaza de la Salvación. His eyes were seared with the sunlight reflecting off the silver stones. The heat appears to liquefy stone, makes the foot trepidatious in its first step. But the man, who wore a saffron caftan and the pointed cap of the wayward converso, must have imagined he could walk on water. He strode confidently across the shimmering expanse of the Plaza de la Salvación, because in the desolation of solar glare he had seen something. It lay upon the deceptive surface either buoyant with illusoriness or the weighty proof of matter.

With his eyes focused upon his objective, the man knew that he stood in full view of the windows that glared back at the naked stones of the pavement. The glass-eyed buildings made up an accusatory verge of the Plaza de la Salvación. But the saffron man was alone. He knew he must be even more readily visible than what he marked with his own eyes. But he followed his gaze with ever more clattering footsteps until his shadow broke over the figure of the prostrated child. Kneeling before the crumpled form, he felt the radiant heat of the stones as a stifling muff around his mouth and nose.

It was not a child, though the size and vellum whiteness of the nude body were deceptive enough at a distance. Closer inspection brought the pubescent and umbrageously contoured maturity of a young woman to blossom. One leg, canted at the knee, gave the body the appearance of a reclining seductress. The violent twist of the head against the grit of the cobbled pavement was the bruise of oblivion into which the face was eternally turned. The stooping figure tried parting the heavy dark locks only to reveal a scalp line like the ragged crack in an egg shell.

If anyone were spying from the surround of vigilant windows, the sunlit figure stooping so investigatively over the body, might have been mistaken for the first flame arising from a pyre. The conical yellow hat was tipped with such flickering intensity. So the saffron man was not surprised to be doused with the shadows of the guardsmen whom he should have imagined had dogged him with their clumsily paced clatter of axes and swords, from the moment he was released from the armoured doors of the Secadora. The man who is forced to don the saffron robe and the conical cap is meant for suspicion. Now he found himself at the scene of a crime for which any man might be suspected. But the man who is already suspected cannot escape conviction.

Do you doubt it, Samaritan?

So who will be his neighbor? The man has been forsaken by his wife and daughters, unless they should be washed in the light of the saffron caftan and thus stained with the hue of public suspicion. They do not wish to be seen. The man's parents are dead, it has been told to him, of shame. His brothers kick dust at his approach. The man's eyes, now fluttering helplessly in the grip of the stoutest guardsman, do not succumb to the dilations of sunlight. The expanse of his loneliness grows ever wider between the quavering lids, if someone would look into his face. To the guardsman, taking custody is not a matter of facing the prisoner. It is a matter of dismantling the rebellious limbs, a binding and a cuffing, denying the head and torso the possession of a body. If the man in the sanbenito were livestock he would be as casually trussed.

Now suddenly aware that the surrounding windows are as full of popped eyes as the cobblestones are clattered upon with the rowdy spectatorship of a crowd amassing around him, the man sees that the man in the sanbenito has no neighbors in the Plaza de la Salvación. The jeering faces and the fusillade of spittle distract him from the clangor of iron shackles braceleting his ankles and his wrists as he is dragged to his feet. When he is stood up and wrenched between the custodial muscle of two armoured guardsmen, and so is fully exposed to the mob's antagonism, he actually cries out for friendship. The parched cry is voiceless however.

The hungry mouth yaws helplessly as the beak of a nested chickadee whose mother's wings are already clenched in the smiling jaws of the cat.

He is of course the wrong man, as you well imagine, Samaritan, knowing what you do of Osvaldo's Alonzo de Zamora's naked criminality in the Plaza de la Salvación. And who is the victimized young woman, whose body might now succumb to your idea of her?

Think of her. She is sister to someone, if only in the bosom of the divine family. Or what can we make of the violently rent black apparel discovered at a short blustery distance from the body, more of a winding sheet than a proper habit, but dyed to the pitch of that most chaste faithfulness in which the nun's body moves, whisperingly as a voice in the dark. The purest chastity is the deepest obscurity is it not, Samaritan?

Can you shed that darkness that we may see who she is in your mind? And perhaps you may see too the possibility that she is your *sister.*

Well I don't dispute it. They are all our sisters as you say. Quite right. In that case why not imagine that your sister so believably sequestered behind the mossy stone wall of the Immaculata is instead mysteriously splayed upon the cobbles of the Plaza de la Salvación as if these stones were two faces—shady and sunny—of the same battlement?

But you say the time of this sister's grief is out of tune with the song of Osvaldo's confession. The evidence of Osvaldo's alleged crime would be mortified by now, a cloud of dust, a stain upon the stones. Nothing more. You challenge the logic of the accusation. You protest that this cannot be the little sister whose broken neck is still being wrung by the compulsive fidgeting of Osvaldo's sweaty hands. Nor would your sister have been a sister to the moment of Osvaldo's deed which, you would say, must have occurred in a dream to him if the discovery of the body waited until now. He could not have committed such a crime without its discovery in a time and a space that cannot be consubstantial with this time, this space.

Ah, Samaritan, you see so many obstacles to the path of the Samaritan.

But these are only logical barriers. There is a better man than the impeccable logician. The blessed soul does not need to reason its goodness like a millstone making flour from rough grains.

Be the better man. Can you not think only that the deflated body of the young woman lying beside her billowing black attire is a sister because she lies dead upon the stones? Is one victim so different from another? Can you not imagine that because the innocent man cries out for a neighbor, that your name has been called? That here is the occasion for your usefulness?

Have you never witnessed the prisoner at the moment of release? The nostrils engorge with air. The skin ripples over cheek bones. Hair grows as infinitesimally as a shiver of air moves the blades of grass. The mouth shines with the drool of a first cut tooth. The color of the eyes becomes more saturated, as if the painter added a fresh brushstroke to the canvas.

Wouldn't you paint the world that way?

I am grateful for your pause. For your introspective reverie.

But then you speak: "And what of the murder," you ask? The denouncer murders no less violently than the accused can be accused. You say that I contradict myself. You protest that if you follow my advice you would merely be Osvaldo's executioner, not the good neighbor of whom I spoke. The denunciation to the Auto da fé ignites a scorching straw. You admonish me that the neighbor does not borrow a life as if it were a loaf of bread.

But perhaps you do not consider that the loaf, in this case, is already infested with worms.

Think of the painter as I say. Touch the canvas like this. Don't let the pyre flicker so fearfully in your gaze. Rather, put some light in your eye at the thought of your helpfulness. Consider that the guilty man may usefully confess, even if they are not the truest words. Yours are more easily pronounced. A "virtuous murder" then. My words in the end. But salubrious enough in your mouth. I can see your wish to form them by the furtive motion of your tongue between such florid cheeks.

So you are converted, Samaritan. So you will become the missing protagonist of my parable of neighborliness? You will shake off the stepfather's grip with these denunciatory words and by that violent shrug, and at the last possible moment, grasp the hand of our saffron man in his hopeless plummet over the precipice you wobbled upon.

And what of Osvaldo? Osvaldo de Zamora will smile. Like the man in the mirror.

I always look to see myself in the wineglass as I raise that convex mirror to my lips. I admit I raise it higher than is necessary, almost above my forehead, licensed as I am by the charade that I am examining the most subtle hues of a vinous decoction, but with the real intent of seeing who is there. Thanks to the curvature of the glass he always looks bigger. He lends himself to inspection. His pouty features give way to the smears of light that wipe away both ears. But the malleable, expressive parts of the face, the nose, the eyes, the mouth, are vividly exposed, even emblazoned with their vermillion dye. It is with an ever sterner expression that he looks back at me. Always a stranger.

I lifted the glass even higher because tonight my gesture was convivial. If *I* were *he*.

"A toast to Isaac!" The voice puckered on my lips.

At last no less than the Pope's physician had declared Isaac to be prodigiously intact. It was decreed: the voice was its own sound. Upon entering the chamber of proclamations, the lavishly gowned inquisitors—the swish of their skirts evoked a queen's retinue passing in her wake—announced that they would permit a demonstration. They would permit us to hear the young man's voice testify to the miracle of his own nature from the curiously bearded orifice. They would marvel no less than if the voice emanated from the nether lips of the frail sex of which it was, after all, the sibilant epigone. They wished to make themselves supine before the bafflements of a divine paradox.

Isaac was, at last, the proof of his miraculous self. He smiled back at the tribunal. He smiled at his brother.

Isaac then stepped to the center of the chamber. He raised his glass to Osvaldo Alonzo de Zamora, as if to make the mirror sound with the clink of it.

Isaac swallowed. Isaac placed the drained goblet upon a marble table top. He stepped into the center of the room soundlessly. He opened his mouth with nothing more to imbibe. And then came the needle-sharp thrust of the falsetto that might even have shattered the mirror.

The smile was brazenly toothed. When the teeth were parted a childhood took flight. The chamber resonated as if it, and everyone who inhabited it, had been turned to glass, we shivered so to the sound of such zealously animate breath.

The fully manned castrato thrilled us with the contradiction. One of the glass figurines in the retinue of the Cardinal's pages actually wobbled and crashed to the marbled pavement. And the note was ascending still. Only the most sensitive ears could breathe the thinness of that exalted air. We exulted from below. Even the black cloaked and crimson capped members of the tribunal might have felt themselves to be sinful petitioners reveling and groveling at the foot of the mountain.

The great wooden doors of the chamber were flung open that the sound might fill the air of the city streets with the buoyancy of soul. Isaac indeed held the note as if it were a taut line barbed in the mouth of a deeply submerged fish that slowly and inexorably would be raised to the surface. I saw the uplifted faces of those around me. Their eyes were as wet with the deep as the eyes of the fish. The frozen footfall of those who passed beneath the arched window of our high chamber was now as audible as the vocable extenuating Isaac's breath beyond mortal limits. I saw Cardinal Mendoza's own mouth round to the amazed circumference of his wide eyes. The puffy, almost purple lips, extruded a long, smooth breath, lathed with awe. The papal doctors' gruff groping after the root of Isaac's manhood seemed to have made his whole being swell to this moment. No one moved until the bubble burst.

Then the Cardinal's arms fell upon my brother's shoulders. I saw what no one else would have understood. Cardinal Mendoza's embrace was Isaac's anointing. It had of course been arranged beforehand and known between them to be a sacrament, though to the holiest of attending eyes the gesture was not even the most nibbling food for thought.

Isaac had solicited his priesthood. Though it would be only a raiment to the outside world, to the converso it would be a belief worn inside out. It was what he wanted. That was all Cardinal Mendoza understood. As the Cardinal's embrace of my brother crushed the slender frame more intimately and his mouth appeared to sip the whorling darkness from Isaac's right ear, I understood that he was pouring a torrent of his own words into that orifice. Cardinal Mendoza was reminding my brother that however much this was to be a masquerade of the cloth, there were still sacred vows that the novitiate must take upon the penance of his blood.

First Isaac must tell no one, though of course the doubling brother would know. Isaac must therefore compel the brother—the brother always knows when the brother is spoken of—to avert his gaze from this mirror. Isaac must never speak when carrying the cloth. He would be no one's confessor but his own. The rites of communion would be devoutly private. Behind the eyes, tightly shut. Or hushed within the walls of the family chapel, that was so deeply buried in the foundation of the palace walls, and only in the family's remotest absence.

"Yes, yes, yes. In the crypt of that silence you can feel free to be the priest."

The sparkle in the Cardinal's eyes flashing above my brother's ear told me what he whispered. He was keen to be the secret abettor of powers he could not understand. I knew the Cardinal did not worry a sinfulness in the bargain, were he even susceptible to such fears.

After all, did not the miracle of Isaac's voice hold that young man accountable to himself without having to be himself? Are not all communions so private? My brother's *and* mine? Mouth and tongue. Our mutual consubstantialities. Our miraculous beings. Who, especially Cardinal Mendoza, needed to divine the reasons why or the meaning how?

I did not drink from the glass I had lifted to Isaac's glory.

I felt a catch in my throat upon seeing the color of my brother's ear darken to its livid brim from the outpouring of the Cardinal's lip. That was a glass too. In its bountiful gleam, I saw what no one was meant to see. I saw the converso priest secretly ordained in the marble carapace of the tiny family chapel buried deeply, deeply beneath our feet. Crypt and bone. I saw the ceremony that would be conducted between Cardinal Mendoza and my brother this very night.

✦ ✦ ✦ ✦ ✦

It would be as intimate as a secret handshake.

This very night.

Isaac's arms would be raised up. Then lowered to fill the armholes of the most holy vestment, in an unmistakably lascivious consummation of his bargain with this patronizing Cardinal. Would there be a solo member of Cardinal Mendoza's retinue in attendance, standing behind them, pursing his cracked lips to the cold metal mouthpiece of a beribboned and badly dented trumpet?

Would the Cardinal utter the service of investiture himself? Or would he ask Isaac to do the blasphemy in his own voice? In the tableau of these two confiders, I could see that I would not be present to hear when the annunciatory words would be mouthed to the empty air, whoever spoke them. The flesh of my brother's soul, cloaked in the black and white haberdashery of heaven's calling, even if the calling voice should be his own, would be belied only by the yellow stockings of the converso, invisible to anyone who would be looking up.

I am looking down on this scene.

And so, I see more.

My brother is roughly stripped of doublet, shirt, pantaloons.

The Cardinal stands behind Isaac. His voice could be streaming from my brother's mouth he presses so closely upon Isaac's naked back. He can perhaps feel the crowning vertebrae of Isaac's spine probing the soft skin beneath his chin. For the Cardinal's head is bobbling upon that spindle where my brother's bowed head gives place to it. And so the Cardinal utters the words. My brother's mouth moves to them, though, bowed as it is, I cannot see the expression on his face. I think of the puppeteer's head tangled in the strings of the puppet. He is attempting to peer out through the gilded proscenium of the stage upon which the wooden clatter faintly resonates.

They breathe as one creature. "Ex Deo...."

Barely a whisper. In the uptake of the next breath the words are rendered indistinguishable from the swish of the garment in which Isaac's narrow frame is enfolded. They are virtually the same shadow upon the glaring marble pavement of the tiny family shrine. When the shadow quavers there is only silence.

Yes, I am looking down on the scene. Isaac stands white as a pillar of salt before the imposing prelate. The white gown in which he has just been sheathed sets off the Cardinal's full-blooded robes. Then out of the blustery agitation of the Cardinal's regalia an even more incarnadine jacket is flourished above my brother's head. As if a wind had died, the garment settles upon Isaac's shoulders. Now, the Cardinal's arms swing brusquely from my brother's shoulders as if hinged to them. My brother is consubstantial with the body that is attiring him. First he finds my brother's hands. They are swiftly cooped into the armholes of the jacket. Then the Cardinal's nimble fingertips capture the buttons of the jacket's breast panel one by one in the rigid nooses of their respective buttonholes. Their stiff alignment, snapping to the attention of thumb and forefinger, leaves the buttons dangling on broken necks. The rounded corners of the high collar, open in the shape of a v where a button might have found its fastening, stand vigilant at the bulge of Isaac's *pomum Adami*. An opening for speech. The Cardinal's right hand chucks my brother under the chin to give the stirring larynx a more labile girdle.

My brother holds his tongue.

And then the Cardinal's hands fall away from my brother's neck to his bony hips. Now the fingers are toiling with the gaping gown, where the satin lash of the robe-tie could be fastened with a brusque encircling tug—one of the hands pulling stubbornly against the other's grip. The Cardinal's grip is tight enough to make the organs of my brother's sex come into relief with the alabaster pallor of something chiseled where he is trussed below the waist. Only Isaac looks down. The tightness of the vestment still preoccupies the frenzied warp and weft of the Cardinal's hands now attending to my brother's thighs and calves. He stoops and rises again. The Cardinal's deft interlacing of two leather straps, dangling garters from the vested portion of the habit, gathers the loose folds of the shiny gown into a sheath for one leg and then the other. So Isaac sees his legs standing apart from one another. The otherwise billowy vestment becomes a sheen over muscled limbs. Isaac feels the torque of the fabric as the tumescence of his whole body.

Is this what causes him to turn his head and lift the smiling words to the Cardinal's eyes. "Is this my body? Is this my blood?"

"This!" was the reply.

The Cardinal seizes Isaac's right hand and forces the sudden fist of it back into the shoulder hole of the doublet he had stripped from Isaac's person only moments before. The other arm follows in the opposite direction. Crossing his arms across Isaac's breast, the Cardinal masters another row of buttons. My brother feels another collar come to rest upon the hackles of his neck.

Then, jabbing his knee into the crevice of Isaac's own jointedness at the knee, the Cardinal drops precipitously lower to snatch the waistband of the silken pantaloons still pooled around my brother's naked feet. One foot lifts involuntarily from the blow behind the knee, and is thus easily snared into a baggy trouser leg. It takes only a stave-like tightening of the Cardinal's grip around the narrow barrel of my brother's chest, for him to hoist my brother's torso with one arm and with the other to snag the other pant leg on the toes of Isaac's other foot, hovering in brief flight. Then an immeasurably short plummet. An almost silent thud to earth.

Then, with another violent genuflexion, a stooping, and a climbing back up into the air, the Cardinal moves to gather the strings of the waistband and to draw the shimmering pantaloons up and about Isaac's slim waist.

Thus was Isaac twice dressed.

"This is your body," Cardinal Mendoza decrees.

"You may carry the priest into the public eye like a stick if you wish, but he stays under your skin. He mustn't ever poke through." The hand that had smoothed the outer garment over the roughly cinched folds of the priest's vestment—flexed so muscularly beneath it—suddenly tenses into a claw. In its grip my brother's genitalia are brought into stony relief against the uncarved bulk of the clothing that wraps him. Isaac is meant to feel the bite of the chisel upon which hammer the cold words of the Cardinal's warning:

"Practice the priest in public and the voice of the castrato will sing in your blood."

✦ ✦ ✦ ✦ ✦

Seeing all is knowing all. I know my brother cannot keep his vow.

Already I see myself recoiling from the sight of what is to be seen in the coming years.

The priest will out.

It begins as a studied dishevelment in my brother's clothing. He learns this dishevelment from a woman. She discovers him in a closet of the cloister from which he daily peers at the secreted world of the monks who patronize his inquisitive presence among them as they do the ectoplasmic paraclete. The fetor of long sequestered flesh fills the closet. Issac's eye widens in the splinter of light that quavers under his thumb where he keeps a grip on the latch. He wonders that there is an inside latch. But before he can reason why, the woman's hand has pierced his sight. She does not knock. She pries him open, latched as he is to the inside of the door. She is immediately upon him, as smothering as the captive air he has been breathing.

She knows this place like a ghost knows its haunt. She is known to the cloister as an unexorcisable demon who stalks the priestly mien. She is no sooner clambering into the closeted space than she is inside the welter of Isaac's clothing. Ferreting hands. Whiff of an underbrush. Her flower-scented hair nuzzles his chin. She has assumed the posture of prayer with such alacrity that Isaac will not catch the flicker of her face before some furtive motion of her arm snuffs the light behind her. The door is shut.

Her hand has found its familiar burrow. But it balks to discover a strange occupant. Her tugging upon the root of Isaac's tumescence extracts only the silken slipperiness of another garment inside the garment she has rent by her hasty foraging. If there were light enough she would recognize the pigment of inflammation which her artful caresses bring forth. It is the incarnadine cummerbund that cinches the priestly vestment to his waistline underneath his outer garb. The cummerbund is crushed in her grip, but protrudes defiantly in the wash of sunlight which floods from the force of Isaac's elbow upon the wooden door. Swung open as it is, the woman can see the door in Isaac's clothing. The silken stalk protrudes like a flame from the window of a burning building. Isaac topples.

He is on his knees. And it is on his knees that the vision comes to him. Dropped to that height and walking nonetheless on those stumps of legs, he is actually pleased to see the priest extruding from the codpiece of his breeches. The woman has shut the door behind her. He thinks her hair is as fiery as the cloth she ignited from his clothing. But he does not wish to turn back. He is more delighted by what is before him. An advantageous slovenliness beckons his begging brain. He rises from the pilgrim's kneel. The miracle has already happened. Standing, he throws open the closet door. He rips open the neck of his shift and a silken plume of priestliness is released into the air like an impatient pigeon.

The palms of his hands, still warm with the flutter of release, cause Isaac to think it will bring him home. He yanks at the cuff of his shift and the blushing undersleeve is revealed. He stoops to the top of his boot and digs for the color that will burn away the sedge drabness of his breeches' leg.

I see Isaac as the idea blossoms in the flush of his cheeks. He will cultivate this dishevelment. No doubt the Cardinal's razor lipped admonition shuttled between his ears as frantically as the mongoose in the box.

"Practice the priest in public and the voice of the castrato will sing in your blood."

But I can see Isaac striding boldly beyond the mud walls of the monastery into the Calle de las Vacas, extruding the vestments from his otherwise somberly garbed gait. He conceals nothing that would not be sealed into the narrow waistcoat and breeches of ordinary mortal life in our ciudad. The hectic flourishes of red and white figure a dervish-like anima escaping the lumbering frame of a man who thinks he will never be dead. But I already see that he is coming for me.

✦ ✦ ✦ ✦ ✦

Even as I watched the Cardinal tuck the crucifix behind the final button of the vested jacket, on the long ago day of his secret and profane investiture, I saw that Isaac would transgress.

He would permit the silken flames to seethe through the unbuttoned orifices and consume the man at the stake. For Isaac wished to become invisible to all eyes that did not dilate feverishly with the luminous image of the priest.

I could already imagine how quickly the flame would burn away the figment of my layman brother. For the eye that stared long enough into that flame the priest would billow into view, fully revealed on a public street, his hands flickering involuntarily with the many fingered signs of holy rites that have been forbidden from his grasp. He would find no pockets in the holy livery to hide his compulsion. His mouth would twitch with syllabic concatenations of a yet inaudible Latin, hammering at the gate of his sealed lips. A vexed and vexing specter.

So the priest who had only lurked behind the ordinary livery of the Cardinal's household, would step boldly forward from behind the bars of the Cardinal's admonition.

Practice the priest in public and the voice of the castrato will sing in your blood.

The outer layers of my brother's lay haberdashery, increasingly unbuttoned, and unbelted, as he cultivated a greater and greater dishevelment, would permit the silken inner layers to shine through in threadbare patches of intent. A tangled wisp of maniple uncoiling from the open collar, the white cincture extruding from beneath the cloacal last button of his waistcoat like the hen's impatient egg, the alb sloughing the grip of his cuffs at both wrists, the golden fringe of chasuble flickering from the open codpiece, would give the appearance of a *chirigota* in carnival. His brazenness would grow. He would cease to wear pants. The skirts of the vestment would spill out from the bottom of his waistcoat, flying about his heels. Isaac would molt.

Until, at last, the priest was fully revealed.

+ + + + +

Who would deny his existence? When the little consort nun joined Isaac in the most lofty apartments of the Cardinal's Palace, he was confirmed in the strength of the illusion, beyond even the Cardinal's powers to threaten it. Who would challenge the severity of the priest who has appointed himself a concubine with such blaspheming candor? I think I have already mentioned our rapier noses. It is the very blade of severity when we choose to use the face for cutting. My brother therefore made a spectacle that dared to be ogled. Astride the stones of the Calle de las Vacas the red and white flickered to the rhythm of his progress.

I was filled with dread to see the specter swooning toward me.

Now I, the surviving brother will be mistaken for the priest. And the fate with which the Cardinal threatened Isaac may rise up on me like my own shadow, from the blazing pavement, whereupon I take another step toward the punishment that awaits me in any case. Regardless that I do not carry the holy cloth upon my back, what I bear before me solicits my doom: the face of Isaac. Who does not know him as the priest? Who will not recognize me as the false priest, even more false for his dying?

Do I not see the passing faces turning upon me grimaces as dark as gouts of mud? The flicker of my brother's face flames in their eyes. Inside their nostrils the thickets of hair bristle. I hear the words I uttered myself as if I need to hear them.

The one who makes an imposture of imposture reminds those who permit the Jew to be the converso that they are such hypocrites.

Isaac did not acknowledge the faces withering in his direction. He shed them like tears in a strong wind. But I am drenched with the sudden knowledge that Cardinal Mendoza's menacing admonition was meant for his own sake, not my brother's. The spittle of disdain would be flicked upon the Cardinal's own head if his indulgence of the priestly charade were to be discovered.

Practice the priest in public...

Now I must take it as the admonition it was meant to be. How else will I know to be ready for my accusers?

Practice the priest...

✦ ✦ ✦ ✦ ✦

I will. The costume will fit. I know. The three leather trunks reeking of incense and containing Isaac's worldly belongings have been delivered to the surviving brother's chamber. The fumes of the thurible swaying on its silver chain make me totter beside my bed where the trunks have been arrayed, as though to provoke a conundrum of choice. I make a short procession before them trying to imagine which contains the incriminating vestments that have fluttered so menacingly in my thoughts.

For all this long recollection of the day of my brother's secret investiture has now been cast in a fresh light by the latest news. I have just had it from the lips of a breathless page. The girl whose skin exudes the crushed grape is *not* to be burned as I had expected. She is to be married.

By Osvaldo Alonzo de Zamora!

I had to think. Would such a mocking of the priest mock more the masquerader or the ritual over which he was to preside? Bringing the question before my mind, my mind's eye, I observed the winking darkness of Cardinal Mendoza's missing tooth when he smiled to think of this charade.

I had to think. But didn't I understand too well already?

Cardinal Mendoza, imagining how he might make it seem that fortune could shine upon brother Fortunato out of the very shadow that had been cast upon his betrothed's well-dyed limbs, had spared the girl's life.

At such moments of inspiration, the Cardinal found himself irresistibly intoxicating. He possessed an inebriate will. His ribald fancy of a nuptial farce was that much more delirious if he imagined the officiating prelate to be the mirror image of the counterfeit priest. The converse visage. Hairs rose upon his neck to think so.

I thought so too.

And so he had planned it to happen. He had visited himself upon brother Fortunato brimming with jubilation. Did his brother's budding warts grow roseate with the radiant tidings? Did he miraculously cast aside his crutch? Were his dry lips parted with joyous song and his tongue become the festive clapper to the iron-forged fate of his crippled physique?

The wine begs the lip's indulgence at such moments. I might have lifted the goblet myself to the salivations of Cardinal Mendoza's announcement.

But perhaps brother Fortunato's reflex was as sobering as my own at the knell of this news, when Cardinal Mendoza embroidered the perversely imagined scene with the details of his deviousness. All was planned. The Plaza de la Salvación would be strewn with straw. "Imagine the crèche instead of the church" the older brother beseeched. "So it first was!" The bride would be trundled to the altar in an open cart used for transporting cheeses over the mountains. Above the waist the bride would wear only the lusciously crushable hue of her skin, that the surge of her naked breasts might better evoke the bursting of the vitis berry at the consummation of its ripeness.

"Who will not be invited? None. All will attend."

Perhaps brother Fortunato's eyes bloodied to hear how the Plaza de la Salvación would be spattered with gouty bouquets of manure. And perhaps the fire in brother Fortunato's eyes would be extinguished when he heard that the altar would be framed up from the dismantled troughs of Cardinal Mendoza's most beloved pig. The Cardinal's flat hand on his brother's back, slapping the breath from him, would no doubt coax the coughing fit that would have landed Fortunato on his knees, his crutch rattling beside him. But the damp coughing would be no match for the Cardinal's resonant guffaws. To witness Cardinal Mendoza trampling brother Fortunato's prostrated spirit with such unremitting mirth one might mistake him for the footless drunkard, whirling in his delirium, for whom all the world is a spinning pinwheel of delight.

"And there at the altar, sniffing the boards where the pig snout exerted its hot breath upon the slops, the erstwhile priest stands ready to perform."

Perhaps Cardinal Mendoza worries, "The role will be new to Osvaldo, though certainly he has seen how the priest is done."

Cardinal Mendoza's thoughts are running now to overtake his most fleet-footed imagining of what the laity might have already surmised of his miraculous protégé. But Cardinal Mendoza knows something the laity do not know: that Isaac is dead of a horsefly. They do not know that one brother survives, the perfect semblance of the other. Death disguises life. Life is death's disguise. "Ha, ha," he murmurs into his goatee. And thus he can continue.

"So the priest at the altar awaits the groom on his crutch, the bride in her cart. The priest is a spectacle to inspire awe. See the crimson cassock sheathing his genuflection at the approach of the nuptial pair. See the chasuble tonguing the breeze that is gathering vortexical force around him. And the appearance of sanctity is crowned, above all, with the *coroza*. The white, conical, pasteboard is a vortex of its own, spiring a meter into the air from the priest's visibly turbulent forehead."

And then Cardinal Mendoza might get to the point, as barbed as the tip of the coroza. "Feel it?" he might ask, his tongue fairly probing his brother's ear. "In your gut, my brother. Do you feel the finger of uncontrollable hilarity beginning to stir? The priest is a figure of fun, is he not? But unless you laugh, the others won't know to. Strain to hear the ominous silence of the coming moment. All rests on your shoulders my brother. Let the first titter rise like the tail of the dog when its snout is dandled by a concupiscent scent of its prey in the wind. The rising wind.

"Tickle, tickle.

"See how the poor priest can't keep his head aloft under the dizzying weight of the coroza. His eyes might pop from their sockets, the pinch of the headgear is so palpable in their teary squinting. Does he clang his head against the high rails of the cheese cart reaching for the bride's hand? You could make yourself cry with laughter if you would just open your eyes to what I see."

I see Cardinal Mendoza's brother as clearly as I saw my own brother's doomed visage in the mirror of memory.

And I think. What would brother Fortunato see but the first bubbles of spittle effervescing on the curling lips of the watchers: their first sips from the cup of cognizance. *Los conocedores.* A bubble of saliva bursts the smile of knowing hilarity. And so the tide of spreading relief will foam with a gurgling hysteria. The mouth and tongue are given to the guffaw as to vomit, knowing what relief it stoppers their gullets with. "Yes, what a relief it is to know one can laugh," Cardinal Mendoza would urge him further.

"Can you dry your own eyes at the thought of the priest crowned with the head-gear of the blasphemer? I think not," Cardinal Mendoza would hiss and squeal.

"The tottering of the priest under the invisible weight of the coroza which has been lined with lead—it is all so cleverly conceived—will be our incitement to *carnival.*" Cardinal Mendoza imagined that the entire Plaza de la Salvación might spasm, as if in some furtively lascivious contact with the lubricious bodily motions to which the priest is subjected by the unbearable weight of his own thoughts. They are trapped like birds in the ever-ringing belfry of his headgear. His spastic gyrations under the weight of the coroza are the first ripples of hilarity eddying across the surface of the Plaza de la Salvación until even the toes of the spectators who stand uncertainly at the furthest periphery are wet with glee.

A vividly imaginable sight. I can see it myself.

But does brother Fortunato laugh? With mouth agape and his tongue a clanging, does he commune with the words which Cardinal Mendoza would whisper in his ear?

"I beg you to see, my brother, how by such carefully provoked revelry we will both be revenged upon the arrogant wine taster…"

"Must I finish the thought myself? At last, the wine taster swallows his own tongue!"

*A*nd so, Samaritan, will you be a neighbor to our cause knowing, as you do now, that Osvaldo Alonzo de Zamora is willing to speak of the priest's duplicities as his own?

Can you doubt that his knowing the little sister of the Plaza de la Salvación to be a sister inspires the feeling of brotherhood that we still beseech you to join by hurling your accusation at him?

Will you be our denouncer?

The saffron man, already emanating the light of the puckering flame to which his armored guardians would press his cracked lips, looks to you for a dousing illumination. The good neighbor, Samaritan, is a link in the chain of brotherhood. Do you not see that the man in the sanbenito and the man toppling beneath the lead-lined Caroza are already such brothers?

If you are indeed to be the Samaritan you will need to know how. How will you know? Only your neighbor can tell you. Do you not see how you and I are already neighbors ourselves? So many questions and answers have passed between us. They might have been our embraces. They have drawn us together into the tightness of this most pressing question: "Will you admit that the sister lying asprawl of the Plaza de la Salvación could be your sister, even if the body is no longer apparent?"

I ask you again. I ask you in the spirit of the neighborliness with which you are now acquainted. Can you stand and strike an accusatory finger into the moist eye of her assassin without the squeamishness of knowing what you are saying? Will your neighborly hand, by such a pointed gesture, convert our innocent wine taster into a river of blame?

Wine into water. Be carried on its current Samaritan. Standing at the prow of your own initiative, peering into the passing depths, do you not see reflected to your squinting sight the rippling image of Doña Fernandina? Be the Samaritan, my neighbor, my brother.

✦   ✦   ✦   ✦   ✦

Can I render an allegory for your persuasion?

There was once a neighbor whose goodness was proven by the unrepentant Jew. The man was a merchant of vinous fruits. He was a man known as covetously for the finery of his haberdashery as for the refinement of his palate. He was a man whose nose was as sensitive as his mouth to the felicitous invisibilities of the most delicate taste. The power of higher perception imbues the same fervor of confidence in the commercial buyer as that which the priest purveys to the hungry communicant for whom the flavorless mash of wafer and grape is as lifeless as a stone.

And this Jew was a liar. The Jew was husband and father to those whose most kindred blood did not itch with a corpuscle of suspicion that he had tainted its holy tincture. To all in this ciudad the wine merchant was known as the most devout of men in whom the Christian soul flourished as a leaf of the natural tree. No wound of grafting was apparent, as is so often detected in the stiff mannerisms of the converso grotesquely distorting his genuflections.

And yet this merchant of the grape bore a nose that cut the air a bit too brusquely.

He might have easily been recognized for one whose flesh is unnamable. Converso does not name. It only marks the body that does not speak to itself. The mind that wanders from its place in time and space. The conversos are the ungainly ones. They might have been born with an extra limb, they are so unsuited to the human gait. Imagine an extra leg. Would you not be tempted to cut it off?

Someone, a neighborly citizen of this ciudad, certainly surmised what I tell you now. The wine merchant was an unrepentant Jew. This is to say that he was circumcised, a fact which not even his faithful wife could know, as she knew nothing else of manhood than what her husband presented to her. She was herself a child of the most devoutly hooded morality.

No: certainly, not a nun!

But yes, he was, in the way of his manhood, shorn of the hood himself. He made no denials. But neither did he make any affirmations. Still he was a man of showy appearance I have already told you. Never one to cowl himself with modesty. When a man flaunts his worldly bearing there are always those who would see more than appears. It puts the object of envy more imaginably within one's grasp to imagine it more covetously. And so someone surmised the wine merchant's secret.

Or someone merely possessed an eye to see. Ostentation is so prone to nudity. Indeed a man glorying in his ownership of a marble basin, intarsied with gold and cresting the back of a bronze and silver dolphin, should always bathe privately.

And so an accusation was made against the luxurious wine merchant. A physical examination was ordered by a prelate of the church in which he was known to bow his head devoutly three times a week. His person was seized by the guards of the holy office. He was revealed to be the person he was: a naked Judaizer, proved to be so by the very organ that fathered two Christian souls, hazarded now to a life as squirming as the wayward homunculus itself. Under the cajoling hand of the Inquisition—waywardness always wants cajoling—the older child was said to have confessed the father's crime without knowing it. The agonizing child could not regurgitate the taste of incriminating falsehood from his tongue.

And so the father made it true.

He slipped a noose around his neck. What the child thought to be false was made true with a tipping of a short stool. Barely the accident of a wineglass swept off the table by a careless swinging of the arm. It hardly made a noise. But the father imagined what consolation might echo in the child's ear. Even a father can be a good neighbor to his son.

Well then, neighborliness requires a hand. It requires a foot. Can you not feel the power that flexes in the palm giving a push, closing a fist? Can you not feel the spring of effort in your arches sprinting towards a fallen prey? The hand that takes the rope. The foot that tips the stool. These are the means. The meaning of it is clear.

So, Samaritan, will you be a neighbor to us in the way of the father to the son, if you decipher the meaning of this little allegory? Follow the example of the hand, of the foot. Thus be a brother to the soul of the Samaritan. Thus know the Samaritan to be your flesh and blood. Was the father's suicide not a virtuous murder? Likewise, if you will ignite Osvaldo Alonzo de Zamora's pyre with your incendiary tongue, you may murder the unvirtuous deed of the stepfather's assassination.

I am the logician of such convoluted fates.

And now you know that the wedding of brother Fortunato to the tight skinned sister of the grape was not a curling wisp of my imagination, though I imagined both more and less of what incarnation would be mine in the spectacular consubstantiation of that ceremony. In such cases *mine* is not as possessive as you might think.

On the nuptial day, the stones of the Plaza de la Salvación were indeed strewn with the straw of the crèche. The color of the sun was as warm to the foot as it was bright to the upturned eye. Those who assembled in the Plaza de la Salvación, however reluctantly, were gilded, one by one, with the radiance of the noon hour until the stones beneath their feet were so eclipsed by the numbers of wedding guests, pressing heatedly against one another, that any sensation of what was underfoot was entirely forgotten, despite how treacherously slippery the stalk littered pavement remained, if one had space enough to lengthen one's stride. So many spectators in the heat of the day undulated the surface of a heaving sea swollen with the vapors of its ablation. If one looked from a distance.

Would that there had been distance enough.

But the bride was *not* trundled to the altar in a wooden cart with wheels the size of cheeses. Nor was the modesty of the bride crushed by an edict of nudity above the waist. Nor did the groom seem to require his crutch. Nor did Cardinal Mendoza bestride the event with unconcealed ridicule from a throne-like perch above the proceedings. He was his brother's brother, by his side and proffering a supporting hand, a halter for the otherwise halting pace of Fortunato's conveyance to the steps of the altar. Nor was the music accompanying this scene a raucous tide of delirium rippling from the middle of the Plaza de la Salvación as though a plunking stone had been tossed.

The steps to the altar were not the apprentice carpenter's roughly hewn wooden gallows-climb to the dais of the Auto da fé, that had become, so ephemerally, a fixture of the Plaza de la Salvación, in the perpetual resurrection of those proceedings.

Rather, the steps to the altar of this day's celebration were sempiternal marble treads leading through the towering bronze doors of the new Iglesia de Santa Teresa. After thirty years of construction, the singular holy edifice to face the immense arena of the Plaza de la Salvación had just one day before been erected to the full lantern height of its brazen dome. The bark-clad wooden scaffolding that still veiled the radiant limestone façade made it therefore impossible to discern, from the depths of the Plaza de la Salvación, any intimation of what the stony face of God might reflect upon the baptismal legion of wedding guests immersing themselves in His shadow.

And yet, the doors of the Iglesia de Santa Teresa smiled broadly. They would accommodate the witnesses to this most mystifying nuptial of the royal brother, whose wart encrusted visage was the most murmured secret of our ciudad, and the girl from a remote and unknown countryside who was rumored to have a maddening vinous liquor coursing in her frantic veins. More profoundly, the blessing conferred upon the wedded couple was to be the official sanctification of the holy shrine. Baptismal for all. Within the benedictory words of the presiding priest two spiritual destinies would suspire.

What mockery of the priesthood would suffice for such blasphemy, I might have asked myself? Only the priest would know.

Did I not inhabit the body of my brother Isaac, as recognizably—such a perfect fit!—as he did the sacerdotal habit he had so shamelessly donned? It was no less a feat of haberdashery to make myself appear to be the priest and so, in that act, divest myself of the thing that is dressed to appear so. So it had been commanded, in any case, by Cardinal Mendoza himself: I would be the priest, on this of all days.

The lofty interior of the Iglesia de Santa Teresa was still redolent of the yeasty spore of fresh stucco, of marble dust, the delicate powdered cinnamon scent of freshly polished porphyry, the soft bite of metal on the tongue that is the tang of newly applied gilt. The commingling of these sensory intimations of a yet unconsummated blessing jostled the crowd overflowing the undulating trompe l'oeil pavement of the cathedral, and spilling out onto the straw littered rougher red stones—betokening only the brazing heat of the oven—of the Plaza de la Salvación. And of course now we understood that the straw was meant to cleanse the soles of the wedding guests whose steps to the still unconsecrated temple would otherwise track the filth of their pilgrimage onto the pristine black and white parallelograms so artfully inlaid as to make the pilgrim unconfident that he could stand steadily upon them.

Is that not where I myself stood, if I could say "I," if I could say "self"? What would have been "mine," then, might have mattered.

But now, "I" was seized and cinctured in the costume of my brother's charade which had been delivered especially to my chambers by the Cardinal's most trusted valet. Was this not proof that Cardinal Mendoza was a conspirator to Isaac's flaunting of the covenant and also a facilitator of the blaspheming ruse to which he had now recruited the innocent brother? After all, "I" was on display before the unsanctified altar, no longer awaiting my own sacrifice. All were waiting on me.

The bronze altarpiece at my back, an architecture that mimed the facade of the cathedral, broken at its midpoint by the apex of a triangle, bore in its central panel the body of Christ. The wriggling form was sunk in such strong relief that the thrusting end of the spear piercing his side struck between my shoulder blades if I took a backward step. Had I turned to the adamantine touch of it I would have marveled to see the disembodied hand shriveled about the shaft of the spear, projecting so far from the scene of the crucifixion that it might have found limber attachment to a body in the tumultuous space surrounding me. But I could not move.

I was etched in a frieze of self-consciousness. For only at this moment did my mind burnish with the realization that this ceremony was not to be a carnivalesque farcing of the nuptial rite which would have been calamitous to the otherwise impressive jugglery of the defrauding priest. I was not to be persecuted in the vestment's of my brother's criminality. The unsteadiness of my footing was not the scaffold's trapdoor trembling on its hinges. This was not meant to be the cruel exposure of the brothers' duplicities to the stinging glare of public ridicule, which would have misplaced the object of blame in any case. That is to say, this was not the Cardinal's connivance to imagine what would palliate the vindictive ire of his most jealously disloyal and suspicious minions. They believed nothing less than that the admonition against practicing the priest in public had been devoutly disavowed by the dispensated brother whom I was mistaken to be. But this event was to be no blinding illumination of an imaginable darkness in which the cowardly brother was hiding himself, as I might have feared.

No. No. No. This was to be an even more furtive concealment in the furling shadows of ambiguation, a balm of cumuli smeared across a scorching sun, a refuge for Osvaldo from the misprisions of the world. This was to be my chance to consubstantiate with the priest, putting all accusations to rest by force of the most unapologetic dissembling. It would be a samaritanism.

The Cardinal, a samaritan.

The faces of the bride and groom would be my testimonials. Already featured to my focusing eye where the couple bobbed distantly upon the steps of the Iglesia de Santa Teresa and, lit as they were with the wick of noon flaming through the open doors of the cathedral, they each showed me the serious demeanor of one who well knows what will happen next. Their eyes were sewn shut against the glare, upon which, having crested the steps, they now seemed to float as though it were something molten. Their noses were hacked with shadow. Their dry mouths hung open like broken windows. Their teeth were shards scraping the billowy breath that seemed to heave against their progress. Brother Fortunato's weight upon Cardinal Mendoza's arm, heavier with each step, was nonetheless buoyant enough to keep pace with the bride whose bonewhite gown, set off against the stain of her skin, was the curling spume of an incoming tide. Behind them a scarlet retinue of guards, axe-heads gleaming over their shoulders, propelled the processional. The solemnity of their approach was as funereal as fate itself. All the better, Osvaldo Alonzo de Zamora comprehended, to conjure the authenticity of the priest.

There he stood, you might say. At the precipitously risen height of the altar steps, almost a figure come alive from the dusky, but violently animate relief of the bronze altarpiece bristling behind him, the priest spread his legs in a stance of bold arrival. To rise so high he had stepped upon the words that were viper-heads of temptation roiling in his brain.

Neither shalt thou go up by steps unto mine altar, that thy
Nakedness be not discovered thereon.

Lifting his arms above his head, and so already possessed of the incensed space that enshrined him, the priest let his voice rise yet higher in a welcoming chant. Cloaked in the mantel of God, he was possessed of the will to be seen.

One would have seen the blade of his resolve shimmering in the slits of his eyes, as the mouth grew more muscular in its exertions. The austerity of the act would be the proof of the priest's authority, if he could whet his will to the ceremony. If he could read the signs that were incised in the motions of his own flesh, the oracular regurgitations of his own breath, he would embody the lie of his priestly mien as a miracle of faith.

Be self-possessed, by another self.

So he was.

Now the officially promised couple were as palpably embodied under the priestly gaze as Isaac's double gave bodily substance to the wispy vestments of the priestly call.

The drooping brown toadstools that clustered upon brother Fortunato's forehead, his cheeks, and the barely existent chin grew erect under the severity of the priest's downcast eyes. The wetness upon the girl's brow, indistinguishable from the droplets that cling to the rim of the goblet where the tongue has lapped, were licked dry by the breath of the priest's invocational words. Thus did he call all of the motley and crowding spectators—their sun smeared faces now querulous with a thousand heterodox wrinklings of the brow and white winged flutterings of the eye—to the uncompromising orthodoxy of the dictum that, anyone could see, sat regally upon his tongue.

Only the face of Cardinal Mendoza, a softly glowing moon wobbling beside his brother's uncomprehending raptness in the thickening dinge of the cathedral, showed no recognition whatsoever that anything was happening. It was for the priest to know what would happen next. Or so Cardinal Mendoza took it on faith. Such would be the test of the priest's recognition that he had been anointed by an act of samaritanism, making him his brother's keeper at last. But the priest's own determination must forge the iron key to that keep.

The vast throng of hungry communicants who had spilled themselves upon the pavement of the basilica, hushed, stilled themselves, imbibed the time with their breath until the spell of an inexplicable intoxication would be upon them.

They watched.

For the moment, the priest's voice was inaudible, though the bride and groom were visibly tangled in an obscure communication that appeared to have been spun from the priest's mouth. The sudden agitation of their conjoined heads evoked the buzzing dismay of the fly in the cobweb. But for the vast crowd of guests too distant even to imagine a sound, the gesture of his hand was word enough, as the priest hooked one finger in the air, brought it tauntingly close to a self-inspecting eye and then slowly, bending his whole person, stooping, caught the hem of his white alb and slowly drew it up his leg. He did this with such anticipation as hangs upon the curtain rising above a stage. The actors are atremble in an onerous frieze of stilled action, awaiting the spark of life which their revelation to the audience will ignite.

The leg that he revealed was white and smooth as milk. Or it was smooth as milk's reflection in the polished blade of the razor that had certainly preceded this journeying gesticulation. For the leg was as hairless as alabaster. Steadiness was steeliness as much for the beading eyes forming their gaze along the imaginable blade's edge, as it would have been for the barbering hand. And as the priest's crooked fingers traveled above the knee, the strenuous effort to bend the knee was palpably balanced against the weight of the one straight leg upon which the priest was left standing. Of course he could not see. But did he not perilously feel the unsteadiness of the questioning pose?

What he could see undoubtedly was that the question was posed in the watery faces of the bride and groom, rippling. A man standing over a flowing brook knows nothing of what will come. Who awaited the answer with more trepidation?

Silence. Incense. Breathlessness, tingling with the spice of that indrawn breath. Darkness was illumined by candlelight that guttered with the extinguishing waves of noontide sun crashing against the open doors of the Iglesia de Santa Teresa. Then the teetering figure of the priest, exposed before the congregation, began intoning the words of the marriage ceremony, as unerringly as all who knew it knew it to be written. He stood the sacred ground.

Perhaps the bride did not have sufficient faith in the feat of the priestly balancing act. Or she was merely impatient for an answer. The bride's hand abruptly lit upon the top of the priestly figure's ever more exposed thigh. A white bird would not have perched itself as unexpectedly in the high and brittle branches of a dead tree. Her hand was steady upon that bare bough.

Willful? Bidden? Divinely ordained?

Regardless, her hand steadied the priest's improbable stance as he continued to gather the hem of the alb into the imminently discoverable crotch where the leg joined the trunk of him, seeable but unseen, where the general murk of incensed air clouding the dome of the cathedral met the nimbus of billowing cloth in his lap. The sight of the bride's hand, more clenched than stroking, but certainly feathering the invisible manhood of the man who was not meant to be so, was tempestuous titillation for the sea of witnessing eyes.

The dilating pupils pull the scalp more tightly to the swell of the concupiscent brain, do they not?

Heads collided in the obscure bustling of enflamed

imagination that pressed one body more impetuously upon another for a better view, producing an involuntary heaving of the pious throng against the alabaster piers of the nave.

Had one possessed the vantage point from which to look into brother Fortunato's face, then one would have seen how the eyes pooled.

But who would have envisioned the bright fish that leapt from those green fringed depths? And yet who did not see brother Fortunato's silvery hand settle whitely upon the hand of his bride as the dove upon the back of its quivering mate? The compact of hands upon the priest's upper thigh, itself more white than the snow in which such birds disappear, did not unbalance that swaying figure. To the contrary. It completed the spectacle that the priest sought to exert. Did the bride and groom know what the priest intended? That their cooing hands would embolden the interrogative mark he wished to describe with this precarious and uncompromising posture?

The priest still stood on one leg so that the other, curving away from it, might write the *quaestio* with his own physique. One might force an answer by flexing a muscle. Or did the ever more tensely gathering congregation possess the only vantage point for seeing things this way?

I wondered: was the priest aware of how this looked? Yes, it was a spectacle for all. He so confessed it to himself, if the physical contortion which held him captive was not confession enough. A tableau unknown, unprecedented, even in a church that has yet to be sanctified, within which dark precinct nothing is yet known. All the better for it to be so, I whispered to myself. To him. All the better to divine what faith and obedience these bodies, now so intricately and portentously arranged by whatever mystery of emotional stagecraft, and displayed to the ever more restive congregation like a gleaming medallion, or a life-sized monstrance, might command. Strangeness persuasively embodied can make the monstrosity of every passing moment more human in the way a hand unfolds itself to receive another hand.

Or would the medallion be shattered, the monstrance defenestrated of its visionary gaze, by the monster of meaninglessness whose anarchy destroys the faithful dreamer's blissful state?

Meaningless and fraught with meaning. Such was the paradoxical burden that teetered with the priest's weight upon one straight leg. Staring into the still upturned faces of bride and groom—purple and brown, blood and the flesh that holds it—the priest stiffened his resolve. By raising his knee barely an inch and observing the rise of the two chins that might have been tethered to his taut gaze, he knew he had prevented the bridal couple from removing their hands from his exposed thigh.

Because he had raised his knee with the tight-rope walker's carefully calibrated effort, he knew that the subtly increased angle would cause their inexplicable grip to slide imperceptibly toward the place where dry bone was anointed with the mystical oils of the body's mobility. Where the hip accepts the leg to be a part of what is indisputably whole, the skin quickens with sensations of an irresistible magnetism. For it is also the place where, under the spell of such sensation, unutterable spirit becomes flesh. There, despite the ruffled hem of the alb that veiled the livening touch of two hands already joined to each other, a raising of the priest's body, as if from nothing, became as apparent as the straightening contours of the silken robe. As it ascended into empty air, the stirring fabric of the priestly vestment became smoother and sleeker, rising to a pinnacle of stringency. Visible. Invisible. Meaningful. Meaningless.

But could such presence be denied? The overwhelming silence of the moment rang with the question. The full authority of the priestly function, rousing its all too imaginably livid head from the depths of an unimaginable groin, imperceptively quivered, despite the chiseled immobility of the kneeling couple and the robed figure still standing so statuesquely on one leg. Now the congregation was weighted with the same motionlessness, as if they had been carved in place to complete the architecture of the church. What could happen amidst such unyielding stoniness? The priest would know.

And so he moved. He relaxed the laboring muscles of his thigh with the brittle suddenness of a breaking bough and recovered his balance on two legs. Thus he observed the no longer conjoined hands of the bride and groom fall like stoned birds lifelessly to their respective sides. He saw that all eyes were still fixed upon the stiff protuberance beneath his immaculate vestment. A stick in the eye. The blood in the starting eyes of the staring congregants was no less tumescent than the bloody stick.

Undeniable. And yet soon to become a mere article of faith. So knowing, the priest summoned all his patience to watch the waning of the glaring protuberance in the astounded eyes of the congregants. The erosion of a monumental rock into a haze of sand on a distant horizon would be no less unbelievable for the stupefying inequality of knowledge and time.

When the white front of the vestment no longer portrayed even a shadow of the formerly inconceivable anatomy that was certainly concealed within it, the blinding vividness of what the congregants still beheld as the conundrum of *what is*, visited upon them all the self-doubts of a man in whose heaving palm a small bird expires, as he uncurls his fingers from the impetuous purpose of capture. "Is this not," he whispered in my ear, "how it is with the priest?" He is meant to keep the mystery.

✦ ✦ ✦ ✦ ✦

Who am I?

✦ ✦ ✦ ✦ ✦

It was at that moment, amidst the first quizzical bows of the congregants, that I caught sight of Cardinal Mendoza's brazen cheeks, the scimitar grin cutting across his face to show the merry sheen of the rouged lips. I saw that he recognized the convincing embodiment of the priestly person in the awefull space opened about him by the ever more stooping congregants. In their back-stepping gavotte, they made it equally apparent that, all hieratic distance notwithstanding, they would never depart from me. Faithful. Had they not witnessed an incarnation indubitably? None would ask *of what*, so long as it remained an outrage to conception, and yet a pleasantly throbbing bruise upon the innermost organs, beyond the reach of a fingertip's sensation. Did Cardinal Mendoza know any less?

No doubt this was an explanation for the disappearance of the bride and groom, props as they were for the theater of illusions in which I now knew my presence was as much a contrivance of the Cardinal's imaginative will as that of the spellbound congregants, who still clenched in their throats the breath of amazement that was nothing less than the feeling of one's tongue suffocating the words in one's mouth. We had collaborated so unwittingly well, Cardinal Mendoza with the priest. Collaborators in the theatrics of light and dark, sound and silence, palpable and elusive flesh, though the gnomic contortions that were the priest's embodiment of himself were my own inspiration.

And so, from that moment, I commenced to live with the knowledge that Cardinal Mendoza had made Osvaldo Alonzo de Zamora a wager against the heretics of his own house and cause. He had schemed to silence his enemies before they could lift their tongues from the bilious pool of their resentments. The sham priest would be made real by the rite of communion, which nothing less than the pendulous sway of the erect penis had now made him rightful heir to. The wine taster made consubstantial with the priest would, by that communion, confound any and all who might be tempted to denounce the house of Mendoza for reckless indulgences of the Jew.

Who would not be saved? Only the girl. Only brother Fortunato. They were both dragged unceremoniously off the stage to be shucked of their costumes and released into the illusionistic perspective of that ever more elaborately staged world where the drama of pursuit and capture is unrelenting.

✦ ✦ ✦ ✦ ✦

We do not know what became of brother Fortunato. But the girl. We know what happened to the girl.

Barely minutes after being cast into the incinerating noontide of the Plaza de la Salvación the roar of her catastrophe suddenly rushed upon our ears as if on the wheels of rolling canon. It has been told that the girl made herself a wick to the candle of her newly liberated body. She bedded herself on the floor of the crèche that was the Plaza de la Salvación, piling the straw high in her lap, vigorously waiting for the two sticks she wielded to cross with enough intensity that they would ignite. The flame that at last thrust its voracious tongue through the doors of the Iglesia de Santa Teresa proved insatiable indeed.

✦ ✦ ✦ ✦ ✦

When the Plaza de la Salvación had ceased to be a glowing coal in the grate of the day, the leather-clad flame-dousers, their feet protected from the still radiant stones by wooden-soled cothurni, stood almost as high as the soot shadowed flames that had scorched the enclosing building facades to the lintels of their charred but still stalwart iron-hinged doors. Carrying enormous iron rakes over their shoulders the brigade of flame-dousers kicked up wraith-like clouds of ash as they commenced to discover what the fire had purified of all combustible substance. They fanned out across the plaza dragging their rakes behind them like nets through a foggy depth. They sifted brass buckles from shoes left in the path of the fleeter foot. They nodded at a nest of carmelized apple cores where they had been piled high in a barrel. They shielded their eyes from the glare of a cluster of silver axe-heads severed from their shafts. Here and there a spray of brass buttons glittered less blindingly, no doubt ripped from a flaming waistcoat flung from escaping arms. They smiled and winked at the skeletal remains of the very iron-framed carts that had hauled the bales of incendiary straw to these hearthstones of the Plaza de la Salvación.

Only one proper skeleton was dredged from the ashen tide, though it might easily have been mistaken for a ravaged concertina, so twisted were the limbs in the black weld of their final convulsion.

But the flame-dousers could not be distracted. They were following the ravaging path of the fire which had merely scoured the Plaza de la Salvación, but had entirely devoured the interior of the Iglesia de Santa Teresa. Leaping from altar steps to altar, inhaling all of the massively framed canvases and shimmering tapestries that described upon the flame-licked walls of the basilica what can rise and what can fall, the fire had only disgorged itself of the bronze altarpiece. The melted bronze formed an impenetrable and deceptively scintillating lake at the feet of the first witnesses, vainly seeking their reflections in it. Only the caved roof beams, large and broad as the rays of sunlight still crashing upon the heads of these faithful explorers, were there to offer evidence of a crucifixion.

"Nothing remains."

From whose gaping mouth would the word *nothing* have extruded itself, as irresistibly as the most undignifying bodily necessity?

As if we did not have to confess it!

From the mouth of the priest, no further word was emitted, where he stood incandescing beneath the brilliant sky light. We see, do we not, the priest serenely illuminated in the very place where the panic-stricken congregants, who had been swept from the floor of the church by the first monstrous breath of the fire, would have forever remembered him to be standing.

Am I not standing there still?

And so, Samaritan, I have read to you the whole of Osvaldo Alonzo de Zamora's confession. Have you now amassed a strong enough army of indignations to oppose all doubts that you are meant to be our neighborly denouncer? Only by words that fall with the weight of the axe head can the sins of Osvaldo Alonzo de Zamora be virtuously murdered. You have been slow to see.

And only now you notice that the hem of my vestment is singed and pocked with cinders. The ashenness of my face is ash indeed. And only now you wax quizzical enough to hazard the question, "Is it you?" "Is it you?" I have told you. I am not myself.

Bid for your innocence, Samaritan. Bid for your innocence with a denunciation that cannot be refused by the Auto da fé. Then we may imagine from whence the answer to your question may at last arise.

As for me, there is only the answering irony. At the bluest height of the flame—that fits my head as piously as a cowl—I, I say "I," will be tasted by the air.

Other Novels by Alan Singer

The Ox-Breadth
The Charnel Imp
Memory Wax
Dirtmouth